JOSEPH T. WALKER UPPER
    700 ALLGOOD ROAD
  MARIETTA, GEORGIA 30062

Deleted 2006

Donated to Joseph T. Walker School
by: David Porter

SOMETHING TO SHOUT ABOUT

BY JOHN AND PATRICIA BEATTY

Holdfast
King's Knight's Pawn
Master Rosalind
The Royal Dirk
Who Comes to King's Mountain?
Witch Dog
published by William Morrow and Company

At the Seven Stars
Campion Towers
A Donkey for the King
Pirate Royal
The Queen's Wizard
published by The Macmillan Company

BY PATRICIA BEATTY

The Bad Bell of San Salvador
Blue Stars Watching
Bonanza Girl
By Crumbs, It's Mine!
Hail Columbia
How Many Miles to Sundown
A Long Way to Whiskey Creek
Me, California Perkins
The Nickel-Plated Beauty
O the Red Rose Tree
The Queen's Own Grove
Red Rock Over the River
Rufus, Red Rufus
The Sea Pair
Squaw Dog
published by William Morrow and Company

Indian Canoe-maker
published by The Caxton Printers, Ltd.

The Lady from Black Hawk
published by McGraw-Hill Company

PATRICIA BEATTY
SOMETHING TO SHOUT ABOUT

FRONTISPIECE BY MARYLIN HAFNER
William Morrow and Company
New York 1976

Copyright © 1976 by Patricia Beatty Uhr
All rights reserved. No part of this book may be reproduced or utilized in any form or by any means, electronic or mechanical, including photocopying, recording or by any information storage and retrieval system, without permission in writing from the Publisher. Inquiries should be addressed to William Morrow and Company, Inc., 105 Madison Ave., New York, N. Y. 10016.
Printed in the United States of America.
1 2 3 4 5 6 7 8 9 10

Library of Congress Cataloging in Publication Data

Beatty, Patricia.
  Something to shout about.

  SUMMARY: The women of a Montana mining town disrupt life when they try to raise money for a new school.
  [1. Montana—Fiction. 2. Frontier and pioneer life—Fiction. 3. Women—Social conditions—Fiction] I. Title.
PZ7.B380544So   [Fic]   76-22185
ISBN 0-688-22078-9
ISBN 0-688-32078-3 lib. bdg.

CONTENTS

1 Our Unexpected Boarder 9
2 By Halloween—or Bust! 31
3 Wiggling Along 49
4 Coward 66
5 A Very Astonishing Surprise, Indeed! 83
6 Miss Emily 104
7 Obstreperous 124
8 Benighted 143
9 A Chair, a Toothbrush, and a Nightgown 160
10 Irreverent 179
11 What Lot? 200
12 Some Other Things to Shout About 224
Author's Notes 251

CHAPTER ONE

OUR UNEXPECTED BOARDER

We four Fosters owned the Whole Shebang.

That meant, of course, that we found out first about everything, or just about everything, that went on in Ottenberg.

Papa came to Ottenberg in June, two days before Davey and Mama and I arrived by stagecoach. He had set up our three tents before we came. When we got off the stagecoach in Montana Territory, we noticed that Papa had already painted *The Whole Shebang, General Merchandise, Albert Foster, Esq., Sole Proprietor* on the front of the biggest tent.

Mama hadn't said a word about the shebang until one evening when we were sitting at supper in the smallest tent, the one we'd be living in. Then, as she lowered herself carefully onto the nail keg she was using as a chair until our furniture arrived from the last place we'd lived, she said, "Albert, don't you think it's a little bit pretentious and undignified to call our store the Whole Shebang?" Because she'd been a schoolteacher Mama used a lot of very big words. I knew what *pretentious* meant from having heard her use it before. It meant that Papa, in her estimation, was getting a bit too big for his britches. She'd told him that more than once, before we had left Silver

Belle, the mining camp in Idaho Territory seventy-some miles to the west of Ottenberg.

Papa answered her as he tried to get more comfortable on his nail keg and Davey and I squirmed on ours. "Everybody out here in the West calls a general store like the one we've always had a shebang. So why not say it in paint, Nora?"

"But not the whole shebang, Albert, my love."

Hearing Mama's words made me tense, as I tried to balance my plate of beans on my knees. When Mama called Papa "my love," I always felt nervous. I knew that what she was saying she didn't mean affectionately. A bean dropped off my plate and rolled onto the dirt floor. Nobody was looking, so I put my foot over it fast and squished it into the ground.

Papa wouldn't back down. "Well, Nora, so far it's the only general store in town. So haven't I got a right to call it the *whole* shebang since it's the *only* shebang?"

"Albert, there will be other stores, you know."

He nodded after he'd swallowed some sowbelly that was pretty hard-chewing. "Yep, if Ottenberg lives there will be. If it doesn't, there won't be. Simple as that."

I sighed along with Mama. Montana Territory's brand-new town of Ottenberg was only a week old. That was pretty young for anyone—even for a baby. Right now it was only a tent town because gold had just been discovered in the hills a couple of miles away. A big tree had blown over in a storm and its roots had dragged up some gold with them "from the bowels of the earth," as Papa had heard it. The men who'd found the tree discovered more gold nearby. If the gold petered out, so would Ottenberg. But if the strike was rich enough, the tent town could

OUR UNEXPECTED BOARDER

become a real one. Otherwise, the people wouldn't stay. They'd drift away to places where there were mines that could make a living for them.

Mama asked, as she ate one of the biscuits she'd baked on a shovel over the campfire just outside the tent, "Albert, how long do you estimate we shall be here in this new place?"

He nodded his head again, chasing a bean around on his plate and finally spearing it with a tine of his tin fork. "Well, I have high hopes for Ottenberg. Old man Ottenberg, himself, told me this very afternoon, when he came into the store tent with his daughter to buy a bottle of bitters for his stomach, that the situation looks good. You saw him, didn't you, Nora? He was the portly gent with the whiskers. Ottenberg says there's lots of gold hereabouts. The Indians have been telling him about it for years, and now it's finally been found."

I saw how Mama pursed her lips before she told him, "I've heard that before, it seems to me. The Indians have told a great many people in a great many places that there's gold here and there—and everywhere." She went on sourly, "Your Mr. Ottenberg and his daughter, too, both looked a bit strange to me. That's the reason I didn't come over to be introduced. Why does she wear those dreadful black clothes? Is she mourning for someone? And her father! The Civil War has been over for ten years now, but he's still wearing his blue Union Army uniform and hat with some sort of insignia on it. My Lord, Albert, it's 1875! Doesn't he know that?"

"He does. He was an officer, a colonel, Nora." That seemed to explain everything in Papa's estimation.

"Well, he isn't in the army now," Davey said. Even

though he was only ten to my almost thirteen, he still had his wits about him some of the time. He looked like me, too. Sort of fair-haired, not too tall and not too short, not quite blue-eyed or green-eyed. He also resembled Papa a little, which was not such a good thing, sad to say. Papa, though he was good, wasn't a person anybody noticed for handsomeness.

Mama was very different. She resembled a queen, tall and dark, and even when she wore an ordinary calico dress without frills and fancies, people turned around to look at her on the street. Although she hadn't been a schoolteacher since she married Papa, you could tell just by looking at her straight posture that she'd been one once. And in most things she got her way, though not when it came to settling down in one place permanently. Mining camps usually didn't last very long—or at least not the ones Papa had found for us to live in.

I could tell from her face that she didn't share Colonel Ottenberg's high hopes for the town named after him because it had been founded on some of his Government homestead land. As far as I could see the only good thing about Ottenberg was that it was only two long, dreadful days' bumpy stagecoach ride from the last town we'd lived in, Silver Belle.

Silver Belle had died, because the silver there petered out before the town could celebrate its first birthday. The town we'd lived in before that had been Wilderness City, also in Idaho Territory. It was mostly wilderness and darned little city. It didn't even live six months, though it was pretty there among the tall yellow pines. As I remembered Wilderness City, it had been almost all saloons except for our shebang.

There hadn't been a school in either Silver Belle or Wilderness City, because there were only a couple of kids in either town and nobody had been able to find a schoolteacher. So Mama taught Davey and me at home when she wasn't helping Papa behind the counter of our store. I sort of liked school, even though my own mother taught it. But not Davey.

My brother hated school, no matter who taught it. When Mama called him in to recite his lessons, he ran away as often as he could. Davey was a fast foot racer, almost faster than I was, and gaining on me all the time. Back in Silver Belle Mama had complained that he was getting to be an "artful dodger." That was a boy character in a book she had read aloud to us, about a boy named Oliver Twist.

While I was thinking about the unhappy life of Oliver Twist in England, Papa interrupted my thoughts. "Colonel Ottenberg claims that he was never in a battle in the Civil War that his side didn't win. He says that he's been one hundred percent right in just about everything he ever undertook, and he swears that Ottenberg will be a real city someday."

"What does Mrs. Ottenberg say to that, Albert?" Mama asked.

Her question made me think about the colonel's daughter, who was maybe Mama's age but, like her father, mighty plump. That day in the store she'd fingered some red-rickrack trimming wound on a spool but had only muttered about it and not bought any. After her father had put his stomach bitters into his pocket and was done talking with Papa, he'd called out to her, "Come on, Emily. I'm through in here."

She hurried out right at his heels. Dressed in black from head to foot, she wasn't one bit handsome to look at, to my way of thinking. I wondered if she was in mourning black because her mother had died recently. Her face was almost as broad as her father's, though with all the white whiskers he had, it was hard to tell where his face ended and they began. Come to think harder about it, Emily Ottenberg looked a good bit like the colonel, which was something that should never have happened to a lady.

Papa answered Mama, "There isn't any Mrs. Ottenberg. The colonel has been a widower for years. There's only his daughter, the one you saw. She agrees one hundred percent with her pa, according to him."

Mama didn't seem to want to talk about the Ottenbergs anymore, and I thought I could see why. Except for the uniform the colonel wore and Emily's strange black clothes, they weren't really very interesting. She said to Papa, "We shall see what we shall see about the length of time this particular town survives, Albert."

They were her last words to him that night about anything much, except to tell him how to unpack our belongings and where to put them.

I whispered to Davey, leaning toward him from the top of my nail keg. "It looks to me like we're going to stay here till the last dog gets hanged. Colonel Ottenberg sure has convinced Papa."

"Yep, Hope, it looks that way to me, too."

And so we stayed. Our stay was educational, even if it wasn't easy. Things worth learning about usually don't come covered with roses. As Mama sometimes says, they are more often loaded down with bricks.

It turned out the Ottenbergs were right about Ottenberg. In a month's time it had turned into a real town. Right away we had city fathers, or so they called themselves, though some of the miners who were city fathers didn't have any children at all.

Colonel Ottenberg, because he was in Ottenberg first and sold land to the people coming in, was head of all the city fathers and elected mayor. The very first thing he did, after he made a speech thanking everyone for voting for him, was to appoint a city council. Papa wasn't picked as one of the members. They were all lawyers except for the town undertaker.

The next thing Colonel Ottenberg and his council did was to decide to build a jail in Ottenberg. A jail was always the first important building a town that lived any time at all put up, according to Papa, who'd grown up in Texas and Kansas. Jails turned out usually to be very, very important places in new towns.

I didn't pay much attention to the jail as it was going up in the center of the town, except to notice that it was being built of bricks while the other buildings were wooden. I'd seen the wagons carrying the bricks arriving in Ottenberg and knew that they were being brought all the way from San Francisco, hundreds of miles from Montana Territory.

Oh, I knew a little bit about bricks. The very word *brick* made Papa look wistful. We had never owned a brick shebang, and that was his dream. But bricks cost far too much money. And the Ottenberg jail was brick because nothing was stronger than that, except maybe for stone.

Davey and I talked about the new building now and then. We called it the Whole Jail. We were poking fun at

Papa for naming the store the Whole Shebang. Papa hadn't backed down on that, though he'd given in to Mama on one thing and had the Ottenberg carpenters make the parlor in our living quarters behind the store larger than usual. Mama liked a parlor big enough for her organ, her golden-oak table, and her six velvet-upholstered sitting chairs. She liked to have company.

There were nine kids in all in Ottenberg by the time the town was a month old. Four families of them, in fact. A miner's kids, a sawmill manager's girl, a lawyer's kids, and a saloonkeeper's dreadful child, Silas O'Hare. But we Fosters were the first of the four boys and five girls.

One day in July I told Mama with pride, "The girls outnumber the boys here. They haven't got even enough for a baseball team, so they'll have to play any game the girls want to play." I was plunking out "Oh! Susannah" on her cottage organ with one finger as we talked in the parlor.

"There are enough boys for cowboys and Indians, you know." Mama was darning a pair of Davey's trousers where he'd fallen and ripped a hole in the knee. "Anyhow, Hope," she went on, "I doubt if any of you children will have so much time to play when September rolls around."

I stopped plunking and with one finger in the air over the organ key asked her. "What's happening then?"

"Oh, school is happening."

"A real one? *A real school?*" I whirled around on the piano stool and then stubbed my toe into the carpet to make the stool stop turning. I hadn't been to a real school in years and years. Well, three years at least. Having your mother who was once a teacher teach you wasn't the same thing as a real school.

"Yes, the mayor and city council have sent back East for an unmarried schoolteacher. They put advertisements into newspapers in several cities. Colonel Ottenberg supposedly heard day before yesterday from a lady who graduated from a female academy in Cincinnati." Mama smiled as she pulled the thread with a ripping sound through the cloth. "I think we might find that interesting. I've been told that there is a lot of ferment coming out of Ohio these days."

Ferment. That was a new word to me. I thought about it while I sniffed the air of the parlor. It smelled fragrant today. I'd gone out of Ottenberg into the hills behind the colonel's house, trespassing, of course, and picked wild syringa. I'd filled the parlor with vases and jars full of the white-flowered branches. It seemed to me that *ferment* had something to do with odors. I asked Mama what the word meant.

"In this case it has to do with thinking and acting among ladies' groups, Hope."

Nothing about smells then. I couldn't say that fermenting ladies interested me very much. Mama had always belonged to some ladies' groups wherever we'd lived. Back home in Oregon, when I'd been quite small, before we'd come east to Idaho and Montana Territories, she'd belonged to drama societies and choral groups. But she didn't do that sort of thing anymore—just altar societies and church charities. I swung back on the stool to the organ, and then as I picked at the notes for the "washbowl on my knee" part of "Oh! Susannah," a thought struck me.

It wasn't about the teacher who was coming here from Ohio. I wasn't about to put my mind to her, because you never could tell about teachers until you'd been with them for a while. Some were good and some weren't, from my short Oregon experience. My question was about the school. "Mama, where's the schoolhouse going to be?"

I'd gone all over Ottenberg yesterday with Margaret Libby, my new best friend, looking at the buildings going up. She was interested because her father's sawmill cut the planks for every one of them. We'd identified a blacksmith shop, a livery stable, barber shop, assay office, and all of thirty-two saloons. But come to think of it, I hadn't spied one building that looked like a schoolhouse. They were easy to spot in Oregon, because they were always large and had a steeple on top for the schoolbell to hang in.

Mama let out a sharp laugh that made me turn around once more. She was snapping the thread off with her teeth, something she rarely did because she claimed a person should never use teeth as tools. She was put out about something. Her voice sounded put out, too. "It's certainly nothing to shout about, believe me. Out of the great goodness of his heart, Colonel Ottenberg has offered to refurbish his chicken coop for Miss Willis."

"His chicken coop!" I knew the coop from visiting his homestead, which was only about a half mile from our shebang. It was a good-sized one that had been whitewashed on the outside. "Mama, what does *refurbish* mean?"

She gave me a sour smile. "Remove the hens and the nests, I imagine, and clean the coop out thoroughly."

"Does the new teacher know about the coop?"

"I doubt that such a dreadful prospect would occur to any delicately reared, well-educated young woman from

Cincinnati, Hope. I'm sure that she expects to find a proper schoolhouse—desks, wood stove, and a bell—all set up and ready for her. It's what should be prepared for her."

"Why won't it be then?" I knew that the sawmill was going twenty-four hours a day making trees into boards for houses and business buildings. There was plenty of time to build a schoolhouse—and wood all over the countryside.

"Because Colonel Ottenberg and the city council have decided that the town's tax money is to be used for other purposes—other more important buildings."

"Other buildings?" I knew about this tax business, because Papa had said he was being taxed for what the mayor called a "building fund." He'd had to pay out a whopping fifty dollars to the town, and he hadn't enjoyed it.

"Yes, Hope, other buildings."

"Do you mean the jail, Mama?"

"Well, it seems the jail is city building number one. Jails are very vital, you know. But so are schools." She gave me a look that was full of meaning. "I have thought for years that if more people went to school for a longer time and if the schools were the very best they could be, there wouldn't be as much need for jails."

This was a new thought. I chewed on it a little, thinking. What she seemed to be telling me was that the more learning a person had, the less likely he was to wind up in a jail.

While I was still thinking, she went on. "Of course, towns need churches, too."

Proving to her that I was following her thoughts, I

said, "What folks don't learn in church, they'll have to get at a school, huh?"

"Yes, or at home from their parents. But all too many don't even seem to get that."

This stopped me, making me peer swiftly over at her. I had stolen pieces of horehound candy for Margaret Libby and myself just the day before from the big jar on Papa's counter. I was a thief. Margaret had warned me that my hand might turn to stone and get stuck halfway down the jar. As I'd sucked the candy to a melted nothing in my mouth, I had been forced to admit to myself that it didn't taste as good as it did when Papa presented it to me as a gift.

Changing the subject, because I didn't want to dwell on my wickedness, I asked Mama, "When will the teacher come?"

"The last week of August."

"Where will she live, the Big Bend Hotel?"

"Lord forbid. That scandalous place. No, she will rotate. That's what the school board and Colonel Ottenberg have decided."

"*Rotate?*" All the word meant to me was run around in a circle or spin the way I was on the piano stool.

"Though she's to be paid twenty-five dollars per month, Miss Willis will board with Ottenberg families, moving to a new one each month. I'd hoped we'd get her with us first, but she's going to the Ottenbergs. Our turn to have her won't come until December, according to the schedule set up for her. But isn't that nice that we'll have her during the holidays?"

That didn't strike me as nice as it did Mama. She'd enjoy having another schoolteacher around for company for a while. But that meant that Davey and I would have the teacher around twenty-four hours a day and at Christmas, too. In any other part of the world, she could go back to her own family over the holidays but not out in the wilds where we were. The Montana snows would be much too deep for that. Our three winters in Idaho Territory had been bitter cold with terribly deep snow—not at all like the mild, green Willamette Valley in Oregon, where we'd come from originally.

I said hopefully, "Doctor Haverford seems to like living at the Big Bend Hotel just fine."

"Doctor Haverford would!" Mama sniffed. "It's got a saloon on each side of it and two across the street. It's the very place for an old bachelor." In her mind an old, confirmed bachelor was one of the worst creatures in all creation.

I sort of agreed about Doctor Haverford. He always wore the same baggy suit of black wool, and he smelled of tobacco and carbolic acid. But at least he said hello to Davey and me and the other kids he met on the street. Colonel Ottenberg was too grand to speak, because he considered himself the town founder. He didn't even nod to children, only to men voters and to ladies because that was considered polite.

While I went back to "Oh! Susannah" I pondered the coming of Miss Willis from Cincinnati and what was going to happen in December, which was my favorite month of the year. Being very closely related to a shebang keeper made for a nice December inasmuch as Papa got Christmas gifts for us wholesale, which meant extra cheap.

As I was glumly considering a Christmas that might not be so merry, our cat Essex came running into the room and jumped up into Mama's lap. His hair was bristling in a ridge over his back. And then, as always, his brother Manchester came growling through the slit in the heavy, red-plush curtains that separated the back of the store from where we lived. They looked just alike, like two big gray trout, but unfortunately they had never taken to one another. They were always fighting. They were supposed to be rat and mouse catchers and watch the cracker barrel and sacks of feed, but so far as we could see all they ever did was watch one another. They'd been a present from Miss Emily Ottenberg and were full-grown when she gave them to us. She said that she had cats aplenty and we needed mousers, but we would rather have picked our own cats.

Papa favored cats over dogs, because cats were neater. He wouldn't allow a dog in the shebang at all. Red-headed Margaret Libby, who owned a brown pug dog, had to stay outside with him or tie him to the side of the store and let him howl. In her estimation our cats were neither useful nor ornamental. I discounted what she said, because either one of our cats could lick the stuffing out of her dog anytime they took a notion to.

After Mama had put Essex down and Manchester had fled when I hissed "Scat, cat" at him, I said hopefully, "Mama, maybe the new teacher won't take to cats. They make some folks sneeze."

"Oh, I doubt if a cat will bother Miss Willis, Hope." I saw how Mama was shaking her head. "But teaching school in a chicken coop certainly could make her less than happy in Ottenberg."

I told her, "It's a big chicken coop."

"But it *is* a chicken coop, dear. That's what matters."

"Mama, why doesn't Papa ask Colonel Ottenberg and the city fathers to build a schoolhouse?"

"He has. So has the preacher and some other men. They got nowhere at all. The colonel's offer of the chicken coop was voted upon and accepted at once—disgraceful as it is."

I nodded. It seemed I was to be "cooped up" in more ways than one this autumn.

The jail was finished by the end of July, and in August another city building was begun—the courthouse. It was fancier by far than the jail, being made of bricks and stones. I overheard one of the lawyers who was on the city council telling Papa that they hoped to put statues on top of it. That would make it the last word in elegance.

Miss Ottenberg was being sent by the town to San Francisco to try to buy a statue of Justice first of all. I wondered what Justice would look like. For that matter, what would a statue of Truth or Freedom or Liberty look like? I had no idea—and neither had Davey.

He and Margaret and I watched the courthouse foundations being built. While we watched the men working we sometimes talked together about the schoolhouse and Miss Willis, all the time wondering about her. We'd heard from one of Colonel Ottenberg's hired hands, who came to our shebang now and then to buy chewing tobacco, that the chicken coop had been cleaned out slick as a whistle. They'd done the job with torches first to get rid of the cobwebs and mites. Then they'd used buckets of water to scrub it and after that buckets of whitewash to spruce it up.

"But it is still a chicken coop," Mama told the hired man.

"Yes'm," was all he said to her.

There was even a newspaper in Ottenberg now, the *Oracle*. It was often my job to read it aloud to Mama and Papa after supper on the three days a week—Monday, Wednesday, and Friday—that it came out. According to the twenty-seventh-of-August issue of the *Oracle,* Colonel Ottenberg had received a letter from Miss Leota Willis of Cincinnati, Ohio, telling what day she'd be arriving. The colonel and the city council and everyone important in town planned to greet that particular stagecoach. I wondered if the Ottenberg Silver Cornet Band would be on hand, too. It was full of bachelors.

There were a lot of unmarried men in town by now, all looking around for single ladies, who were very hard to come by in any mining camp. Back in Oregon Papa had hired lady clerks to measure out the yard goods for customers, but not here in the territories. He was told they either spent all their time flirting with bachelors, who rarely bought any yard goods, or they quickly made their pick from the crop of lonesome men and left their job to get married. Papa hired men clerks when he could find one who didn't want to dig for gold. Mostly though he and Mama waited on customers, or in a pinch, me.

The day Miss Willis arrived, the Silver Cornet Band wasn't gathered, because it was the middle of the day and they were all working. But a lot of other people were there: the city fathers, the town bachelors who weren't at the diggings, and the nine of us kids who would soon be going to school. Davey and Margaret and I and the other kids were right up front in order to get a good look at our new teacher, Miss Leota Willis.

Davey and I hadn't dolled ourselves up to meet the teacher the way Margaret Libby had. She was wearing her white dress with the blue sash and a floppy straw hat, as well as shoes. Another girl, who was shy but hoped to be teacher's pet, was carrying a bouquet of wild flowers for the teacher.

I figured I could judge Miss Willis's character by the way she got down out of the stagecoach. Stagecoaches bruised people's bones and jarred their teeth. And many of the drivers were mighty cussers. If Miss Willis came down smiling, that ought to prove she had a very good disposition.

I held my breath as the stagecoach, which was half an hour late, came jerking and swaying down Ottenberg's one street. When I saw the driver, I knew for a fact that Miss Willis had gotten an earful of interesting language. It was old Thompson, the wildest cusser in the whole territory, according to Doctor Haverford.

Ottenberg's street was full of mud puddles. In Oregon, which was a very civilized place, they would be called small lakes. The driver pulled up with the stage straddling what had to be the largest and deepest puddle of them all. The collapsible coach ladder was going to end up right in the middle of the water!

I heard Mama, who was standing behind me on the porch of our shebang, mutter under her breath, "That Thompson! Isn't that just like him, though?"

A miner, who looked more than a little bit drunk, waded out and unlimbered the stagecoach steps from where they folded on the outside. He stood in the puddle as if he expected to lift the passengers out over the mud. I knew his game. He wanted to make Miss Willis's acquaintance that way. I chuckled to myself. I hoped she weighed two hundred pounds.

She didn't. The miner's very first words told me that she wasn't fat. "Come on out, little lady," he said as he opened the door.

After a moment a lady appeared at the door, as small a lady as I'd ever set eyes on. She wasn't even as tall as Margaret, who was just five feet, one inch. Miss Willis wore a gray traveling costume and a black straw bonnet with white birds' wings on its top. Her face was as white as blackboard chalk and her hair dark red. Her features were sort of sharp and her round, darkish eyes weren't missing a single thing as she gazed out upon Ottenberg. Then she looked down at the waiting miner standing in the puddle, and from him to the stagecoach steps.

Finally she spoke to him. "Remove yourself, please, from my way, my good man."

Surprised, he stepped backwards, and to my amazement she stepped down—all the way down and into the puddle. She waded through the water just as if it hadn't been there at all, while Colonel Ottenberg came rushing forward, too late to help her though.

"Welcome to Ottenberg, my dear lady," I heard Colonel Ottenberg say in the loud voice he used when he was being mayor.

"Is this all there is of it?" she asked him. Oh, she had a schoolmarm voice all right. It carried just fine.

"As of this moment, ma'am, it is, but we're growing fast." He was smiling at her now.

Miss Willis turned around and looked over the welcomers as though taking a count of heads, then said, "My carpetbags and valises are on the stage."

"Yes, yes," said the colonel, sounding a little annoyed that she wasn't more impressed with his town. He told her, "My buggy's over there across the street. I'll take you to my house so you can rest up."

"Where is the school building, sir?" were her words.

"You'll see it on the way to my house."

Davey poked me in the ribs with his elbow. Schoolhouse, ha! Naturally I passed the poke on, poking Margaret, who scowled at me. The saloon owner's pug-nosed kid, Silas, let out a hooting, then a hissing sound. His eyes were glittering so much he looked like a cat with its gaze on a crippled mouse.

"You be quiet, Silas," Margaret told him. Silas was greatly in need of schooling in the estimation of just about everybody in Ottenberg. I thought he was horrible, but Mama said he should be pitied because he was "motherless." I could understand why, if she had to put up with him day and night.

He went on hissing while Miss Willis lifted up her already muddy skirts ever so carefully and picked her way across the street on narrow paths between puddles to the buggy. Her coming to town meant that Silas's fun and freedom would be over for the rest of the year, so he naturally hated the idea.

By now other people had stepped down out of the stagecoach, too. Three I recognized as frequent customers at our shebang. They'd gone out of town on business before winter hit the territory, when all travel came to an end. But the last one out of the coach door was a stranger.

A thin man, he was dressed in a pepper-and-salt suit that looked so new it was stiff. He walked calmly through the puddle, too, because Mr. Thompson still hadn't moved the coach. Once he was on dry land, the stranger looked around as if he was waiting for someone to meet him.

That someone turned out to be red-faced Doctor Haverford, whose grin was spread so wide that it showed off every one of his big gold teeth. I watched him come up to the young man, grab his hand, and shake it and shake it. For a minute I even thought he was going to hug him. And then the doctor pointed toward Mama and Papa up on the porch of our store. He and the stranger came toward them, laughing and talking. Naturally Davey and Margaret and I followed them out of curiosity.

On the porch, I heard Doctor Haverford tell Mama, "This is my young friend, J. Marah. He's going to be Doctor Marah one of these days real soon. He's come here to study some more and get practical experience under me before he takes his examinations for his M.D. degree any day now."

That was interesting. So—doctors had to pass tests, too.

"How do you do, Doctor Marah?" Mama said. "I'm Mrs. Foster. This is my husband, Albert, and these are our children, Hope and David."

I studied Doctor Marah while I nodded at him. He had pink cheeks and glossy dark hair and a broad smile. He surely was young looking. For a very interesting minute I thought he was going to kiss Mama's hand, something I'd read about once in a book but had never seen done to a lady. I was disappointed that he didn't. I sniffed Doctor Marah a bit, too, wondering if all doctors smelled of carbolic acid like Doctor Haverford. He didn't. He smelled of lilac or lavender or something like that. Lilac vegetal, maybe; we stocked that in the shebang.

"Doctor Marah's looking for a place to board," said Doctor Haverford. "I don't think the Big Bend Hotel's going to suit him very well. He's got a lot of my medical books to read, and it's too noisy there for him to concentrate. Besides he has a very delicate stomach and inclines toward dyspepsia. That kind of stomach appreciates good home cooking. How about you Fosters taking him in?"

I saw how Mama eyed Doctor Marah while she thought it over. Then she said, "Albert, what do you think?"

"Well, it's up to you mostly, Nora. You have to do the extra work."

"That's so." Mama nodded, then smiled. "Would five dollars a month suit you, Doctor Marah? We'd planned to have a boarder in any event come December, so we might just as well start a bit earlier. I hope you will like my cooking. It's nothing fancy, mind you. Perhaps you medical men expect dumplings and angel-food cake at every meal?"

"Not me, Mrs. Foster. Five dollars sounds just fine." He had a nice soft tenor voice. "What you offer suits me."

"He doesn't look one bit dyspeptic," Margaret whispered in my ear.

"Uh-huh." Well, I was suited, too, with Doctor Marah. I knew that Mama would cook fancier meals just because he was boarding with us. There was another reason why I favored having Doctor Marah in our place right now. We had room for only one boarder. If the new doctor stayed on with us, we could probably be spared having Miss Willis at Christmas. She'd have to move on to her January family in December. I couldn't honestly say that the way she'd sloshed through the puddle had made me feel easy in my mind about her. It appeared to me there was something determined in her. Maybe she was one of those fermenting ladies from Ohio all right.

Davey must have got the same idea because while she was wading he'd started to hum under his breath, "Pass Under the Rod." That's what some teachers used on unruly pupils—a rod.

What's more the girl who'd waited with Davey, Margaret, and me hadn't gone forward with the welcoming bouquet of flowers. The last I saw of her she was still clutching them in her fist and staring at the new teacher.

Only Silas had approached Miss Willis. He'd started to run after her so he could stick out his tongue and tell her the school was a chicken coop. But old Colonel Ottenberg, who was pretty nimble and strong for a man his age, fixed Silas just fine—and very swiftly, too. As Silas tried to duck under the colonel's arm to pull at the teacher's sleeve, the mayor grabbed him by the collar and plunked him down right in the middle of the puddle next to him. It all happened so fast that Miss Willis hadn't even noticed. I had to agree when the lady behind me said, "That was a very commendable action on the part of our mayor."

Dr. Haverford had laughed. But Doctor Marah watched, then looked away as if he was disgusted. That was the right word for Silas all right. *Disgusting!*

CHAPTER TWO

BY HALLOWEEN— OR BUST!

I decided quite soon that Doctor Marah was the sort of boarder families ought to take in, and it wasn't only because he'd displaced Miss Willis either. He lived in the little room behind our parlor next to Papa's and Mama's room and was quiet as a mouse. Either he had his nose in the medical books Doctor Haverford brought from his office, which was over the Union Town Saloon, or he was keeping office hours, or he was out on calls with the old doctor. When Doctor Marah was in for meals he ate everything Mama put on the table and always complimented her on whatever it was—even if it was mostly beans. Like everyone else in Ottenberg, we ate a lot of dried food because it was easy to ship and kept a long, long time.

Mama liked the young man, who wasn't really supposed to be called doctor yet because he was only a medical student. We called him Doctor Marah anyway. He didn't smoke bad-smelling cigars. Unlike Papa, he didn't even smoke a pipe. Doctor Marah was a good sort. He never kicked up a fuss about anything, not even about the amount of noise Davey and the O'Hare boy made when they ran through the store into our living quarters, and he never said a word when Manchester, the cat, took to sleeping on his bed every night.

I wished I could say that Miss Willis was easygoing like him.

Mama had been right as rain about the chicken-coop schoolhouse. Miss Willis hated it.

We all hated it once we'd started to school. And no wonder! Of course, it wasn't really big enough for ten people. Most schools put only two pupils together, but we had to sit three squeezed at a desk. Two kids at one desk were bad enough, because one could reach out and punch and pinch the other one. But three were just dreadful. I was in the middle between Margaret Libby and my own brother. No one at any school anywhere ought to have to share a bench with her own brother, particularly a left-handed one, who jabbed you in the ribs with his elbow every time he picked up his pencil. He sat so close there was hardly enough room for me to kick his ankle, to make him keep his elbow down. Margaret wasn't any fun either. She had a habit of humming joyfully to herself while she did arithmetic, almost as if she liked that awful subject.

There was a little black potbellied stove in the coop. It wasn't lit with a fire yet, but now that it was early September it would soon have to be. The stove was much too close to both the kids' desks and Miss Willis's. If we built a fire in it, we'd be roasted, and if we didn't, we could freeze to death come January. During the winter it could easily go down to thirty degrees below zero, the way it did in Idaho Territory. Oh, we Fosters knew this part of the country all too well. If it didn't snow by

Halloween, we would be very much surprised—and more than pleased.

Davey and I hadn't been within hearing distance, of course, when Miss Willis had first seen the chicken coop she was to teach in. But Mama had heard all about it from the wife of one of the school-board members who had gone off with Colonel Ottenberg and the new teacher the day she arrived.

No, Miss Leota hadn't been one bit taken with the new desks and her chair and the pupil benches one of the town carpenters had made out of prime lumber, or with the shiny blackness of the new stove Papa had sent for from Portland, Oregon. It hadn't impressed her at all that the hen roosts had been taken out and the whole coop whitewashed on the inside as well as on the outside or that Miss Emily Ottenberg had made an embroidered curtain out of turkey red cotton for the coop's window. Miss Willis wasn't fooled for a minute that her schoolhouse was something other than a once-upon-a-time chicken coop. Although she'd attended a fancy female academy, she'd lived for a time on a farm not far from Cincinnati, so she'd been in chicken coops before.

What she said to Colonel Ottenberg and the schoolboard member that first day, according to his wife Mrs. Prescott, was enough to singe any man's ears. Miss Willis called her husband, Mr. Prescott, and the city fathers and Colonel Ottenberg "men bent upon deliberate deceit, scoundrels of the deepest dye, monsters of misrepresentation and scalawags." I knew what *scalawag* meant because Papa used the word for Davey and the O'Hare boy quite often whenever they came out with some sass.

Yes, some of the men in Ottenberg were scalawags when it came to the matter of the schoolhouse. But this turned out to be one more battle Colonel Ottenberg won. Miss Willis stayed on because she'd signed a contract with the school board while still back in Ohio, suspecting nothing.

She could resign, of course, and go home to Ohio before the snows started, but as Mama explained to all of us at supper, "It's too late for her to get a teaching job anywhere else. Poor little dear, she's so miserable."

Poor me, was what I was thinking at that moment. I hadn't had an easy day at school. Margaret had hives and had scratched herself, making me want to scratch, too. Davey had sniffed and snuffled because he was coming down with a head cold. Added to that, Miss Willis was in a snapping mood. She'd snapped at every one of us by three o'clock and let us out early, saying she had a pain in her brain, which was probably a fancy Ohio way of saying we gave her a headache.

I watched Doctor Marah across the table while Mama was feeling sorry for Miss Willis. Doctor Marah had polished off everything on his plate and had rolled up his napkin ready to shove it into the napkin ring. He was as neat as could be, unlike Doctor Haverford, who always had flecks of tobacco all over his clothing.

Doctor Marah said to Mama, "I have a great deal of sympathy for Miss Willis. It's a shameful thing that she's stuck here in Ottenberg, teaching in a chicken coop." It sounded to me as if he didn't take much to the town either.

Davey asked him as he finished the last bit of his plum-preserve pie, "Do you want to fly the coop, too?"

I didn't think it was much of a joke. I was tired of jokes about coops. So I didn't laugh along with Papa.

Doctor Marah only smiled politely and said, "No, David, I have faith that things will change in Ottenberg one of these days."

"Not while Colonel Ottenberg is mayor," Mama said.

"More than likely not, Mrs. Foster."

Doctor Marah turned to Papa, who was lighting his pipe as Mama got up to pour the grown-ups some coffee. "Mr. Foster, I heard today that the next building the city expects to put up when the courthouse is finished is a town hall."

"Yes, sir, that's what it'll be. You can read all about the plans in tomorrow's paper. The editor came in today and told me all about it. The rumor's truth, in this case."

"That's what I thought." Dr. Marah took out his silver pocket watch, looked at it, sighed, and said to Mama, "Thank you for another excellent meal, Mrs. Foster. I don't think I want any coffee tonight. Please excuse me." He set his napkin ring down and left the table.

"Now what do you suppose was the matter with him?" asked Papa, taking his pipe from his mouth, surprised.

Mama gave him his coffee, then sat down with her cup. "I think perhaps I can guess what's wrong, Albert."

"Well, what is it? I never saw Marah beat such a fast retreat from the table. Usually he sits around and jaws for a while before he gets at that big pile of doctor books of old Haverford's."

"It's that town hall, my love."

I tensed myself when I heard those two little words. Mama kept quiet for a long minute looking down into her steaming coffee, then she said, "Albert, I believe that Doctor Marah and Doctor Haverford hoped that the men who run Ottenberg would use the tax money to build a hospital next. We need one badly, the way the town is growing. We've got ourselves a jail and the courthouse is coming along nicely. We're even being sent a judge from the territorial capitol next month. These buildings are perfectly fine, of course, and necessary at the moment."

"And made out of brick, too, Nora."

"Yes, brick and stone, very expensive things," Mama said softly. "But our schoolhouse is a made-over home for laying hens. It is a terrible place for the children to be in case of a fire. And we have no hospital. We have no real church, only a tent so far. And except for our family's set of Charles Dickens and the McGuffey Readers and some arithmetic texts at school and a Bible here and there, I doubt if there are any other books in town."

"Doctor Marah has those big books he's reading," Davey piped up.

Mother ignored him. "We need a library, too, Albert."

It was my turn to be wishful, so I added, "I'd like a museum while we're at it."

Papa laughed. "What would you put in it, Hope?"

Davey supplied the right answer, "Colonel Ottenberg and Miss Emily."

"Stuffed," I added.

Mama said, "That's scarcely a Christian sentiment, children. Besides, I don't think a museum is quite as vital as a school and a hospital at this moment."

Papa drew on his pipe, thinking. "You're right, Nora, I suppose, but the money's been voted for the town hall, so it will be the only building constructed before next spring. We can't very well build during the winter when the snow's deep. All we can do is finish the courthouse and town hall on the inside during bad weather." He reached over and patted Mama's hand, then told her, "It isn't as if it's going to be a big town hall, Nora. Just the right size for Ottenberg—sort of small."

"Yes, Albert. *Small!*"

During the second week of school in September something mighty interesting happened in our town. It certainly wasn't anything we'd been expecting. And it was something that involved all of us at school—not just something that had to do with grown-ups. That alone was enough to make it very, very exciting.

Early one afternoon, while Davey was reading out loud from his McGuffey Reader, stumbling over the big words the way he always did, there was a knock on the door of the coop.

Miss Willis looked up, exasperated. That's a big word I'd just learned and one I liked very much these days. It was easy to guess why she felt that way. She probably thought it was Miss Emily again, wanting to ask her something, the way Miss Emily did just about every day. Listening to her was a strain, because Miss Emily had a habit of talking all the time. Even when people were talking to her she kept right on. She never stopped.

I suppose that Miss Willis was eager for next month to arrive, when it would be time for her to move in with Reverend Gardiner and his wife. They were to be her October family. The Gardiners were only just married, but they were willing to board the teacher all the same. Mama said that Reverend Gardiner, who was interested in education, might be appointed by Colonel Ottenberg to the school board.

I was eager for October to roll around, too, so that Miss

Willis could shed herself of the Ottenbergs. I was hoping her disposition might improve living with the Gardiners.

While I was thinking of that during the second knock on the door, Miss Willis spoke to me, "Hope Foster, please see who is at the door."

I got up obediently, determined not to smile politely if it was Miss Ottenberg again. But this time, glory be, it wasn't! The caller at the chicken coop was a long-shanked man in a black frock coat and wide-brimmed hat. He was so tall that he had to stoop once he got partly inside the schoolhouse.

He had a very deep voice that boomed from wall to wall. "Is *this* supposed to be the schoolhouse?"

Miss Willis got up from behind her desk. I thought she looked startled. As for me, I went back to my seat, tramping on Davey on the way, so I could sit down.

"This place is a disgrace to the territory." Not waiting for Miss Willis to say a word, the man continued. "My name is Cassell, William Cassell. I am the Montana Territory Superintendent of Schools."

"Superintendent of Schools? There *is* one way out here!" Our teacher's eyes were shining with what I guessed was amazement, or maybe it was tears, though Miss Willis didn't strike me as the type to shed many tears.

"There is indeed, and I intend to see that Montana Territory becomes very well aware of it. I've just ridden in this morning from parts south of here. I left Helena some weeks ago, making the rounds of the places in the Territory that might conceivably have schools."

Miss Willis positively beamed at him. It was like daybreak. She said, "Well, sir, you have no idea how glad I am to see you. Shall we go outside and talk? As you can see, you are a bit too large to be accommodated with ease in here."

True. There wasn't room for Mr. Cassell to come all the way inside the coop. There wouldn't really be room for another first grader, in fact.

Miss Willis squeezed by us and as she reached the door told us, "Don't chatter and don't hit anyone. Study for your next recitation. I'll be right back and do remember that I'm just outside the door with the Superintendent of Schools."

It looked to me as if she was almost shooing Mr. Cassell off the coop step, so eager was she to talk with him.

Of course, none of us studied. We talked but in whispers, so neither of them could hear us. Though Miss Willis wasn't tall, she wasn't one bit shy about spanking a pupil's hands with her ruler when he or she disobeyed or sassed her. Still, I had to admit she was fair and didn't hit just anybody for anything. But she'd passed a couple of us under her rod all right—most of all Silas O'Hare, who always deserved it because he was an unholy terror.

And Silas didn't obey her now. He generally knew when to do his bedevilment. Being put down into the mud puddle by Colonel Ottenberg may have dampened his boots and britches, but not his ornery personality.

He got up off the bench and trampled over a third-grade girl and a second-grade girl to get at the window. They didn't dare yelp in pain for fear that Miss Willis would hear them and come back inside. They had to suffer in silence.

There he stood with his pug nose sticking through the curtains, spying. His dark hair stood up in spikes all over his head, like a porcupine. The town barber had told him last week that he wouldn't cut his hair anymore for fear he'd lose his temper over Silas's smart remarks and snip off the tops of his ears instead. Silas's shirt was dirty and his pants torn. I knew he didn't have a mother to look after him, but as far as I could see there wasn't one thing lost or forlorn about him. If there'd been any other boys his age in Ottenberg, Mama would have forbidden Davey to play with him.

While he was spying on the teacher, Margaret Libby whispered to me, "What's a State Superintendent of Schools?"

"I don't know, but he must be important if he comes from Helena." I knew that the capitol of the Territory had been Virginia City in the beginning, but just this year it had been switched to Helena.

Davey said hopefully but softly, "Maybe Miss Willis will let us out early because of her visitor."

Margaret told him, "Don't get your hopes up. My mother says 'Blessed are they that expect nothing for they shall not be disappointed.' "

I hated that saying. My father used it, too, and so did Doctor Haverford. It was just the sort of thing grown-ups loved to say.

I glanced at Silas, who was still peeking outside, hoping that someone would ask him what he was seeing so he could feel important. I hoped nobody would.

But then one of the girls he'd walked on to get to the window asked, "What are they doing out there?"

Silas turned around, pleased as all get-out to tell her with his lips all puckered up, "They're hugging and kissing each other."

She wouldn't believe him any more than I would, which

showed me she had sense even if she was only in the third grade. "I don't believe you, Silas. Miss Willis wouldn't kiss anybody!"

"Wouldn't she though? He's a man, ain't he?" Silas wanted to shout but didn't dare. That proved to me that Miss Willis and the Superintendent of Schools were nearby.

I whispered to him, "You're going to wind up in jail for all the rest of your days, if you don't get hung or drowned before."

He made a terrible face at Margaret and me, showing his lower teeth. "You'll be in the jailhouse before I will, you nanny goat."

After he'd cruelly insulted me with nanny goat, he turned to the window. Then all at once he came back, trampling the girls again, and sat down as if he'd done nothing wrong at all. What a horrible boy he was!

Just at that instant Miss Willis opened the door of the coop. She stood on the top step talking to Mr. Cassell. I thought she sounded more cheerful than I'd ever heard her as she said, "So you'll talk to Mayor Ottenberg and the others before you go on to look at the Horse Thief Creek School?"

I couldn't hear exactly what he said—his voice rumbled so—but by the way she acted, it must have been what she wanted to hear. She shut the door and came back to her desk, beaming. She told us as she sat down, "Children, there are going to be some alterations accomplished around this town, and very soon, too." Miss Willis pointed at me. "Hope Foster, tell me the meaning of what I just said."

As a storekeeper's daughter, I knew what *alterations* were. Mama altered too-long, ready-to-wear trousers for men customers all the time by cutting off the bottoms. I stood up the way I was supposed to. "I think you're saying there'll be some changes made." I grinned hopefully at her. She was in such a good temper that she might dismiss us early, after all.

Yet she didn't.

Margaret had had the right of it when she'd talked about expecting nothing and not being disappointed. So I wiped the smile from my face and sat down, wondering what the changes would be and what Mr. Cassell from Helena would have to do with them. He had certainly been fired up about the fact that Ottenberg had a made-over chicken coop for a schoolhouse. I wondered all the rest of that afternoon what he would have to say to Mayor Ottenberg and what Mayor Ottenberg would have to say to him.

That night Mr. Cassell came unexpectedly to our she-bang, along with Reverend Gardiner and Miss Willis. We hadn't expected visitors, so Davey and I had to put away our stereopticon viewer to clear a place at the table in the parlor and vacate two chairs. Mr. Cassell was scowling. Reverend Gardiner, who was a short man with a round, pink face, seemed more sour than I'd ever seen him, and his little dark-haired wife had tear marks on her cheeks. I stole a sharp look at our teacher while Davey went over to haul one of our cats off the sofa so Miss Willis could sit down in the spot the cat had got warm for her. Miss Willis hadn't been crying. She looked hopping mad, to my way of thinking.

First, the preacher introduced Mr. Cassell to my parents and apologized for dropping in. Then he started a conversation with Papa while Mama and Davey went out to the kitchen to make fresh coffee for everybody. "We've just come from seeing the mayor and the council and school board in a meeting specially called owing to Mr. Cassell's presence here," Reverend Gardiner said. "We demanded a proper schoolhouse."

"Did you get one?" Papa asked him.

"No, our visit came to naught."

I knew this was a fancy word for zero.

Mr. Cassell spoke up next. "It seems those who operate Ottenberg are firmly decided on erecting certain city buildings before they get around to a school fit for something other than laying hens."

"Yes, they are," agreed Papa. "A jail, a courthouse, and a town hall, all of them to be made out of brick."

"And the courthouse will be decorated with a statue of Justice, too," came bitterly from Mrs. Gardiner. She asked Papa, "Do you have any idea what that statue is costing the town?"

"No, ma'am, I do not. It wasn't ordered from my store."

"Well, let me tell you then. Miss Emily told me last week, after she got back from her trip. It will be shipped here direct from the sculptor's studio in San Francisco."

"What did it cost?" Papa was a patient man, ready to let Mrs. Gardiner tell him in her own time.

"Nine hundred dollars cash, a scandalous whole nine hundred dollars." She leaned back in her chair and folded her hands in her lap.

Papa whistled.

As for me, my jaw dropped in amazement.

Mr. Cassell, whose hands were resting on his knees, was looking directly at my father. "Mr. Foster, I am told that you are one of the leading citizens of this community and that you are the father of two pupils of this poor exploited woman."

I suspected he meant Miss Willis; she had pupils and Mrs. Gardiner didn't. I wasn't sure what *exploited* meant. When I had time and he wasn't in his room, I'd look the word up in the dictionary that Dr. Marah had brought with him from Maryland. I doted on dictionaries lately.

"Yes, sir, both Hope and David are still in school," Papa answered.

Cassell continued. "As a storekeeper, you must keep abreast of new developments in today's industry?"

Looking puzzled, Papa told him, "Yes, sir, I try to. What exactly did you have in mind?"

"I take it you know about the preconstructed buildings that can be purchased, shipped by train or wagon, and erected wherever the buyer chooses?"

Papa nodded. "I do. I received a folder from Chicago about that sort of thing not long past. Very interesting it was, too."

"Do you have it handy?"

"Maybe." Papa spoke to me over his shoulder. "Hope, the folder ought to be in the little drawer under the coffee-bean grinder."

I picked up the second kerosene lamp in the parlor, the one Mama had lit in honor of our guests, and went out into the shebang on the errand. The folder was just where Papa had said it would be. I glanced at it to make sure before I gave it to him. Yes, it had sketches of buildings in it.

"Well now, Mr. Foster," Cassell asked, "what does it have to say? Does it mention a schoolhouse in it?"

Papa got his spectacles from the table next to the pile

of slides of the Egyptian pyramids Davey and I had been looking at with the stereopticon viewer. "I'll run down the list of prices for you. Yep, here it is. A one-room house shipped out to this part of the West from Chicago costs $175, a railroad station costs $600, and a shebang like mine $800. Hmmn. Yes sir, here's a genuine schoolhouse, with a school bell included, for the sum of $1250. Expensive, huh?"

"Would that be made of wood or of brick?" Miss Willis wanted to know. Her voice sounded eager.

"Out of wood, ma'am. Everything for sale in this folder is made out of wood, including the church."

"A church? A church, too?" Reverend Gardiner spoke wistfully.

"That's right. A church costs $4000, but that price includes a spire."

"A spire!" Dilsey Gardiner breathed, wistful also. I doubted if she or her husband looked forward to holding church services all winter in a tent. It was a big tent, and I knew from living in them that tents could be cozy enough, but a tent couldn't compare to a church with a spire.

"Let's get back to the matter at hand," Mr. Cassell said. "I propose, Mr. Foster, that you send for one of those presawed schoolhouses at once."

Papa lifted his eyebrows. "What will I use for money? Will the Territory send me the money?"

Cassell shook his head. "Not right away, I'm afraid. The legislature has met this summer, voted money for schools and school necessities in other towns, dissolved, and the members have gone home. What I suggest to you is this. Send for the schoolhouse on a cash-on-delivery basis and, in the meantime, collect the money for it. You will be repaid, I assure you. When the legislature meets again in April, they will vote the funds for you. I'll see to that."

By now Mama had come back, sat down, and taken up her knitting while waiting for the coffee to boil. "Where do you suggest we get the money in Ottenberg, Mr. Cassell?" She'd come back just in time to hear Papa reading off the building prices in the folder from Chicago.

"However and wherever you can, Mrs. Foster. Theatricals, basket suppers, church fairs—the usual sort of thing."

"That would take years, Mr. Cassell."

Just then during the silence that followed Mama's statement, I heard the front door of the store open. It had to be Doctor Marah, who was the only person besides Papa to have a key. I went out to meet him while the people in the parlor started to talk about ways of raising money.

"It sounds to me as if your mother has guests, Hope," Doctor Marah told me. He was always very careful not to intrude on our family company.

"In a way they're guests." Then I told him what was going on.

He listened in a way I found thoughtful, and said, "You know, Hope, you children should be in that new schoolhouse by the time winter gets a good grip here—mid-November, at least. That place you're in is as drafty as a sieve. You could all catch galloping pneumonia. I think I know how you could come up with that much money within several weeks' time."

"You do?"

"I believe so, but it'll take some effort and courage on the part of the ladies of Ottenberg."

"The ladies?"

"Yes." He smiled at me by the light of the moon coming through one of the shebang's windows. "You'd better let me tell them myself."

So Doctor Marah and I went into the parlor together and when Papa introduced him to Mr. Cassell, the doctor-to-be spoke straight out, bolder than I'd ever heard him before. "Hope has informed me of your problem here. What I suggest is that Mr. Foster order a schoolhouse at once for immediate delivery. Inasmuch as the powers-that-be in Ottenberg are not willing to pay for it out of tax money, my advice is that all citizens who are interested in having a decent building for Ottenberg's children to attend school in go out and collect the necessary funds at the earliest possible moment."

"Collect?" asked Reverend Gardiner, who, in his job, made a specialty of collections.

Miss Willis, who'd been sitting rather crumpled on the sofa, came straight to the point. "From whom, Doctor Marah?"

"From the most prosperous places in Ottenberg. The saloons. At the last count I made there were thirty-six of them. But that was last week. There are probably thirty-eight by now."

"Saloons!" Mrs. Gardiner exploded. Her cheeks had turned pinkish.

Mama dropped a stitch in her knitting and the needles stopped dead in their tracks. Miss Willis was sitting bolt upright. As for me, I was rooted to the floor, amazed at the very thought.

Doctor Marah didn't seem to notice what was going on. He plowed right on. "Yes, Mrs. Gardiner, you heard me correctly. I think that if you start immediately, you could have a new school building erected by Halloween. Men in saloons are inclined to be quite generous when it comes to worthy causes. Perhaps that comes from a feeling of generosity or more possibly from the glowing effects of whiskey and beer."

No one said a single word. We were all too astonished.

I saw Davey standing behind Mama's chair with a look on his face that let me know he was tickled to death at the prospect. He had never been in a saloon but had always wanted the chance.

Doctor Marah said next, "I suggest that you get at it quickly, without a lot of harmful delay. As I say, in my opinion, you should aim to have the cash on hand by the thirty-first of October. The schoolhouse could go up very swiftly. You should gather donations while the weather's still good."

"Halloween or bust," Davey put in under his breath. Mr. Cassell, who was sitting next to Mama's chair, chuckled softly. The chuckle told us, each and every one, that the State Superintendent of Schools was on our side and that he had faith that the deed could be done.

"You good people of Ottenberg can manage it," Mr. Cassell told us in his deep rumble. "I have faith in you ladies and gentlemen. The whole Territory could be talking about Ottenberg's enterprise and remarkable interest in education by Christmas."

CHAPTER THREE

WIGGLING ALONG

There was a long moment of silence, while everybody thought about going into saloons asking for money. I decided that this wasn't anything anyone had ever done before; the idea took a lot of getting used to.

"Well, now," said Papa, who generally broke up the silences in our family when somebody was in a pout. Not that we were in a pout at the moment; it was just that we were shocked. Yet the more I thought about Doctor Marah's suggestion, the more breathtaking it became. Papa spoke to the young doctor, "You think mighty boldly."

"Drastic diseases call for drastic remedies," Doctor Marah told him. Our medical boarder turned his head to our teacher. "Miss Willis, I don't believe that you personally should go into saloons."

This irked her. "Why not, sir? After all I have to suffer with the children in that terrible chicken coop, too!"

"Because, Miss Willis, your collecting in the saloons could tempt the city fathers to accuse you of behavior that was not circumspect."

"What does that word mean?" Davey asked the doctor.

"Yes, tell him, Doc," came from Papa, who generally didn't pretend the way most grown-ups did that he knew what a big word meant when he really had no idea. That was one of the things I liked about Papa.

"It means to behave yourself," the minister, rather than Doctor Marah, explained. Of course, Reverend Gardiner would know the meaning of that word.

Miss Willis laughed a bitter sort of laugh that was really more like a snort. "I know what the word means, all right. I doubt if there's a schoolteacher, man or woman, in the entire country who doesn't. Teachers never go into saloons, because teachers do not drink alcohol in public."

Davey could ask some very shocking questions at times. "Does that mean that they drink where nobody can see them?"

"Davey!" scolded Mama.

"No, Mrs. Foster, don't chide David. Many a teacher has drowned his sorrows over things far less annoying than a chicken coop for a schoolhouse." Miss Willis nodded toward Mr. Cassell. "I have not taken to drink as yet and have no such intentions." She frowned, shaking her head. "You know, it isn't right, though, that the rest of you make the saloon visitations, and I don't help."

"The doctor is right, Miss Willis," said the Superintendent of Schools.

"Yes, I suppose he is." Miss Willis gave Mr. Cassell a rare smile.

I guessed that she hadn't found much to smile about in Ottenberg so far, but there seemed to be some improvements ahead for her—if we could only collect enough for a school. My, but $1250 was a lot of dollars!

Mama picked up her coffee cup, took a deep swallow, and said, "It's the thirteenth of September now. It seems we'd better start on our project at once."

"We'll have to get a wiggle on." This was the first time I'd really said anything in front of all those grown-ups.

It just burst out of me, because the more I thought about it the more interesting and thrilling Doctor Marah's idea became. I completely forgot myself in front of Mr. Cassell and Miss Willis. Papa had always cautioned me about talking out of turn in adult company, though he never had come straight out and said, "Children should be seen not heard," the way Margaret Libby's father always did.

Mrs. Gardiner backed me up right off. "Yes, Hope, get a wiggle on is correct." She turned to her husband next to her. "What about calling the Ladies Aid and the Altar Society together tomorrow at our house?"

"Dilsey, dear, Miss Ottenberg belongs to both organizations," Reverend Gardiner said, blowing out his cheeks.

"She will be invited to come to the saloons with us, Matthew. If she refuses to join us, that will be her choice."

I saw the little dimple in one of Doctor Marah's cheeks deepen as he told the minister's wife with a grin, "No, you certainly must not leave any of the Ottenbergs out of your invitation."

Because it wasn't a Saturday or Sunday, Margaret Libby and I didn't get to go to the ladies' meeting at the Gardiners'. But we talked about it at morning recess.

"I doubt if my mother will do it even for a new schoolhouse," she told me. Mrs. Libby was dead set against alcohol.

I couldn't see why that should stop Mrs. Libby from collecting cash in saloons. She wasn't going to drink in them—only ask for money. But I didn't tell Margaret what I was thinking. There wasn't any cause to annoy the Libby family. They might be inclined to make a donation. I hadn't told Mama or Papa yet, but I'd been thinking that other people besides saloon drinkers and saloonkeepers might be inclined to chip in for a new schoolhouse. We could even put a big glass on the counter of our shebang with a sign for it asking people who wanted to give donations for the new school building to drop their dollars and dimes in. I didn't think anyone but kids should put in less than a dime.

I told Margaret, "Oh, I'm sure there will be other ways for people to raise money and your family will be happy to help with those, won't they?"

"Probably so, Hope."

Mama reported on the meeting at the supper table after dessert. Seven ladies of the Ladies Aid and six of the Altar Society had said they'd help collect for the school. The other ladies were afraid their husbands wouldn't let them go into one saloon, let alone into thirty-eight time after time, until the $1250 was collected. But because they believed in the cause, they were willing to risk their husband's wrath.

"How do you plan to go about it, Nora?" asked Papa. "Will you tackle all thirty-eight dens of drink at once?"

"No, Albert. We shall go every other night to the same place, and rotate our visits in groups of twos and threes. That way we shall give each other moral support."

"Good idea. Then the men won't get tired of seeing the same old faces all the time." Papa nodded at her over last night's copy of the *Oracle*.

"The ladies who will be taking up a collection for the new school building are not old, my love."

"All right, I'll grant you that." I saw him raise the paper higher and knew by that gesture that he was hiding a smile behind it. Mama never did like hearing that word *old*. I couldn't see why ladies felt that way, but I supposed when I got to be her age I'd find out.

Just then Doctor Marah came between the long, red plush curtains from the store. He was carrying Essex in his arms. He'd probably scooped him up off a counter top as he'd come in. The cat liked napping on counters while he watched mice run by below on their way to gnaw at the grain. Doctor Marah had missed supper tonight. Probably he'd been out on a call somewhere. He never talked much about his medical matters.

He sat down across from Mama, settling the cat on his lap, and asked, "How did you fare today in your meeting, Mrs. Foster?"

She told him what she'd already told Papa, Davey, and me, but added, "I'm to begin Saturday night at the Shoo-Fly Saloon along with Mrs. Gardiner and Mrs. Prescott. From there we three go on to the Dolly Varden and the Oro Fino Saloons. The rest of the ladies will cover the other saloons. We all drew lots to see which saloons we'd go to."

"The Shoo-Fly? Isn't that Tom O'Hare's place?"

"It surely is," Papa put in.

The doctor looked serious as he said, "Mr. O'Hare's the real reason why I missed supper. Doctor Haverford and I had to patch up two of the Shoo-Fly's customers who'd got into a fight. Mr. O'Hare had dealt with them in his own way, and because of that we were sent for—or rather Haverford was—I tagged along."

Papa asked while Davey listened, hanging on every word, "What did O'Hare do? How did he deal with the fight?"

"With a gun?" blurted Davey.

There was one thing you could say for sure about Ottenberg. It wasn't exactly full of books, but it had more pistols and rifles and shotguns that I'd seen even in Idaho Territory, which was also considered the "wilds of civilization." Papa did a good trade in selling Winchester rifles and Colt revolvers, although he claimed he didn't much fancy the gun business. Gunshots at night made Ottenberg's one street a mighty noisy place. It wasn't that the miners were out so much to kill one another; the men were just full of good spirits and bad whiskey, according to Doctor Haverford.

Doctor Marah gave my brother a melancholy look. "Not this time, David. There's entirely too much of that sort of thing out here as it is. Too many guns and far too little sense about them, though most of the men seem to be just skylarking. The quarreling miners in the Shoo-Fly did have weapons, but luckily they hadn't got around to using them yet. So Mr. O'Hare used a bung starter to break up the fight. Not gently but all too well, in fact. He hit one miner on the back of the skull and the other on the side of his head."

I knew what a bung starter was. It was a sort of wooden hammer more than anything else, used to open barrels. One of those striking a person's head ought to discourage him from getting into any more trouble.

Mama said, "Well, I find it rather hopeful that Mr. O'Hare's not feeling the need of using anything worse than a bung starter to keep the peace in his place. I don't know the gentleman, but he sounds like a reasonable person."

"A mallet on the skull isn't exactly what I'd call reasonable, Mrs. Foster, even when necessary," Doctor Marah put in calmly, still stroking the cat, who doted on him. "Don't expect too much of O'Hare."

"But Mr. O'Hare has a poor little child in that chicken coop," Mama said.

"And that's where that small scalawag belongs, too, in a coop if not a cage," said Papa, as he handed the newspaper to the doctor. "Look at the bottom of the first page, Doc. There's a judge due to come here and take up residence soon. We're getting to be a real town, and with two doctors, five lawyers, an undertaker, a dentist, and some fine brick and stone municipal buildings."

"And what a mayor!" I said. Then I asked Mama all at once, "Was Miss Ottenberg at your meeting?"

"No, she went out four days ago on the stagecoach bound for Portland, to look at some hardware and furniture for the courthouse." I saw how Mama glanced at Papa out of the corner of her eye. He'd expected to get the furnishings and spittoon business for the town buildings, but it seemed the mayor and city fathers and Miss Emily thought differently.

Trying to sound unconcerned in front of Doctor Marah, Papa went on, "We've almost got ourselves a city now."

"And with thirty-eight saloons in it!" Mama started her chair rocking. There was a look of contentment on her face. I'd never have believed she'd speak of all those saloons as if they were good things. "Ah yes," she murmured to herself. "Our first stop will be Mr. O'Hare's Shoo-Fly. He will understand what we are doing, and perhaps he will influence the other publicans."

I'd heard a lot about Republicans but nothing about "publicans." I wondered if they were the same thing, but then I remembered Silas's saying that Mr. O'Hare was a Democrat. Later I'd go look up the meaning of *publican* in Doctor Marah's dictionary. I was sure I could spell it and was pretty sure that it meant saloonkeeper, but it would be fun to find out for sure.

The doctor spoke to Mama. "I wish you luck with O'Hare. Would you happen to have any coffee left in the pot?" He put Essex down onto the floor.

Mama asked as she got up, trailed out to the kitchen by the cat, "Will you go out with us Saturday night, Doctor?"

"I think it would be wiser if you went without me. I had hard words tonight with O'Hare about his overuse of the bung starter, and he called me a 'beardless pup and a meddling nincompoop.' My attitude toward his violence seemed to annoy him greatly. I'd be delighted to contribute ten dollars toward the building fund, however."

Ten dollars! That was twice what he paid Mama each month for board. We Fosters certainly didn't think of him as a nincompoop or pup, though come to think of it, he didn't have any beard. He was neat as brand-new pin, not even mustachioed. The town barber sure must do right by him every time he shaved and trimmed his hair, or maybe Doctor Marah was an expert shaver, himself. For a time I'd been concerned that Doctor Haverford's careless ways of living would rub off on Doctor Marah, and he'd get to act like an old bachelor, too, growing a beard and sleeping in his clothes. But so far he'd kept his standards up just fine.

Mrs. Gardiner and Mrs. Prescott came together to get Mama at eight o'clock sharp on Saturday night. Mrs. Prescott was a tall, thin lady with fair hair and a long freckled face, not one bit pretty but very pleasant. Right now she looked worried about something. So did the minister's wife, Mrs. Gardiner, who'd put on her Sunday-go-to-meeting, rose-flowered bonnet, tied under her chin with peach-colored ribbons. I supposed she wore it to give herself courage.

I noticed Mama had put on her best bonnet, too, the one with violets and snowdrops mixed all together over the crown. She was wearing her fancy purple velvet gown with the fringed polonaise.

"Well, ladies, are we ready?" Mama wanted to know, as she stood in our parlor, drawing on her white gloves.

"I'm not at all sure, Nora." Dilsey Gardiner's voice was quivering.

"Stop wavering, my dear," Mama said to Mrs. Gardiner.

Mrs. Prescott added, "The faster a thing is started, the faster it's finished." She always favored mottoes.

I was standing up because grown-ups were in the parlor, and Mama said, "Hope, go out, please, and tell your father to come here and see us off."

I knew where Papa was, playing cribbage with Doctor Marah out in the shebang. The ladies had come to our side door—the way they usually came when calling on Mama—rather than traipse through the store. Out I went, interrupting the game, and after Papa and Marah had laid down their cards, we all returned together.

The doctor, who was smiling, said, "I must say that you ladies look determined enough to get your way in anything you want. You look to me as if you could lick your weight in proverbial wildcats."

"Well, kittens perhaps," Mrs. Gardiner said.

"Good luck, ladies," said Papa. Then he told Mrs. Gardiner and Mrs. Prescott, "I ordered the schoolhouse C.O.D. today by mail."

Mrs. Prescott breathed, "The deed is done! The die is cast!"

I watched as the three of them exchanged looks. It was time to go. Mrs. Gardiner sighed as she started bravely for the door in the wake of Mrs. Prescott.

"Wait a minute, please." Doctor Marah sounded on the brink of laughing. "Why don't you take Hope with you?"

"We have hope already," said Mrs. Prescott looking bewildered. She didn't have much imagination. I'd noticed that people who fancied mottoes generally don't.

"Hope?" Mama understood and turned to look at me.

"Yes, Mrs. Foster. There can be some pretty rough men in those saloons, you know. What they might be tempted to say to you I'm quite certain they wouldn't say in front of a child."

A child—me a child? I was ready to tell them that I had just turned thirteen and certainly was no child. I glared at Marah, but he wasn't looking at me.

Mama asked me, "Do you want to go along?"

I pondered for a minute, then nodded. "Yes, I'll get my bonnet, too." After all it was right that I should go. I spent long hours cooped up in that chicken house. I could tell better than anyone here how bad it was in there. It was my duty to go. More than that, here was my opportunity to see what went on in saloons. The only views I'd ever had I got from peeking under the swinging doors when I passed one.

Doctor Marah's words floated after me. "Hope, find something that you can collect money in. The ladies have forgotten to bring anything with them."

I stopped as I reached in my room for my bonnet, which was dangling from its strings on a peg. As I tied it on, I tried to think of something to collect money in. The money would be all coins, of course. People in the territories didn't believe that paper money was real. The container would have to be strong enough to hold metal. I left my room and went to Mama's and Papa's bedroom.

I wished Mrs. Gardiner would have had the good sense to bring along a wicker collection plate from the church. I considered Mama's sewing basket. No, too light. Papa's spittoon beside the bed was clean but pretty vulgar for such a noble purpose. The wash basin was so large that it would make us look greedy. There it was—Papa's shirt-collar box. It was made of plain black tin, with a tight-fitting lid, and was exactly the right size. Because I knew he wouldn't mind my taking it, I dumped the collars and collar buttons onto the top of the chest of drawers.

With the box in my hands and my bonnet tied tightly under my chin, I rushed out to join the ladies in the parlor. I even made a little curtsy as I gave the box to Mrs. Prescott, who was the oldest lady there and the wife of one of the first members of the school board to be appointed. The Prescotts were noble people. Mr. Prescott had forgiven Miss Willis for what she had called him. He seemed to understand now why she'd said "scalawags," among other things, when she first saw the schoolhouse coop.

"Onward, ladies!" said Papa, as he turned to go back to

the cribbage game with Doctor Marah, who had already left the parlor.

It was a nice night, though the sharp tweak in the air would let anybody who wasn't a stranger to the Territory know that autumn was truly on the way.

Mrs. Prescott must have felt the tweak also. She repeated what Davey had said, "Halloween or bust!"

"Pray to heaven that we don't have an early winter," said Mrs. Gardiner, who'd been born and raised in Wisconsin and who knew about long, cold winters, too.

"Yes, that could really ruin our hopes, Dilsey," Mama agreed.

I wanted to say that Mrs. Gardiner ought to take up the problem of the weather with her husband, since praying was in his line of business, but I didn't. The older I got, it seemed, the harder it was for me to keep my mouth shut when I had something on my mind. I could barely wait until I was old enough to let out my thoughts and opinions. Right now I'd like to tell Doctor Marah that he should have come with us. After all, the idea to collect in saloons had been his, and he'd also thought of the money box and of my going, too.

As we all stood beside the shebang hesitating to step out into the street, I listened to the sounds of Ottenberg on a Saturday night. Oh, that was something to hear! All thirty-eight piano players seemed to be playing a different tune. They were all so loud and so mixed up that I couldn't make out any one of them for certain.

"Remember, ladies," said Mrs. Prescott from in front of me. "Music has charms to soothe the savage breast." Yes, that had to be another motto.

"Oh, I hope so, Annabella," Mrs. Gardiner replied.

Mrs. Prescott stepped out onto the newly nailed-together boardwalk. One by one we followed her to a spot in front of our store. There we encountered Colonel Ottenberg walking along with hands folded behind his back, busy being the important mayor. He took off his black army hat and bowed deeply. "Good evening, my charming ladies."

"Good evening, Mr. Mayor," they said one after the other. As for me, I didn't say a word. He'd never said one to me. Besides, I doubted if he'd included me in his greeting anyway.

He stood there with his hat off, looking up at the stars and the waning moon. "Beautiful night, isn't it?"

Just at that moment a man came riding past us on horseback yelling. Two other riders came shouting after him. Dodging the holes in the street, the three of them raced down to one of the saloons at the end, reined in their horses, and jumped down.

"Yes, it—" but Mrs. Gardiner never finished agreeing, because just then the swinging doors of the nearest saloon opened and a man was pitched out to the sidewalk where he landed on his face. He didn't move a muscle.

"—is beautiful," Mrs. Prescott finished Mrs. Gardiner's sentence. Just as she did, somebody somewhere fired a rifle. You could hear it echoing around the hills behind Ottenberg.

The mayor gave up after that. He shifted his gaze from the sky to the new jail. He didn't ask, as I'd expected, what brought our foursome out strolling on a Saturday night, when most ladies stayed safely behind closed doors. He simply put his hat back on and muttered, "Good night." Then he crossed the street full of dried-up ruts and holes to take up a position in front of the jail. From there Colonel Ottenberg had a fine view of the new courthouse, which was already finished on the outside and half done on the inside, and of the rising walls of the building that was to be the new town hall. I supposed the sight of his fancy new buildings comforted him.

It certainly didn't comfort Mama, who burst out with, "Look at that old coot across the way. I wish to heaven I could vote, so that next time he's up for office I could cast my vote against him."

Mrs. Prescott spoke to me, not Mama. "Hope, did you know that women can vote in Wyoming Territory, right next door? They've had the vote for six long years."

I knew that, of course. Miss Willis had talked about it in school when we sixth-graders had studied about America. Davey hadn't been much interested, but little as he was Silas surely had been. He'd said straight out, "Women shouldn't ever vote." And he'd scowled as he spoke.

I'd scrooched around on my bench to glare into his face, and Miss Willis hadn't tried to stop me as I'd demanded, "Silas, what makes you say such a mean thing?"

"Because my pa says it. He says that when women can vote, they'll vote right away to stop men from drinkin' whiskey and beer, and when that happens, he'll go out of the saloon business."

"What's wrong with that?" I asked him. "My mother says there's a saloon in Ottenberg for every twenty-five persons, man, woman, and child. And women and children don't go into saloons!"

"You bet they don't, nanny goat." Silas had very dark blue eyes, set deep in his face.

"Hope Foster! Silas!" Miss Willis wisely tried to stop

us before I grabbed a handful of Silas's hair and slammed his face into the top of his desk, so full of wrath was I.

I was remembering that run-in with Silas, as Mama and the other ladies and I started toward the Shoo-Fly Saloon, which was on the same side of the street as our shebang. It wasn't much of a place on the outside, but then no saloon in Ottenberg was. The Shoo-Fly was also made of wood with a false front. The words:

> The Shoo-Fly Saloon
> Spirits and Beer
> Billiard Parlor

were painted on the front in black-and-green letters.

The four of us stopped outside. I watched Mrs. Prescott as she took the top off the collar box, squared her shoulders, and said, "Take a deep breath, all of you. It clears the head and lungs. Mrs. Foster says that Doctor Marah recommends it before starting any unusual or demanding undertaking."

I did as she said, of course, wondering if this meant the ladies would march in singing hymns, for deep breathing was the same exercise church people did before they sang in the choir Sunday mornings.

Mama parted the swinging doors and entered first, walking as tall as she could. Mrs. Gardiner and Mrs. Prescott went in after her. Taking another deep, dizzying breath, I followed them into my very first saloon.

I couldn't say much for the Shoo-Fly. It was only one big room. At one end was a dark-colored wooden bar with a mirror behind it, and a lot of bottles set on shelves under the mirror. I saw several unpainted wooden tables and a long narrow one with a green top and little colored balls on it. I knew it was the billiard table. A few chairs were set out on a sawdust-covered floor. A rickety little stairway led upstairs over the bar. From what Davey had told me that was where Silas and his father lived. There was also an outside staircase leading to their living quarters.

As for the Shoo-Fly's people and the saloon decorations, I got only a glimpse of them. The men were miners and businessmen—most I recognized by sight—and they were standing around at the bar or sitting at the tables. Nobody was playing billiards. Nobody seemed to be doing much of anything, as they listened to a runty bald-headed man playing "Nelly Gray" on the piano. It seemed to me that everyone looked more sad than gay, and I didn't think that was only because the song was so mournful. Nobody was paying any mind to the elk, grizzly bear, and deer heads on the walls, or to the paintings of plump ladies in white dresses with wreaths of red roses on their heads, and bunches of purple grapes in their hands, leaning on casks of beer. The painted ladies were looking down on the men smiling, but they were the only faces in the whole place that looked happy.

I didn't know whether Mrs. Prescott as the wife of a school-board member or Mama would speak up first.

And thanks to Mr. O'Hare, a gray-haired, gray-bearded man I'd seen once or twice inside our store, I never found out. He'd been leaning on his bar, too, but the minute he spotted the four of us standing around just inside the doors, he came roaring out from behind the bar. It all happened so fast I couldn't understand at first what he was yelling at us. He took Mrs. Prescott by one arm and Mrs. Gardiner by the other, swung them around, propelled them to the doors—and shoved them outside. Quick as a wink he was back for Mama and me. Grabbing us the same way, I heard him say, clear as could be, "You blasted, bedamned women, you get out of here. I keep a good saloon and I won't have no females in here."

My, but he was powerful. In no time at all Mama and I had joined Mrs. Prescott and Mrs. Gardiner on the boardwalk. All told, we hadn't been inside the Shoo-Fly for more than ninety seconds.

And we hadn't collected one red cent for the new schoolhouse!

CHAPTER FOUR

COWARD

"Well, I never in my whole life!" Mrs. Prescott exploded, as she settled her bonnet more firmly on her head.

"Good heavens," came weakly from Dilsey Gardiner, who as a minister's wife was sure calling on the proper place.

I didn't say anything. Neither did Mama. We Fosters just stared at one another.

"Now what will we do?" Mrs. Gardiner asked the other two ladies.

"I really don't know." Mama turned around to stare in disbelief at the saloon doors, still swinging back and forth.

Mrs. Prescott spoke up finally. "Nora, we should go right back in there. We should have the courage of our convictions and let nothing daunt us." Her dander was up all right. She was trembling all over with fury.

It was finally time for me to say a motto, too. "Blessed are they that expect nothing, for they shall not be disappointed." I pointed at the empty collar box in Mrs. Prescott's hands.

"You are faint of heart, Hope."

Perhaps. Or maybe I was just being smarter than the ladies. I'd had a very good look at Mr. O'Hare's face as he rushed us out of the Shoo-Fly. His hair was gray, but it was still spiky like his son's, and he certainly had Silas's horrid little eyes. Because I knew Silas, I figured I knew his pa. "Like son like father" was a good motto, too.

Mama spoke after a long period of thinking. "There are two other establishments on our list for tonight yet. Let's go there while we reconsider the Shoo-Fly."

"All right, Nora. We'll brave them first," agreed Mrs. Prescott.

Little Mrs. Gardiner didn't say anything. She only pulled her shawl tighter about her as if she were cold. I don't know how the others felt, but I felt that Mr. O'Hare's eyes were boring holes in our backs as we walked up the street. More than likely he was laughing at us and probably making his customers laugh at us, too. It was a very uncomfortable feeling, which after a while changed to anger. Mr. O'Hare didn't have to be so rude about getting us out of his place. He could've told us to go, instead of grabbing us and shoving us out bodily.

I was wary of the other saloons now, but the good welcome we received at the Dolly Varden, which was named both after a trout and a girl in a Charles Dickens' novel, and the Oro Fino, renewed the courage of all four of us. Once we'd explained our mission the men were very generous about dropping coins into Papa's collar box.

One of the Oro Fino dance-hall ladies, who wore a green spangly dress and had bird plumes in her bright red hair, began to weep over the idea that we kids had such a bad school building. She even took the collar box from Mrs. Prescott and went from miner to miner, calling each by name. "Cough up, honey, for them poor little chicks of kids."

After thanking her, we left the Oro Fino and went back to the shebang to count our collection. Nobody suggested we go back to the Shoo-Fly for a second try. Mrs. Prescott even crossed the street farther down, rather than pass in front of it. I couldn't say that I wasn't thankful to her.

Inside the store we found Davey along with Silas. The boys had been into the pickle barrel, which I supposed was no worse than my getting into the candy jars with Margaret. I gave Silas, who certainly wasn't any friend of mine, my most evil look and told him in front of Mama and the other ladies, "Your pa wouldn't even let us speak our piece about what we wanted in his saloon. He threw us out. And he laid hands on us to do it."

"Bodily," agreed Mrs. Gardiner.

Silas bit off a big hunk of one of our dills before he said, with his mouth full, of course, "My pa don't hold with womenfolks goin' into the Shoo-Fly."

"Why not?" I demanded before anyone else could ask him politely. Politeness was just wasted on him. "Did your pa think we wanted to drink anything in that awful place or play his billiards?"

Silas shrugged. "Maybe you might." He swallowed the pickle bite. "How would Pa know? Anyhow, he don't ever serve women and don't have dance-hall girls around neither. There's even a sign up over the bar that says *Female Trade Not Wanted Here.* Didn't you read it? If you'd've asked me first before you took off tonight, I'd told you not to go to the Shoo-Fly."

I countered with, "You knew what we planned to do." That was true. He had listened at school while we talked about the ladies going out Saturday night. I pointed my finger at him, wishing I could jab him in the eye with it. "You could have come out with it before now. Just for that you can go over to the Shoo-Fly and collect from your pa for the school. We never even got the chance to tell him what we wanted."

At these words, Silas jumped off the top of the pickle barrel and pointed to his chest with the pickle he had in his other hand. "Not me. My pa'd thrash the tar out of me if I did that."

I asked Mama another question. "Do you think Davey could go?"

She asked Davey, "What about it, David?"

He looked doubtful for a minute, but then he took the box, which Mrs. Prescott gave him after she'd dumped the money out on our yard-goods counter. I knew he had always wanted to get a good look at the inside of a saloon, too, but still he was dragging his feet when he left the shebang. Silas went dashing after him, eager to get away from us. But when he got to the door, he turned around and stuck out his tongue.

"Urchin!" was Mrs. Prescott's only word, but it was too mild.

My brother was back even quicker than I had expected. Wearing a long face, he tilted the box so all of us could see: it didn't have even a dime in it. "Mr. O'Hare said that the Shoo-Fly wasn't any place for kids either," he said.

"Did he throw you out, too," Mama asked him with an angry red color rising in her cheeks.

"No, but he held one of the doors open for me, so I had to leave fast. I sure didn't get much of a look at the place."

"At least, he wasn't manhandled," said Mrs. Gardiner.

"Apparently not." Mama glanced over my head at the big old grandfather clock we'd dragged all the way from

Oregon with us and told the ladies, "I've got the coffeepot on. We'll have coffee and doughnuts while we wait out here for our sisters."

I knew these sisters were really the other church ladies who were out collecting at the remaining thirty-five saloons. I surely hoped they hadn't run into saloonkeepers like Mr. Tom O'Hare. Come to think of it, there hadn't been ladies in the Shoo-Fly for the miners to talk and dance with. I wondered why and when O'Hare had turned against women. After all, Silas had to have had a mother. Anyhow, there was no arguing the fact that O'Hare had behaved very rudely toward all of us.

So we waited for the sisters. When they finally straggled in, Doctor Marah, Papa, and Miss Willis were on hand to greet them. They sure had a strange group of things to collect cash in: a wicker basket, a soup bowl painted with pink roses, a measuring cup, and even a ribbon-decorated tambourine. Its owner explained it by saying, "I played a gypsy in a theatrical production back home in Connecticut when I was a girl. I knew if I hung onto it long enough, I'd find a use for it." After she'd put the money inside it onto our counter for Mama to tally, she shook it so that the metal things along the side clinked. Because Mama was the treasurer of the Ladies Aid, she'd got the job of counting up the schoolhouse fund. And because Papa was married to Mama, he got the job of keeping the cash. Luckily we had a heavy metal safe in the shebang.

Altogether the saloon money came to nearly $100 in silver and gold. There were also a couple of tiny gold nuggets that we could get weighed in the assayer's office.

As I'd predicted, there wasn't one piece of paper money at all.

Papa shook his head admiringly over the money. "I have to admit that the drinking men of Ottenberg are mighty generous." He put the money into a metal box and took it to the safe.

Miss Willis had watched as every coin was counted. Now she said, "Yes, at this rate we'll have all the money we need before the thirty-first of October without any trouble at all." She looked over at Doctor Marah and said, "Your idea seems to be a very workable one." Oh, she seemed to think that all had gone smooth as silk, but she hadn't heard about the Shoo-Fly yet. We'd agreed earlier not to talk about it or Mr. O'Hare until all the ladies had come back.

After they had arrived, Mama told the story, but she got some help from Mrs. Prescott and Dilsey Gardiner and some noises and facial expressions that fit their tale from me. To wind up the story the way it should be, I grabbed Mama and Mrs. Prescott and showed them how Mr. O'Hare used bodily force to throw us out of his saloon.

Most of the ladies exclaimed, "Well, I never!" That was about the strongest expression ladies I knew seemed to use in public. I thought it was pretty feeble, myself.

Miss Willis had more to say on the subject. "That O'Hare man has a child in the chicken coop. He should have been delighted that you ladies were striving to get a better environment for his Silas."

Environment. I knew that word from having looked it up in Doctor Marah's dictionary. Miss Willis used it quite a bit at school when she was referring to Ottenberg and the chicken coop. I had thought at first it was a cuss word because of the way she used it. But then I found out what it really meant—which was nothing more than what was around a person wherever he was.

Mama had kept very calm. She said, "Miss Willis, that is the way of it. Mr. O'Hare simply will not permit females or children in the Shoo-Fly."

"What about men then?" The teacher's eyes had fallen on Doctor Marah, who was leaning against a counter. He didn't seem to hear her. He went on stroking his chin and staring up into the ceiling of the shebang, where Papa hung harness pieces, horse collars, and other things to save space on the floor.

Papa caught part of what she was saying as he came from the safe. "What about me, Miss Willis?" He was grinning at her the way he sometimes grinned at small, helpless ladies when they got mad. It was an annoying habit of his.

Miss Willis didn't get mad, but she came straight to the point the way schoolteachers were inclined to. "Mr. Foster, why don't you and Doctor Marah and Doctor Haverford and Reverend Gardiner go to this saloon and ask Mr. O'Hare and the other men inside for contributions to the new school building."

Papa said slowly, "Well, I suppose we could do that. How about it, Doc?" He turned to face Doctor Marah.

I watched Marah shrug his shoulders. "I doubt if I'll be any asset to you. O'Hare and I have had words already, but if you want me to come along with the rest of you, I'll come."

"Good, then we'll slate it for tomorrow night if no medical emergency comes up for you and Haverford."

Marah nodded while the ladies nodded, too, glad of the men's offer of help. The women had made their plans to hit the saloon trail again tomorrow evening. Personally I had my doubts about collecting every single night until Halloween. It might annoy the other saloonkeepers and miners and could even kill the goose that was about to lay the golden egg. I surely hoped all of the other ladies were making it as clear as Mama was that our collecting was "only temporary."

Then Doctor Marah asked my mother and Mrs. Prescott, "Ladies, what do you plan to do if Mr. O'Hare says no to us, too?"

"Well, I don't exactly know, Doctor." Mrs. Prescott was wrinkling her brow with thought. "I suppose we shall simply forget about him."

I said, "But if we get the money for a new school, Silas will get to go to it, too, and his pa won't have helped us."

Papa told me, "That's true enough, Hope, but that's the way things work out in this old world a great deal of the time. A few folks work very hard, and their work benefits those who won't raise a finger. In life, it's generally only a few who really go out and cut the mustard."

"Amen to that," came from Mrs. Prescott.

The last person there I expected to more or less agree with me was Mrs. Gardiner. But she said, "Mr. O'Hare shouldn't be allowed to get away with such rude and ruffianly behavior." I guessed that she hadn't been married to her minister-husband long enough to learn to turn the other cheek. She wanted O'Hare to pay for what he'd done. So did I. I was breathing out revenge. My arm hurt where he'd grabbed me.

Doctor Marah chimed in too. "I agree with Mrs.

Gardiner. He should not get away with it, but it seems he has."

Miss Willis got back into the conversation. "I can't help you do it, of course, Doctor Marah, because of my delicate position, but back in Cincinnati I saw some very effective action taken against a storekeeper who behaved badly. The ladies were in a great ferment about him, let me tell you."

"What did he do?" I asked, wondering what had made the Cincinnati women "ferment."

"He beat his wife."

I said, "Aha!" This answer called for that very powerful word.

There were quite a few more ahas from the sisters. Then Mama asked the important question, "What did the Ohio ladies do?"

"They all brought chairs with them and sat down in a body in front of the storekeeper's establishment. They never said a single word to him or to anyone else—or even to each other. They left a path so customers could go in and out and as they came and went, the ladies simply stared at them, accusing them silently with their eyes."

Davey, who'd kept quiet up to this point, asked, "Were the customers men who beat up on their wives, too?"

"No, David, surely not all of them," Miss Willis explained carefully to him, just the way she did at school. "The customers were made to feel guilty because they were buying merchandise from a wife beater. Let me tell you the scheme certainly worked. Scarcely anyone would buy from him. Finally he closed up his store and left town for want of customers."

Davey asked before I could, "Did his wife stay in Cincinnati?"

"No, she went away with him." Miss Willis sighed mournfully.

Papa wasn't sighing. He was scratching his side-whiskers. Very slowly he said, "Well, ladies, let's hope that it doesn't come to that. Are you still going to ask Miss Ottenberg to join your collecting? I hear that she's due back from Portland tomorrow afternoon on the stagecoach. Having her along should add some weight to your worthy cause."

"Uh-huh, all two hundred and one pounds of her!" my brother informed us. "I watched her from behind the flour barrels when she weighed herself here on our feed scales last week. Colonel Ottenberg weighs two hundred and twenty pounds."

"Davey!" Mama tried to scold him, but she couldn't help laughing. "All right, Albert," she told Papa. "We'll call on Miss Emily and ask her to join us. What with all her gallivanting around to San Francisco and then Portland, we haven't had a chance."

After that the sisterhood didn't hang around much longer. Full of doughnuts and sloshing to the gills with coffee, they went home and we Fosters and Doctor Marah went to bed.

While I was lying under the quilts, listening to autumn rain falling on the roof, I got an interesting idea. I'd talk it over tomorrow with Margaret Libby after church. It would appeal to her, too. It wasn't very often girls got to see any excitement in Ottenberg, and I had some in mind!

* * *

Because it was grown-up business, I didn't get to go with Mama and some of the Ladies Aid ladies to speak with the newly arrived Miss Emily that Sunday afternoon. But later I surely did hear all about it from Mama.

Even though it was Sunday, Colonel Ottenberg had called a meeting of the city fathers in the first room of the courthouse to be finished. So Miss Emily was at home alone when Mama and the other ladies went calling.

At first Miss Ottenberg had been very friendly and offered the ladies tea, but when she found out that they were planning to collect money for the new schoolhouse by visiting saloons, she changed her tune fast.

"She seemed shocked," Mama told Doctor Marah, Papa, and me.

"What did she say, Nora?" Papa wanted to know.

"She said 'Under no circumstances whatsoever could I ever go into a saloon anywhere. What will my father say? He'd disown me, and I can't have that happen.'"

Personally, I thought being disowned by the colonel might be a good thing, but his daughter didn't seem to think so. She was strange. A person would think from her size and her face that she was like her father, but inside she wasn't. She was timid, where Colonel Ottenberg was sure of himself and bold.

Doctor Marah asked Mama, "What did Miss Emily say about giving you money for the fund? Did you ask her to contribute, herself?"

"Yes, and she refused straight out. She said that she had no money to give."

"Perhaps she hasn't, Mrs. Foster."

"Oh, Doctor, it doesn't seem very likely. I swear she refused to contribute for the same reason she refused to go collecting with us. She's afraid of going against her father. I think we can count Miss Ottenberg out of our actions from now on."

My father let out a laugh that rang all over the shebang. "She can't say that she wasn't invited to add her weight, though," he said to all of us.

I didn't go out with Mama and the others that night. I told Mama I was feeling feverish in the chest and might be coming down with a cold. It wasn't exactly the truth, though what I'd planned with Margaret made me feel feverish all right. I was going to wait until the coast was clear of church ladies and until Doctor Marah, Papa, Haverford, and the preacher had left. Then I would hoot like an owl, which was the signal for Margaret to climb out of her bedroom window and join me.

It wasn't part of my idea to get caught by anybody. I listened from behind the parlor curtains until I heard the four men shut the front door behind them. Then I got my shawl and went out the side door after I had peeked to see that Davey was asleep. He didn't figure in my plan for Margaret and me.

From the store it was only a little ways to the Libby house. I hurried across the street, as quietly as I could, and went behind the line of houses on the west side of Ottenberg and slid between the Libbys' and the Prescotts'. From that narrow space I hooted twice. Before I could get out the third owl hoot, the sash window of Margaret's room was up and she was flinging a leg over the sill. I grabbed her hands and helped get her down.

"Did they really go?" was her excited whisper to me.

"You bet they did. Come on."

Together we crossed the street with our shawls over our heads, hoping not to be recognized, dodging horses going north and south and avoiding mud puddles at the same time. We made it to the side of the Shoo-Fly without being hailed or challenged for being out so late, and there everything was just the way I'd arranged it earlier that day. The two O'Hares hadn't been near their big rain barrels, so they didn't notice that I'd put the lids over them and set some boxes beside them to use as steps.

I'd placed the barrels on each side of the saloon windows, nice as you please, for Margaret and me, so that we could stand and look inside without being seen. We could hear, too. Like most of the saloons in Ottenberg, the Shoo-Fly had been built in a big hurry because no one knew for sure how long the town would last. The windows didn't fit into the walls too well, and there were slits between the clapboards, as well as knotholes aplenty for good eavesdropping. The window wasn't exactly clean, but we could see through it if we leaned our elbows against the boards on each side of it and craned our necks.

I sucked in my breath after the first look and whispered, "There they are." Yes, Papa and Reverend Gardiner and the two doctors and a whole bunch of people, mostly the same men I'd spotted there last night, were standing around. I looked harder. Just about every man Jack in there, except for my father, the preacher, and the two medical men, was wearing a gun at his hip. I wished that Margaret and I had been at our posts from the very beginning, but even though we had arrived late there was plenty to be overheard now.

O'Hare wasn't just talking; he was thundering. Margaret and I heard him clear as any bell and three times as loud. "Foster, you tell me you got two kids in that there chicken coop and I got my one son in there, too. That don't cut no ice with me that you got two kids to my one kid in school. I don't see that what a school is or where it is matters one damn. A teacher on one end of a log and a kid on the other end—that's a good enough school for me and it don't cost much. I didn't have no more than two years of school, and I done just fine in bus'ness everywhere I've settled. I don't see no need for a fancy, fandangled schoolhouse from back East for the kids here. Mayor Ottenberg's buildin' will do just fine until there's more kids here in town and we really need a bigger place."

I heard Doctor Haverford tell him, "Tom, the snow's due here before long. There probably won't be any more families coming here this late in the year."

"Well, Doc, as folks say, 'after the winter comes the spring.' That's the time for a new school—next year." I watched Mr. O'Hare take a big brown bottle down off the shelf behind him, uncork it, and pour from it into five glasses set out in front of him. Two were little ones. The other three were bigger, the size of glasses people drank milk from. "Here, gents, just to show you there's no ill feelings on the part of Tom O'Hare, 'cause I don't want kids or females or anyone else collectin' for a school in my saloon, I'll pour a free drink for all."

He shoved the small glasses toward Doctor Haverford and Papa, took one of the big ones for himself, and flicked a hand toward the other two. "Help yourselves, gents." The other two large ones were for the preacher and Doctor Marah, it seemed.

I saw my father and the old doctor drink their little glasses in two gulps. Then while Margaret gulped too—so loudly I could hear her—we saw Mr. O'Hare down his large glass without stopping once for breath. After he'd wiped the whiskey off his mustache with his coat sleeve, he said very loudly, "Come on, you two gents, show me that you're men, too."

Reverend Gardiner was shaking his head and we heard him saying, "No sir, wine is the strongest beverage I ever take."

"Come on," roared O'Hare, laughing. "The Bible don't say a single word against the drinkin' of whiskey."

All the men in the Shoo-Fly laughed along with O'Hare, all but my father, Marah, and Haverford.

"No, Mr. O'Hare, the people of ancient Israel didn't know about whiskey," said Gardiner pleasantly, as he pushed the glass back to the saloonkeeper.

Mr. O'Hare was still laughing as he took the preacher's glass and drank it down, too. When he'd finished it and set it down, he stuck his head over the bar and said, "All right, little Doc, you come next. How about you havin' a drink with me? I'll do better than a free drink. I'll make a wager. If you drink down three a these dainty glasses with me every time you come in here and leave without being carried out, I'll let you collect for the new schoolhouse anytime, you beardless pup, and I'll kick in a five-dollar gold piece to boot."

Teetering on my barrel with excitement, I reached out to Margaret to pinch her on the arm. This was a crucial moment.

We waited. She waited. So did everyone else watching Doctor Marah, including Papa who put his hand on the young doctor's arm. Doctor Haverford took a step nearer to him at the same moment as if he wanted to say something, but before he could Doctor Marah brushed Papa's arm off, shook his head at O'Hare, and turning around walked quickly out of the Shoo-Fly. The drinkers and the saloonkeeper laughed till their sides must have felt like splitting. The piano player, who was laughing, too, struck up the tune, "Shew! Fly, Don't Bother Me." My father, Haverford, and Reverend Gardiner stared at Marah's disappearing back, then turned around and slowly followed him out.

Margaret and I got down from the rain barrels and stood together, whispering.

She asked me the one question I didn't want to hear. "Golly, Hope, wasn't it Doctor Marah who said that the ladies should collect money in the first place? Wasn't it *his* idea that you told me about?"

"Yes, it was."

She went on, "Even though my mother doesn't like him to do it, I've seen my father drink three glasses of whiskey almost as big as that on Saturday nights."

I told her, "My papa doesn't. One glass is plenty for him."

She was quiet for a long moment, then said, "Of course, we have to remember that Doctor Marah surely wouldn't ever hang around in the Shoo-Fly very long if he came collecting, and he would have to drink very fast. My father takes all night to drink that much!"

Margaret, being a true-blue friend, was trying to make me feel better about Marah's not drinking, but it didn't work. There was no getting around the facts. Doctor Marah had let the school fund down. He had let the sisters down. Margaret knew it and I knew it. After all, Doctor Haverford had drunk with O'Hare. It wasn't that medical men were against drinking whiskey. Doctor Marah didn't have that excuse.

Margaret and I waited alongside the Shoo-Fly until we saw Marah and the three others walk past. Then, without them seeing us, we came out onto the boardwalk and peered after them down the lantern-lit street. They were on their way to Reverend Gardiner's house just beyond the Big Bend Hotel, I suspected. We saw the four of them nod to Colonel Ottenberg, who was walking around in the rain with his black Union Army officer's cape over his blue uniform. He was out again tonight, keeping an eye on his town.

"Good night, Margaret," I told her from beside the Shoo-Fly.

"Good night, Hope."

While she crossed the street to crawl back through her bedroom window I went to find Mama and tell her what we'd just seen. Of course, I'd have to explain how I knew what had happened just now inside the Shoo-Fly, but because of my valuable news she would probably not punish me for fibbing about a fever and leaving Davey alone in the house for a little while.

The upshot of the whole thing, as I saw it, was that Doctor Marah was a coward—for a doctor and for a man.

CHAPTER FIVE

A VERY ASTONISHING SURPRISE, INDEED!

Mama wasn't back yet, so I sat out of sight with Manchester lying beside me on the sofa, snuggled up to me to keep himself warm. There was a nip in the air again tonight. I heard Mama tell her sisters good-night out in the shebang after they'd left their collections with her. She came through the curtains to the parlor, humming.

When she caught sight of me, she asked, "Hope, what are you doing up? I thought you said you had a fever. Were you playing the organ, fever and all?" She looked disapproving.

"No, Mama, I went out after you and Papa did."

She frowned at me and, her bonnet in her hand, asked, "Where did you go?"

"Out with Margaret Libby. I don't have a cold. Please sit down. I have to talk with you."

"What's so very mysterious, child? You look as if you just saw a ghost. Don't you spoil my good mood now. We took in a pretty fair sum again this evening. I hope what your father and the other men collect in the Shoo-Fly will bring it up over a hundred dollars again."

"It won't. Mama, they didn't get anything in there."

"*What?*" At last she sat down. Manchester jumped off the sofa and leaped up into her lap.

I was sitting down across from her, so I could see her face in the light of the lamp while I told her what Margaret and I had seen and heard going on in the Shoo-Fly. I finished with, "Doctor Marah's a coward. Margaret thinks he is, too."

Mama let out so deep a sigh you would have thought it started at her ankles. "Hope, did it ever occur to you and Margaret that Doctor Marah might have good reasons for not doing what Mr. O'Hare demanded of him? O'Hare wanted to get him very drunk and, if possible, very sick, too, to embarrass him."

I cried to her, "Well, if Doctor Marah has good reasons, he'd better tell everybody what they are. I know that it isn't because he's against alcohol, because I saw him drink a glass of wine with you and Papa at dinner today."

"Some people don't like large amounts of straight whiskey, Hope. It poisons them."

"Mama, it didn't poison Mr. O'Hare. I watched him drink two big glasses."

"Oftentimes a snake is immune to his own venom. I doubt if Doctor Marah or the town's heard the last of this, unfortunately." She shook her head. "From what I saw of Mr. O'Hare, I'd predict that he has it in for Marah. Poor man. Well, no matter what, Doctor Marah has friends in your father and me, and you, Hope, will treat him politely even if you do consider him a coward."

"Yes, Mama, but I still think that he is one."

Three days later we Fosters and everyone else in Ottenberg who could read learned that Mama was right in her prediction. Mr. O'Hare was truly bent on tormenting Doctor Marah, who had never said one word to Davey or me about O'Hare's treatment of him in the Shoo-Fly. Papa told Mama in private what O'Hare had done. She told me that Marah had never mentioned it to her either, and I could certainly see why.

Mr. O'Hare followed up his insults in the saloon by an advertisement he took out in the *Oracle*.

Wednesday night everyone read:

WANTED
One Beardless Meddling Pup
of a Quack Doctor and Coward
to Get Out of Ottenberg—or Else—
and Leave on the Next Stage Going Anywhere
Thomas X. O'Hare, Prop., Shoo-Fly

Well, that was clear enough to me. It meant that O'Hare wanted Doctor Marah to leave town. Other people, older than I was, read even more into it. Papa told us all that O'Hare hoped Marah would get so angry over the insulting notice that the doctor would challenge him to a duel. And if the two didn't duel, they'd at least have a fistfight. *Quack*, I knew, was the worst word you could call a doctor because it meant he didn't know his business.

Every man spent the rest of the week talking about the notice. Some of the men who came to the shebang asked Papa straight out in front of Mama and me what Doctor Marah was planning to do about Tom O'Hare. Papa had to tell them that he had no idea. Nobody knew. Doctor Marah was keeping his own counsel.

Though I longed to ask him, I didn't either. I wanted to hear him say just once that he aimed to "fix O'Hare's wagon" when he got good and ready. But he never talked about that night in the Shoo-Fly with me or with anyone else that I knew about, though he could have talked about it secretly with Doctor Haverford. No, Doctor Marah walked quietly about town the same as before, not seeming to notice that folks whispered behind his back and sniggered at him. The rest of the time he spent in his room, studying medical books. Only one thing had seemed to change: he never came out anymore at night when the sisters returned from the saloons with the money to put in our safe.

I came out in my nightgown and wrapper every time to see how well they had done. I took note that not one lady ever mentioned Doctor Marah by name.

By the end of our first week of collecting, which was on the twenty-fifth of September, the ladies had taken in over $400. That was mighty good going. That Saturday night Mama gave the women not just doughnuts, but pound cake and coffee to celebrate. Papa and I were there for the cake, too, but not Doctor Marah who stayed in his room.

As a way of testing him, I had invited him to come out into the store. But he had some sort of excuse for keeping to himself. Some things had arrived on the morning stage for him. One was a big horsehair trunk with his name on it, and the other was a large, thick, brown envelope with red-wax seals on the back of it. He told me briefly while I was trying to get him out into the shebang that it was his examination to get a license to practice as a bona fide doctor. Looking at the size of that envelope made me feel almost sorry for him—coward though he was. I'd surely hate to take any test that came in such a big thing.

He got right at the examination papers that next day,

Sunday. He didn't leave his room once, and, on Mama's orders, no one went near him. She took his food in on a tray after telling me that he was writing out the examination and shouldn't be bothered by Davey or me.

I asked her, "Mama, what about that piece Mr. O'Hare put in the *Oracle*? It's been days since it came out, and Doctor Marah hasn't done one single thing about it."

"What he does is his business, Hope, not ours."

"Mama, isn't he going to do anything at all?" Davey and I were getting teased at school by Silas—and not only by him—about our "lily-livered boarder." Right now I would rather have had Miss Willis living with us than Marah, who had seemed so nice at the start.

Margaret's father and mother had let it be known, after the newspaper notice appeared and after they'd waited in vain for Marah to do something about it, that they would never consult Marah as a doctor for so much as a sore finger. I knew that many other folks in Ottenberg felt the same way.

Doctor Marah mailed his examination off to wherever it was supposed to go Tuesday morning, while I was at school suffering from Silas's torment in the chicken coop. It wasn't until Wednesday night when I read the paper that I learned what else Doctor Marah had done on Tuesday. He'd taken out a newspaper advertisement, too.

It read:

> The Town of Ottenberg Is Hereby Informed
> That I Have No Intentions, Whatsoever,
> of Engaging in Any Violent Actions
> With Any Man Hereabouts or Anywhere Else
> *J. L. Marah*

Papa hadn't brought the paper to the supper table for me to read out loud tonight. He showed it to me out in the shebang so as not to embarrass Marah.

After I'd read it, I asked, "Papa, what will Ottenberg folks do now? They'll really think he's a coward after this."

Papa was chewing on his mustache. "Hope, there probably won't be a man in town who'll go to Marah as a doctor now. He might as well get on a stage and leave before he gets snowed in."

Mama was in the store with us, dusting the counters with a feather duster. She said, "My love, it seems to me that you are forgetting some of the other citizens who might have some very different ideas about this whole affair."

"Who would they be, Nora?" I thought he looked surprised.

"The women. I know that at first the ladies didn't like it when Doctor Marah didn't reply to O'Hare and welcome a fight, but I think I can guess how they will react to this second notice. The women of this country hate having their men shot dead in duels, and it's no wonder when nine times out of ten the duels are fought over something stupid. Fistfights are very little better, and what do they prove? Do they convince the loser of his errors? Not that I have ever noticed. I, for one, plan to congratulate Doctor Marah on his very good sense. I intend further to talk to every woman I know and tell her he should be praised not condemned. What he did by refusing to fight is even more courageous than going out to challenge O'Hare with a pistol!"

Papa told her, "Nora, the only patients he'll ever have will be women."

"What's so wrong with that, Albert? Women and children and babies. I'm sure that they will be enough to keep him occupied. What's more, he'll never have to dig a bullet out of one of those rough men or patch up injuries from saloon fights. That ought to be something nice for him."

Papa asked her, "You've been jawing with that Ohio schoolteacher a lot lately, haven't you?"

Mama was enjoying this conversation. I could tell from the little smile that was making her lips twitch now and then. "Why, Albert, of course we talk to Miss Willis. She is one of the most intelligent women in Ottenberg. She has many interesting things to say about her life back in Cincinnati. Sometimes she even lectures to us when we can get together with her. Mrs. Gardiner and Mrs. Prescott and quite a few of the others and even Reverend Gardiner agree with her. Women should have a right to speak their minds. They should own their own property and have the right to vote here in Montana Territory, too. They'd see that strong laws were passed against dueling. They'd see that there wasn't shooting in towns, and they'd probably legislate the saloons out of business. That would be something to shout about, indeed!"

Papa laughed out loud. "Next thing the ladies will be taking the same kind of jobs men take."

"What is wrong with that, my love, if the women are as capable as the men."

Papa opened his mouth to reply, but just at that moment the bell of the shebang jangled and he had to go help a man who wanted a pound of coffee beans and a horse collar. He went off muttering, "Ferment, ferment," to himself, making Mama giggle, which she seldom did.

I asked her, "How does it feel to be fermenting?"

She stretched her arms to the ceiling and smiled. "It makes one feel very much alive, Hope. It's truly as nice being in love with an idea as to be in love with a man."

"Hmmn." I had never been in love with either thing yet. There certainly wasn't any boy in the chicken coop who caught my eye.

I thought about fermenting as I looked at the glass jar on the counter that had held licorice sticks until the ladies had begun collecting for the school. Now on the side of the jar was a sign I'd lettered saying that this was the "right place" to drop coins for a new schoolhouse. Even though it was a big jar, its bottom was already covered two inches deep with silver. Well, I suppose I had been fermenting in a way, too, when I made the sign. I'd even drawn pale blue forget-me-nots all over it to remind people not to forget to give the jar the change left over from their purchases in our place. Doing that had given me a pleasant feeling, but I doubted if it was love. As I thought about it, though, I decided I could fall in love with the idea of going to school in something other than a chicken coop!

The ladies went on collecting and collecting and I went out with them three times more. It seemed to me that all I learned from my saloon visits was that saloons were pretty much alike. I couldn't really see what the men who went to them saw in them. They weren't at all interesting.

But something truly interesting took place the first Monday in October, which was the fourth, something other than a rejoicing Miss Willis finally moving all of her things out of Colonel Ottenberg's and into the Gardiners'. The late-afternoon stagecoach from Helena arrived in Ottenberg, carrying another passenger, who, like Miss Willis, had been expected for some time. Naturally there was a welcoming group out on the shebang's front porch to watch the important passenger get off the stage.

At last Ottenberg was getting the judge we'd been promised from the territorial capital. I watched him closely, having wondered all day at school what a judge would look like. He wasn't a big man the way I'd expected. He was sort of small and skinny, wore a long, black frock coat, and a black plug hat sat atop his going-gray hair. He wasn't young, though. That fit my idea all right. Everybody knew that judges were always more than thirty years old and were supposed to have more common sense than most other folks.

The lady with the judge wasn't as old as he was by a long shot. She was pink-cheeked and yellow-headed, dressed fit to kill in a fur-trimmed, dark-green traveling cloak and green bonnet with black plumes. She even had a beaver-skin muff to warm her hands in. I couldn't tell at first if she was the judge's daughter or his wife until I heard Colonel Ottenberg, who was, of course, the official town greeter, call the judge, "Judge Bokman" and the lady, "Mrs. Bokman."

Clearly the Bokmans were very important people. Even surly Mr. Thompson, who hated just about everybody, pulled up his stagecoach and horses with some care so as not to make the Bokmans step down into a mud puddle, the way Miss Willis and Doctor Marah had. I even saw Thompson sort of bow on the coach's seat and lift his hat to Mrs. Bokman, who smiled up at him.

Mama, Mrs. Gardiner, and Mrs. Libby, who was holding the Libby pug dog to keep him from running out to snap at the hooves of the coach horses, were standing just behind Margaret and me as we perched on the shebang's railing.

Mama said softly to the other ladies, "I never saw a lady traveling in such a condition."

Naturally I took a closer look. Aha! Mrs. Bokman was going to have a baby. If the baby was born in Ottenberg, it would be Ottenberg's very first baby. This was something else to look forward to. I wondered which would arrive first—the Bokman baby or the new school building.

Mrs. Gardiner spoke up. "Thank heavens, there's a house ready for the Bokmans. Their furniture has arrived from Helena, too. It would be dreadful for Mrs. Bokman in her condition to have to stay in the Big Bend Hotel. My husband's going to offer to help them get settled into their house."

Mama was murmuring almost as if to herself, "I wonder what Judge Bokman will think of a chicken coop for a school."

"Oh, I'm sure that he will make a donation to help us." Obviously Mrs. Prescott understood what Mama was driving at. All Mama thought about was getting cash for the school, and about Mr. O'Hare and Doctor Marah, wondering what the saloonkeeper's next move would be.

The next Sunday I walked home from church with Doctor Marah and Davey. It had been cold in the church tent that morning. Though it had stopped raining and the sun was out, the heat wasn't enough to dry up the mud puddles in the street. At noon the ice was still white over their tops.

Doctor Marah had been quieter than usual that weekend. He hadn't even come out into the parlor to hear from Mama how tickled the ladies were with their Saturday-night collection, which had netted them over $200. They were really gaining on that $1250, all right.

I had changed my opinion about Doctor Marah a little bit after talking with Mama about fighting. In other words, I was speaking to him. As we neared the shebang I asked him, "Are you sick?" I suspected that doctors got sick sometimes, too, though they surely ought to know what ailed them and treat it fast.

"No, Hope, just apprehensive." He gave me a sidelong glance and a smile as he walked around the big puddle Davey was eying to see if the ice would hold his weight.

"What does *apprehensive* mean?"

"Worried, fretting, expecting the worst."

"Oh, Mr. O'Hare you mean?" He must know that I knew that O'Hare hated him because of the advertisement in the *Oracle*. I'd never let on that I'd spied on what had gone on in the Shoo-Fly that night.

"No, not the worthy Mr. O'Hare this time." He laughed. "I am referring to my examination. I hope I passed it."

I told him, "Well, I can understand that." I was sure that I did understand better than most adults. After all, they were out of school and didn't have to take tests anymore. I told him this, too.

He nodded at me, then said, "Well, Hope, there are other sorts of tests in life, too, you know. They aren't all taken with a pencil and paper." He stopped all at once and asked me, "What do you think about this business between O'Hare and myself?"

He wanted *my* opinion? I guessed if he wanted it I'd better give it to him. I was flattered. "I think you did right in not getting mixed up with him. What did you do in the first place to rile him up so much?" I had figured there had been more to it than Doctor Marah's telling O'Hare what he thought of his use of the bung starter.

"I told the sheriff I thought O'Hare ran a pretty unruly place and should have been brought to account before this. I wanted him arrested but he wasn't. He nearly killed that miner with the bung starter. At the time it appeared to me that he hit him unnecessarily hard, almost as if he took pleasure in it. The man could very possibly never have regained consciousness. As it was, Doctor Haverford and I had to send him by stagecoach to Virginia City to a hospital, and we heard later that he reached there more dead than alive. He was little more than a boy."

"And Mr. O'Hare has it in for you because of that?"

"That seems to be enough for him."

"Silas hates me, too," I told the doctor.

"Like poison. He hates every girl in town," said Davey, who'd caught up with us after deciding not to stand on the icy puddle after all.

"Being hated by Silas O'Hare is a compliment," I told Doctor Marah. "I like being hated by him, but I still mind when he calls me nanny goat."

We had stewed chicken for Sunday dinner. While I was helping Mama to clear off the table, I told her about my interesting chat with Marah, who was now out in the shebang by the stove playing cribbage with Papa once more. We stayed open for business on Sunday afternoons like everyone else in town. Essex was out there on the doctor's lap again. Our cats seemed to favor him even more than they favored me or Mama.

I said, "Mama, I don't think Doctor Marah's such a coward anymore. It takes courage, I guess, not to let somebody make you do something you don't want to do."

She understood what I was trying to say. "Hope, sometimes that takes much more courage than to do what they want. You know if you refuse them, you run the risk of their anger. By the way, what are you going to do this afternoon?"

I'd had my organ practice before dinner, and I had thought of going to the Libbys' to see what Margaret was up to, but had decided against it. I'd been reading in our set of Charles Dickens yesterday and in a book borrowed from Miss Willis. From those books I had written out a list of twenty new words I didn't know. I could spend a happy half hour looking up the words in Doctor Marah's dictionary. I could even spend the rest of the day learning new words, because I had a tendency to get stuck in dictionaries. I just adored dictionaries.

Doctor Marah's room was neat as could be, as always. The bed was made, the curtains pulled back, and the window opened to let in the sunshine. His horsehair trunk had a closed padlock on it, not that I would have really peeked inside. His slippers were set just so under the bed, and the top of his chest of drawers was neatly arranged with a hairbrush, a comb, a glass for his toothbrush, and a bottle of lilac-scented hair tonic.

I sat down in the chair at his table, next to the big stack of medical books Doctor Haverford had loaned him, pulled the dictionary over, and hunted up the first word, which was *equivocate.* It pretty much meant to lie, to tell falsehoods. I thought that was certainly a roundabout way to say it. The next large word was *hirsute.* All it really meant was hairy. I sat back in the chair thinking of all the hirsute men in Ottenberg—Colonel Ottenberg, Mr. O'Hare, Doctor Haverford, Reverend Gardiner, Mr. Prescott, and even Papa, who had a mustache as well as muttonchop whiskers. Doctor Marah seemed to be one of the very few totally clean-shaven men in town. No beard, no mustache, and no sideburns. He never even looked particularly whiskery.

I glanced at the top of his chest of drawers again, curious now about his razor, which I must have overlooked. It had to be the sharpest in Ottenberg to give him such good shaves. I plucked a hair out of my head to test the razor's sharpness. It ought to cut right through the hair.

When I looked again, though, I couldn't find any razor there. So I went across the room to peek at his pitcher and wash basin, expecting to find it there and the mug of shaving soap along with it.

They weren't there—neither one of them.

Nor was the razor in his black-leather doctor's bag, which was set on the end of the bed. Good heavens, did Doctor Marah carry his razor with him the way other men in Ottenberg wore their guns? Was he really scared of Mr. O'Hare or of some of the miners and not letting on to us that he was afraid? An unfolded straight-edge razor could be a dangerous weapon.

This was something I felt Mama should know about, so, leaving the dictionary open and with *obstreperous, benighted,* and *irreverent* still not looked up—along with fifteen other words from Dickens—I went out to the kitchen.

Mama had got all the dishes into our big metal dishpan by now and was pouring hot water from the teakettle into it when I said quietly so Doctor Marah, who was out in the shebang, wouldn't hear me, "Mama, I can't find Doctor Marah's razor anywhere in his room. There doesn't seem to be any shaving soap either."

"What do you want those for, Hope?" Mama was giving me a very strange look as she held the teakettle in the air.

"I wanted to see if his razor was as sharp as I thought it must be to give him such a close shave every day. He never has nicks on his face the way some men do." Reverend Gardiner had only a wispy mustache, and he always had court plaster on the rest of his face because he wasn't such a good shaver.

"No, he doesn't cut himself and he doesn't go to the barber." Mama finished pouring the water into the dishpan, put the kettle back on the stove, and said, "So you've noticed that?" She asked me, "Have you also noticed how the cats act toward Doctor Marah?"

I stopped to think. The cats were almost always on him or on his bed. Before he'd come to live with us, they'd both slept with me. Neither of them had ever had much to do with Papa or Davey.

"The cats like him, Mama."

She nodded. "Yes, they came out of a litter Miss Emily raised, remember. Remember what she warned us about when she gave Manchester and Essex to us."

Miss Ottenberg? I harkened back to our first days in town. Miss Emily had come calling with the two almost-grown kittens in a basket under her arm. You could hear them growling and spitting at each other inside. She'd said at the time that though they were "gentlemen cats," they were partial to the company of ladies, more partial to them than to men.

Colonel Ottenberg didn't care for cats at all. He'd never once played with the kittens. Miss Emily had, though. And because of her the cats fancied ladies over gentlemen. Personally, I had suspected the colonel of stepping on their tails and not really giving a hoot. Or maybe his stomach was so large that he couldn't even see a cat under him when he walked around his house.

I pondered Miss Ottenberg's remarks in my mind and from them went to the mystery of the razor and soap. An idea came into my mind, but it was so wild I pushed it right out again.

Mama must have known what it was, because she told me as she put her hands down into the dishwater after the silverware, "Yes, child, you are quite right. Doctor Marah is a woman."

The suddenness of it made me sit down with a plunk beside the kitchen table. Of course! Soft pink cheeks, no beard, a very neat room, gentle voice, and good manners.

"But why does he—I mean she—wear men's clothes and call herself Jay?"

"Hope," Mama explained quietly, "she doesn't call herself Jay. You have misheard or misunderstood. She uses only the initial J, remember? Her real name is Jeanette Louisa. She passes herself off as a man because she feels she has to in order to become a doctor. It is almost impossible for a woman to become a medical doctor, you know. Medical schools admit men but almost never women, though the women may be just as qualified."

I asked, "Does Doctor Haverford know about her?" My head was swimming with this remarkable and very astonishing piece of information.

Mama smiled at me. "Of course, he knows. She is his great-niece. She comes from a family of doctors. Her father's a doctor in Maryland and so are her two brothers. She's studied medicine along with her brothers, though she's been forced to do so at home and pretty much in secret. No hospital would take her on as a beginning doctor, so she came out here to get some practical experience working with Doctor Haverford the way other young doctors get experience in city hospitals."

"Oh, Mama, did you know from the beginning, too? Did Papa know?"

"Not at the very start. But Doctor Marah told both of us the first week she was here after she'd sounded us out enough to be sure what our reaction would be. Your father was shocked at first, but I talked him into being pleased, too, about her courage and enterprise. We have never told a soul that she is a woman. It has not been easy for her, believe me!"

"Then she isn't dyspeptic?" I wasn't concerned about Papa.

"Not one bit. She wanted good, plain food and a clean room, and Doctor Haverford knew she would get these things here. More to the point, she required privacy that the Big Bend Hotel could never give her. There are no private baths there, you know." Mama was looking rather sadly at me. "Hope, won't you keep her secret, too? She's got enough to worry about, given O'Hare's persecution and her very difficult examination, without being afraid that you'll tell that she's masquerading as a man."

"Oh, yes!" What a secret! I was very flattered. My goodness, to be asked to keep such an important secret went right to a person's head. The more I thought about it the more thrilled and excited I got. Then I asked Mama, "Why won't men let ladies become doctors?"

"Jeanette says it's because men think that women are too delicate and squeamish for that sort of work. Yet we women take care of very sick people who are confined to bed and sometimes dying, and we wash and lay out the dead for burial."

That was true. The ladies were the ones who nursed sick people. That always seemed to be women's work. Davey had been terrible to deal with when he'd had the chicken pox last spring. Mama had had to bathe him in water filled with laundry starch several times a day to keep him from scratching himself bloody. And how he had complained. And when Papa's foot had been run over by the wheel of a dray wagon in Silver Belle, he'd been in bed and tended to by Mama for two whole weeks.

I said, "I think it's terrible that women can't be doctors if they want to. I think it's dreadful that Doctor Marah has to dress like a man so people will think she is one."

"It *is* terrible."

My mind raced ahead, recalling those notices in the *Oracle* and of how Mr. O'Hare, out of meanness, had set out the big whiskey glass for the doctor. I told Mama, "I think Doctor Jeanette Marah's got to be the bravest woman I've ever known."

Right then I wished I could rush out into the store and fling my arms about her and tell her what I felt about her. But I couldn't do that. That would make her wonder, and she'd suspect I knew she was a Jeanette. And I'd thought for a time that she was a coward. No wonder she didn't drink any of O'Hare's whiskey. She'd probably never had a drink of whiskey in her life and naturally wouldn't have a head for it at all. If she had taken the three glassfuls O'Hare offered, it might have made her say or do something that would've let folks know she wasn't a man. Rather than risk that, she let herself be insulted and made to look like a coward. And she'd had no choice but to let the men of the town refuse her as a doctor, because she wouldn't go out with a gun to shoot Mr. O'Hare. But she hadn't left town—the way O'Hare told her to.

The more I pondered the more excited I became. I was so fired up with the news that I just had to do something, something important that would show how I felt about Jeanette Marah and make it up to her for my thinking she was a coward. But what could I do? I couldn't tell the whole town how remarkable she was.

And then in a flash, I knew. Something Miss Willis had said not long ago came to mind. "Could I borrow this chair for a while?" I asked Mama. It was only a kitchen chair, not one of the parlor ones with the green velvet seats.

"Of course, you may. What do you want it for? To sit out on the front porch like Davey and watch the world go by?" She was smiling at me. The porch was Davey's favorite perching spot. From there he could see just about everything that went on in Ottenberg.

"I need it, Mama." That was all I said. Taking my shawl off the wall peg, I put it on, grabbed the chair, and ran out the side door.

Davey was on the front porch, all right, sitting on the rail with Silas, admiring the miners' horses that were hitched to the rail, while the men went from saloon to saloon Sunday carousing.

"Hey, nanny goat, where are you goin'?" Silas shouted after me, as I went past him.

I turned my head and stuck my tongue out at *him* for a change. He'd find out soon enough where I was bound if he kept his eyes on me.

I took the kitchen chair to the front of the Shoo-Fly Saloon, put it down right next to the right side of the swinging doors, and sat in it. Then I put as fierce a glare on my face as I felt I could keep up for any length of time. I truly meant to make the miners who went inside to drink O'Hare's whiskey feel uneasy in their minds by my accusing and disapproving stare.

Unfortunately, the first person to come along was Silas, himself. Once he'd seen me sit myself down in front of his pa's saloon his curiosity about me had got the best of him.

He asked me, teetering on his heels with his hands in his pockets, "What do you think you're doin' sittin' out here on our property, nanny goat?"

I could have told him that he'd been sitting out in front of my property with my brother, but instead I decided to annoy him more by being mysterious. It always annoyed boys when girls acted mysterious, so I told him, "Fermenting, only fermenting."

That would fix him. If Davey came tagging along, I'd ask him to go back home and fetch the collar box. I didn't want to give any of the miners who dared pass me the idea that I'd refuse a donation toward the schoolhouse.

The second person who came along after Silas went inside the Shoo-Fly wasn't my brother or a thirsty man either. And certainly not anybody I could get a donation from!

Alas, it was Miss Emily Ottenberg, sailing down the boardwalk like a great big ship, dressed in her long black coat and black-feathered bonnet. I braced myself for her. I wished she would ignore kids the way her father did, but Miss Emily talked to children. My goodness, how she talked!

It certainly wasn't my lucky day to be doing something for Doctor Marah. First, I'd got Silas O'Hare and now Miss Emily. Just about anybody in town—except Mr. O'Hare himself—would have been a more welcome sight to me.

CHAPTER SIX

MISS EMILY

I'd almost decided to take the glare off my face temporarily, so she wouldn't notice it. After all, she wasn't one of Mr. O'Hare's customers. But I'd thought better of it when I recalled how she felt about collecting for the new school and kept right on glaring. I wasn't one bit sure of Miss Emily. I thought there might be more up her sleeve than her fear that her pa might get mad at her for collecting with the Ladies Aid and Altar Society. Maybe she wanted to keep a close eye on the teacher and the school. And with the school on Ottenberg land so close to their house, she certainly could do that easily enough. Maybe she wasn't pleased either, because we didn't like her chicken coop.

In her husky, softish voice, the sort a lot of fat ladies have, Miss Ottenberg said to me, "Hope Foster, whatever are you doing sitting out here in the chill in front of this saloon?"

Oh, I'd expected her to ask me that, though it was none of her business. I was tempted to tell her that I wasn't sitting down at all. That was only her imagination playing tricks on her. What I was really doing was running up and down the street, flying a kite. But if I told her that, she might look up into the sky for the kite. So I said instead, "I am sitting out here to embarrass Mr. O'Hare."

"Why would you want to do that, child?" I had taken

her interest all right. I was afraid that my answer would, but I didn't want to be caught lying to her and get in trouble with my mother.

"Because he was very rude to Mama and some other ladies from the church and rude to me and because he was extra rude to Doctor Marah."

"Rude to the nice young doctor?"

"Yes, ma'am, he told him to get out of town and hinted that he wanted a fight with Doctor Marah. First it was all because of a bung starter Mr. O'Hare had, and then it was about the school, you see."

"No, I certainly do not see. What *are* you talking about?" Her big face was crumpled into a frown. She cocked her head to one side to get a better look at me. "Why are you looking like that, Hope? You'd think you'd swallowed a peck of alum."

"If you really want to know, I'll tell you but it will take a while," I told her.

"Well, sometimes I would like to know what is going on around here."

And then that crazy sort of two-people-talking-at-the-same-time conversation began with her. She couldn't help it, though it got me to talking faster and faster and louder and louder. While I told her how I felt about the saloon visits to the Shoo-Fly and the insults to us and notices in the *Oracle,* she talked about her latest out-of-town trip and the things she'd ordered on her father's behalf for the "little city's" latest civic building and the statue of Justice, which was being shipped direct from San Francisco by its famous sculptor.

I didn't think that she was much interested in what I was saying, even if she had asked me about it. But then she never wanted to listen to anybody. While I was talking and she was talking, I found it very hard to keep up my glaring at men passersby. But I rattled away about the talk in town of a possible duel between the doctor and the saloonkeeper until, all at once, I noticed that I was doing all the talking.

Miss Emily had actually stopped jawing. She was standing poker straight, staring dead ahead of her. All at once, though, she moved and looked straight down into my face and asked me sharply, "Did you say 'duel,' child? Did you say that word, or did I just think I heard it?"

"Yes, ma'am, I did say duel," I replied. Apparently she didn't read the *Oracle*, and her father hadn't told her what townfolks were saying about Doctor Marah. Good heavens, didn't Colonel Ottenberg talk to her at all? Could that be why she talked so much without listening to other people?

"A duel? Oh, dear, not that!" I saw her reach into her jet-beaded reticule, fish around inside it, and come out with a tiny bottle of smelling salts, the kind we sold in the shebang for delicate ladies given to fits and swooning. She sniffed from it, then asked, "What did young Doctor Marah do? Did he challenge the odious saloonkeeper?"

Odious? A large word, that one. I wondered how to spell it but didn't dare ask her. Instead I kept my mind on our talk. "No, ma'am, Doctor Marah refused to fight anybody in any way. He said so in the notice he paid the *Oracle* to print for him."

I saw her draw in her breath. "Thank God, he did. That must have taken great courage on his part."

My goodness, I certainly never expected to hear Miss Emily Ottenberg say such a thing. I was liking her now for the first time and beginning to think there was more to her than just her size!

Then I told her how the men in town were refusing to have Doctor Marah treat them for their ailments.

"So you are endeavoring to embarrass men who enter the Shoo-Fly because you, Doctor Marah, and the church ladies have been embarrassed by Mr. O'Hare?" To my surprise, Miss Emily was nodding her approval at me. And she wasn't smiling. As a matter of fact, she looked very grim around the jaws, where the muscles were working hard.

I told her, "Well, the preacher was embarrassed, too. He didn't drink the whiskey either."

"Good for the reverend." I saw that her dark eyes were fixed on the tree-covered hills rather than on me or on the town named after her father. She added almost in a whisper to herself, "I once knew a very fine and much-beloved young man who went out and got himself killed in a duel. Shot through the heart, he was." She sounded choked up at the end.

All at once I guessed why Miss Emily was a spinster and why she always dressed in black. Yes, she was in mourning. She must have been in love with the young man who died in the duel. I didn't ask her about him, because it really wasn't any of my business, though I knew it would certainly be very interesting to find out. Instead I said to her, "We Fosters think duels are very foolish."

"They are, indeed, Hope. All they prove is that there are two fools ready to fight when one fool in the world is plenty. Before long such dreadful things will not be done in this land. They are illegal now, you know. But foolishly proud men find secret places to hold them in.

And duels must be fought in absolute secrecy lest the duelists and their seconds, the men they bring with them, be arrested. Oh, yes, they still take place in the woods or behind the barn or cowshed." She sighed a sigh that sounded more like a wheeze and smiled a smile that was more sad than gay. "Hope, it appears to me that you are a girl with a conscience and a will to make the world a better place. I like that in you. What would you say if I pulled up a chair, too, to let Mr. O'Hare know what I think of him? I shall go borrow a chair from the milliner across the way."

I was speechless. I'd much rather have Margaret or even Miss Willis for company. But it wasn't my boardwalk or my saloon. So I said, "Please do sit down with me." After all, she was lots more important in Ottenberg than I was. Mr. O'Hare would be wary of her where he could just overlook me. "But don't go to the hatmaker's after a chair. Take mine. I'll go get another one. Sit down here, please. I've already got it warm for you."

I got up, before she could say anything more to me, ran down to our store's side door and into the kitchen. There I told Mama, out of breath, "I have to have another chair."

"What did you do with the first one?" She sounded bewildered as if I chewed up chairs outside or was playing some sort of game with them with some other kid from school. Well, in a way I was—but it wasn't with a child—it was with Mr. O'Hare. And I never would have dreamed in my wildest dreams that Miss Emily would be a partner in my plan.

I told Mama, "I have to have one for myself. Miss Ottenberg is sitting on the other, out in front of the Shoo-Fly Saloon."

"Why on earth is she doing that?" Mama had been stirring something in a pot on the stove. Now she put the spoon down and took off her apron, all the time looking at me as if I'd gone crazy.

"She's going to help me do what I'm doing," I answered. By now because she hadn't said no, I had a second chair under my arm and was ready to take it out of the kitchen, too.

"Just a minute, Hope. What are you doing with Miss Emily?"

"Sitting down, that's all." So I had to tell her everything, though I didn't want to take the time to do so. The words rushed out of me. "I think Miss Emily's lover was killed a long time ago in a duel, and she wants to do something about it. I think she's on our side now even about the new schoolhouse. She thinks Doctor Marah has been insulted enough by Mr. O'Hare."

"Good heavens!" Mama stood looking at the chair I was holding, and then she said, "Perhaps an ally has fallen from heaven. Miss Ottenberg! Good heavens!"

I watched her go to the hat rack of deer antlers, take down her everyday bonnet and cape, and grab hold of a third kitchen chair. She came right out the door after me.

I called over my shoulder to her, because an idea had just hit me, "Mama, while we're at it, shouldn't we get the collar box, too?"

"No," she called to me. "We can't make miners feel guilty and at the same time ask them for money. I doubt if they would give us any."

I couldn't see her point. As far as I was concerned, the men who passed by us to drink in the Shoo-Fly could pay a toll to get inside. And after they came out full of whiskey, they could put some more money into the collar box. That should ease their consciences!

After we were both out in front of O'Hare's saloon, I saw how Mama smiled at Miss Emily, who had just very recently refused to help the ladies in their cause. Miss Emily sat with her hands folded in her lap and only nodded at Mama, but then she smiled too, and said, "Good afternoon, Mrs. Foster."

Mama ranged her chair across from Miss Emily, next to the one I put down on the left side of the swinging doors. We were stationed on both sides now. We sat there, the three of us, sometimes nodding at each other but always ready to glare down any man who came along the boardwalk from either direction and appeared to be heading into the Shoo-Fly Saloon.

Quite soon along came a red-shirted miner toward us. Because he had a beard that was an unusual combination of brown, black, and red, I knew him by sight as one of the men I'd seen inside the Shoo-Fly from my place on the rain barrel that night. I drew my eyebrows together, stuck out my lower lip, and bestowed my very worst glare on him. Miss Emily's eyes were fixed on him, as though he were a bug climbing up her bedroom wall, and I supposed Mama was looking at him in the same cold way.

Though the miner gave the three of us a strange lingering and bewildered glance, he passed in front of us through the swinging doors and into the saloon. We had failed our first test, but there were others to try. So we sat quietly waiting for the next man to go in or come out. We knew there were drinkers inside. We could hear them talking and the piano playing.

Just as I was about to ask Mama how long she thought we ought to stay when business out on the boardwalk was so slow, Mr. O'Hare, himself, poked his head out between the doors. He had a large cigar between his teeth. It was waggling up and down as he gazed first at Mama and me, then at Miss Ottenberg. Then he shook his head and asked, "Would either of you ladies out here like a glass of beer?"

Miss Ottenberg gave O'Hare a frosty look and snapped, "Mrs. Foster and I would most certainly not!"

"Maybe a small snort of whiskey then?" He was laughing at us, all right, being polite as all get-out and at the same time poking fun at us.

Mama didn't rise to his bait. She said as sweetly as I'd ever heard her speak, "Why Mr. O'Hare, I thought it was against your policy to serve alcoholic beverages to ladies?" She smiled up at him.

He was ready for her. "Inside my place it is, but I wouldn't want to be called cheap and not offer a drink to ladies who camp on my doorstep like they wanted somethin'."

"Yes, Mr. O'Hare, we do want something," replied Miss Emily.

"What'd that be, Miss Ottenberg?" He'd moved out between the doors, showing off his gold-and-black brocaded waistcoat with the big gold chain across it. There was some sort of yellow animal fang hanging down from it.

She said, "Your absence, sirrah."

I was stunned at her three words. They weren't many in number, they were just right all the same. Mr. O'Hare opened his mouth and closed it tight as if he was just as stunned. I only wished at that instant I had the collection box with me. I could have added insult to injury by holding up Papa's collar box. I wondered what Mr. O'Hare would do. I was sure that he wouldn't try to throw our chairs, with us in them, bodily out into the street. The boardwalk didn't belong to him as far as I knew. He could pick Mama and me up all right and put us out into the street but not Miss Emily, who was as big as he and Mama rolled together.

I asked Mama as O'Hare popped back inside to safety, "What do you think he's going to do now?"

"I don't know, Hope, but there will be something. We can rely on that."

I'd taken notice of the redness of his face as he turned away. He wasn't only hopping mad; he was embarrassed. I figured that he wouldn't come out, himself, again. He'd send somebody.

The somebody was Silas. He came out with his hands in his pockets, glaring, too. But his glare was for me, not Mama and Miss Ottenberg. He said to me, "My pa says that he knows what you and everybody else out here are up to. You're trying to keep miners from comin' into the Shoo-Fly. He says there's a name for that. It's called 'obstructin' bus'ness.' He says if you keep it up, he'll deal with you proper."

I tried to sound just as sweet as Mama had, "You tell your father for me that he's picking on an innocent child. I am only sitting here with my mother and a friend enjoying the sunshine. It's very pleasant. And next time we come to sit here, we'll bring our fancywork."

"There'd better not be a next time, nanny goat." And he went back inside to carry the tale to his pa.

"Poor child," said Miss Ottenberg. "O'Hare sent a boy to do a man's work. That's typical of such a man, you know. That sad lad."

"Hmmph," I exploded. "You should have to sit near Silas on a warm day in a chicken coop. He hasn't taken a bath all year." Oh, this was my chance to tell Miss Emily a thing or two. "That's a terribly small building for a schoolhouse. I'm within arm's reach of Silas all day long. And he pulls girls' hair whenever Miss Willis isn't looking."

"He's all the more to be pitied then." She wasn't going to rise to a debate about the schoolhouse with me. Well, I'd tried. I couldn't find it in my heart to pity Silas. I happened to know he had a bathtub, because I'd watched it being carried up the outside stairs into the Shoo-Fly earlier in the summer. There was also a Chinese laundry in town now. The O'Hares weren't poor. The only reason Silas was so dirty was because he wanted to be. Mr. O'Hare was dreadful, but at least he wasn't dirty.

We three went on staring and glaring at the miners and Ottenberg businessmen who came and went. One of them grinned questioningly at us and raised his eyebrows, but the other two didn't. They just went past quickly, looking away once they'd had a glance at the expressions on our faces. Both of them avoided our eyes, which were very accusing, I thought.

After we'd been there a couple of hours, as I reckoned it, Miss Willis came by walking with Doctor Marah, who certainly did manage to look like a man.

The teacher said, "I came to your place, Mrs. Foster, looking for you." Then she spoke to Miss Ottenberg, and I thought her voice sounded cooler. "Good afternoon, Miss Emily."

Miss Ottenberg replied, "Good afternoon. If you are wondering what Mrs. Foster and Hope and I are doing sitting out here, we're letting Mr. O'Hare and the men who frequent his saloon know what we think of him for his deplorable treatment of Doctor Marah. For your sake, young sir, we are trying to embarrass Mr. O'Hare."

I thought Doctor Marah looked a bit startled, but the words came out smoothly enough. "Well, thank you, Miss Ottenberg. It is very kind of all of you." I saw how the doctor glanced at Mama and me. I smiled and nodded, reassuring Marah that it was all right. We knew what we were doing.

Miss Emily spoke to Miss Willis. "Leota, do tell me how you like living with your October family."

Aha! I saw it all clearly. I was beginning to understand Miss Ottenberg more and more. She must have wanted to hang on to the teacher for company. I was sure that she was lonesome living with the colonel. He couldn't be much company now that he was so busy being mayor, but I doubted if he ever had been. And she was scared of him. I was very sorry for her at that moment. What would happen to her because she had sat with us? This couldn't be kept a secret from her father for long.

Miss Willis answered, "I like it very well, Miss Ottenberg." She turned to Mama. "Oh, Mrs. Foster, the Gardiners have had a good idea. There's going to be a square dance next week to raise funds for the new school."

I heard my mother say, "That's good news, indeed. It

should bring in quite a bit of money, especially from folks in the town who never go to saloons for an evening's entertainment." She moved her chair about to look at me. "Hope, how about making a nice sign to put up in the store about the dance?"

I liked making signs, so I agreed, of course. I'd draw some pictures on it and maybe get Margaret to help me with it.

Then the teacher said good-bye to the ladies and me and with Doctor Marah walked on to the Gardiner house. Being intelligent, neither one of them had gone to get chairs to sit down with us. Mr. O'Hare wouldn't have hesitated to lay hands on Marah.

As twilight came on, Miss Emily said a very bold thing, which showed Mama and me that she meant to keep on with what she was doing. "Mrs. Foster, tell me, what time do you suggest we take our vigil tomorrow?"

Mama hesitated, then said, "At about three in the afternoon, Miss Ottenberg. I think there may be more of us tomorrow."

I said, "But I have to go to school, Mama!"

"You will be dismissed at four o'clock, won't you?" Miss Ottenberg wanted to know.

By golly, that was an invitation if ever I heard one. Yes, they wanted me to come, too. I resolved that I would be there with my chair right on the dot of four fifteen.

Yes, Mama was right. It wasn't just Mama and Miss Ottenberg when I arrived with my chair the next afternoon, after a very hard day at school. There were enough ladies to make a real aisle on each side of the entrance to the Shoo-Fly. I saw Mama, Miss Emily, Mrs. Gardiner,

Mrs. Prescott, and two other ladies I knew by name who went out nights to the saloons collecting. I sat beside Mrs. Gardiner on the right side of the swinging doors. I figured she might need me to help her. She had a sweet little face, so I doubted if she was much good at glaring.

I was primed to glare my worst, all right. My trouble at school had been with Silas O'Hare, as usual. But it was different today. He hadn't once called me nanny goat or hit me or pinched me or even pulled my hair. As a matter of fact, he hadn't said a word. Miss Willis kept her eyes fixed on him all day long. All he'd done was clench and unclench his fists every time he looked at me, which seemed to be most of the time. More than that, he'd told Davey at recess that his pa was getting ready to do something about those "pesky women" that would, according to him, "make all of Ottenberg sit up and take notice."

I leaned over and asked Mrs. Gardiner, "Has O'Hare come out yet?" What Silas had said worried me. He meant every word of it. I was expecting Mr. O'Hare to keep popping in and out from the moment we sat down outside.

"Not yet, Hope."

"Have a lot of men gone inside the Shoo-Fly since three o'clock?"

"Only four of them. Five others looked as if they had it in mind, but when they saw us they went on up to the Dolly Varden."

"That's good." I noticed that Mrs. Gardiner was knitting something. It looked too small for her or the preacher. She saw my glance, held up the needles and knitting, and said, "It's for the Bokman infant, Hope."

She wasn't much of a knitter. The part she'd already knit was grayish, not white the way the unused yarn was.

That meant she'd worn it halfway out already, by ripping it out to pick up dropped stitches. White yarn that was knitted over and over again got gray, no matter how clean the knitter's hands were.

I asked, "What's Mrs. Bokman like?"

"She's a lovely person."

That told me nothing at all. That's what most ladies Mama knew said about just about every other lady. I was about to ask what was lovely about Mrs. Bokman when suddenly the Shoo-Fly's doors opened again and out came Mr. O'Hare in a long brown frock coat. He was all dolled up today.

He moved out into the center of the aisle of chairs, folded his arms, and said, "I'm givin' you ladies five minutes to pick up your chairs and clear the walk in front of my establishment. If you don't I'm goin' to take action you won't like."

"And what would that be, sirrah?" asked Miss Emily.

"Be here when the five minutes is up and you'll find out!"

She stood up. "Mr. O'Hare, why on earth should we do what you ask us?"

"You'll do well to obey me, Miss Ottenberg." He was looking very determinedly at her.

"Obey you? I'm not married to you, am I? Why must I obey you?" She was taller than he was and larger, too, as she looked down on him.

Oh, but I wished she'd said that loud enough for all of the town to hear. That was something to be shouted out, not said in a low voice. She hadn't raised her voice much, but what she said worked. Mr. O'Hare went back scowling into the safety of his saloon, and we gathered in a cluster around Miss Ottenberg whose face was pink as a pink peony and just as big, to boot.

"What's he going to do now?" asked Mrs. Gardiner.

"I have no idea, Dilsey, but we are going to hold fast here whatever he does," Miss Ottenberg told her. I saw that Miss Emily's hands were trembling in spite of her brave words.

"But we only have five minutes. Do you think he means what he says?" Mrs. Gardiner went on.

"I believe that the man does. Back to your chairs, ladies. And don't let him see that we are frightened of him."

Well, I was, and though they didn't show it, I knew the others were, too, by the way they pressed their lips together. I watched the little gold watch pinned to the bosom of Mrs. Gardiner's bodice. Five minutes wasn't a very long time. When I wasn't looking anxiously at the hands of the watch, I was anxiously watching the doors of the Shoo-Fly.

Five minutes after his father had gone back inside, Silas came running out of the doors, past the chairs and across the street. I saw him leap up onto the boardwalk in front of the jail, go to its door, open it, close it with a loud bang behind him.

"Oh, dear," wailed Mrs. Gardiner softly, putting down the baby knitting into the embroidery basket beside her chair. She stood up with her hands pressed against her chest.

"Sit down, Dilsey, dear," said Mrs. Prescott.

Mrs. Gardiner sat down with her gaze fixed on the jail, just as mine was. In fact, there wasn't a single one of us who wasn't staring in that direction.

Finally Silas reappeared. With him came a big man wearing a black hat and dark-blue shirt with a star on his chest. He was the sheriff.

"Ladies, keep your seats no matter what," warned Miss Ottenberg.

I didn't know about the others, but every step the sheriff took toward me made me feel more like getting up and running home. I knew him. He was Henry Sherman, someone we'd known when he was also the sheriff of Silver Belle. He seemed flustered as he came up onto the boardwalk, with Silas tagging along behind him like the little tattered tail on a big kite. "Howdy, Miss Ottenberg. Howdy, Mrs. Foster. Howdy, ladies." He didn't seem to know what else to say to us.

Miss Emily helped him out. "Henry, you came over here for a purpose. Speak your piece."

He mumbled, "You ladies got to quit doin' what you're doin'—stopping men from goin' in and out of the saloon."

"We aren't stopping anyone at all, Henry," replied Mama. "We haven't touched a finger to a single gentleman who's come past us."

"You've stared at 'em, though. It's been making the men nervous."

"A cat can look at a king!" That was Mrs. Prescott with another motto.

"That's right, ma'am, a cat can," said the sheriff, "but you ladies can't block the way here. If you don't leave right now, I'll have to run you in."

"Aren't you at all interested, Sheriff, in why we are sitting out here in the cold?" asked Miss Emily.

"Your reasons don't matter so much to me as the fact

that you're here now. I think I know why, though. You're mad at Tom O'Hare 'cause he won't give no money to that new schoolhouse."

Miss Emily said, "Sheriff, that is not my primary reason. Primarily, I am letting every man in town know that I highly disapprove of the manner in which Mr. O'Hare has treated young Doctor Marah. I do not approve of open invitations to fighting."

Mama spoke up next. "We agree with Miss Ottenberg that the idea of dueling is dreadful. That feeling is part of our being here, too. We are also going to continue collecting for the new school building as usual this evening, and tonight I predict that there will be some of us sitting here, as we are right now. Mr. O'Hare hasn't asked us yet why we are here and what we want, and we certainly know from past experience that we cannot go into his place. It isn't fair that we shouldn't be allowed to let him —and the men who are his customers—know our exact reasons."

"Amen to that," said Mrs. Gardiner.

The sheriff ignored what all of them had said. "Ladies, you just got to disperse. Disperse—or else."

In a whisper I asked Mrs. Gardiner, "What does that word mean?"

Her face was grayish white, like the milk in a churn after the butter had come. "It means if we don't go away as he says, he is going to put us in jail."

I squeaked, scared now, "I'm only thirteen!"

The sheriff heard my squeak and turned to me to say, "I don't mean you, kid. Just these here ladies." He put his hands on his hips and told Miss Emily, "Please don't give me no trouble, Miss Ottenberg. Go on home peacefully."

She was on her feet, looking eye to eye with the sheriff, who was her size. "Do you expect me to give Mr. O'Hare such an easy victory, Sheriff Sherman?" There were red patches in her cheeks, and her voice rang out louder than I'd ever heard it before.

He took off his hat to wipe his forehead. "Miss Emily, am I going to have to get your father to make you leave?"

"If I go at all, I will go peaceably, but I will certainly not go anywhere if you bring my father here."

"Won't you ladies please disperse to your homes?"

"No, sir, I don't think we will." Mama was fired up, but her voice was still as sweet as could be.

Sheriff Sherman put his hat back on. "All right then, you don't leave me no choice. Everybody sittin' out here, except for this kid Hope, is hereby under arrest."

I couldn't believe my ears or my eyes either as the ladies cheered and got up, one by one, to stand in a row beside Miss Ottenberg. It was a grand and glorious sight as she stepped down into the street with her black parasol tucked under her arm. I watched the other ladies go down off the boardwalk, Mama last of all. She called back over her shoulder as she walked arm-in-arm with Mrs. Gardiner toward the jail, "Hope, take the chairs back where they belong, so Mr. O'Hare does not take them into that saloon of his. And while you're delivering the chairs to our house, tell your father where I am."

"My pa don't want your old chairs!" Silas hooted after the ladies. I saw him put his fingers into his ears and waggle his hands at her and the others.

I got hold of our two chairs first, then before I picked them up I told him, "Oh, go inside and tattle to your publican pa. You tell him why we're out here."

The word *publican* got Silas. He didn't know what it meant. He thought it was something very bad, so he dashed into the Shoo-Fly past the sheriff, who was shaking his head, taking his time to follow the ladies, who were halfway across the street, skirting the mud puddles.

Obeying Mama, I headed for the shebang as fast as I could go. I figured it would be up to Papa to get messages to Reverend Gardiner, Colonel Ottenberg, Mr. Prescott, and the other menfolks as to where the women were. It would come as a big surprise, I was sure of that.

On the way home with the chairs I met Doctor Haverford coming out of the Oro Fino Saloon. He looked as bad as ever—or maybe worse. I thought his complexion was more purple than usual.

"Where are you going, Hope?" he asked me, not seeming to notice the chairs. He hadn't passed while we were seated in front of the Shoo-Fly.

"Home to tell Papa that Mama's just gone to jail!"

"*What?*" I saw him reach for the barber pole to steady himself.

"Yes, sir." I stopped long enough to tell him how noble Mama and the other ladies and Miss Ottenberg were being for the sake of the school and especially for Doctor Marah. Naturally I kept it quiet that I knew that Doctor Marah wasn't a gentleman but a Jeanette.

"Well, well," Haverford mumbled in his beard. "That's one way to deal with violence. I suppose any way that avoids meeting force with force is good in my book, good in any doctor's book, that is."

I told him, "I suppose so. I've got to get on home." I grabbed the chairs I'd set down to save my strength when he'd hailed me and started off again.

But Doctor Haverford called after me, "How much cash is there in the kitty now for the school?"

"Over seven hundred dollars. We're more than halfway there. Mama and I will go out again tonight collecting." A rich mine owner had given Mama nearly two hundred dollars in nuggets day before yesterday and that had helped swell the fund.

He went on shouting at me, "If you need company tonight when you go out collecting, call on me. I'll go with you."

Him? Why would I need him?

And then the whole thing finally struck me. Good heavens! I halted in my tracks, a chairback in each hand. Mama was in jail! And so were the other ladies who collected with her. If she was in jail, how could she go out collecting for the school tonight?

What would Papa say? What would Colonel Ottenberg say about Miss Emily's being in jail, the new jail that he was so proud of? I was sure he'd never figured on that. I stooped down a bit, jerked a chairback under each one of my arms, and began to run home fast as my feet would take me over the boardwalk.

CHAPTER SEVEN

OBSTREPEROUS

I didn't wait for Papa to ask me where Mama was. I came right out with, "Mama's in jail and so are her best lady friends—and Miss Ottenberg."

Papa was weighing out some coffee beans into a sack for a miner, who had a thick black beard. The news startled Papa so much he let the sack drop to the floor. Coffee beans rolled across the boards in every direction.

"Nora? *In jail?*"

"Oh dear," came from the miner. Considering how serious the situation was, it seemed a pretty feeble comment from such a hirsute man.

I gave him a fierce glare and said, "You have the look about you of a man who drinks at the Shoo-Fly Saloon."

He nodded. "I have been known to go in there now and then."

"Well, I would appreciate it if you would stop it. It's because of Mr. O'Hare that my mother's in jail. He got the sheriff to arrest the preacher's wife, too."

"Ye Gods! What's going on in Ottenberg?" The miner was doing better. Now he had spoken like a man.

"Mr. O'Hare will live to regret this," I said to Papa. "The sheriff claimed the ladies were obstructing business. I was with them. They didn't lay a hand on anybody."

"How come you aren't in jail with them?" asked the

miner, who hadn't yet lifted a finger to pick up his coffee beans.

"The sheriff says I'm too young to go to jail." That would fix him.

The miner finally left without his coffee beans as I asked my father, "What're we going to do about Mama and the others?"

I saw that he was chewing on the ends of his mustache, which meant he was worried, and he was frowning, to boot. He said with a wheezing sound, "Hope, I'm afraid this is what comes of listening to tales of Ohio fermenters. As I see it, your mother is my concern but not the other women."

"What?" I flared up like a piece of kindling wood with kerosene poured on it. "Aren't you worried about Mrs. Gardiner and Mrs. Prescott and Miss Emily?"

"Of course, I am. But I'm not their husband or their father. Their men will have to get them out of jail—probably have to bail them out."

"Bail? What's that?"

"Go look it up in Doc Marah's dictionary, Hope. It's too complicated for me to tell you about right now." I watched him take off his storekeeper's long muslin apron and put on his coat, muttering about all the cat hair on it.

He went on, "You go tell Reverend Gardiner and Mr. Prescott the glad news. Ask them to go see the menfolks of the other ladies. I'm going to see Colonel Ottenberg and then Judge Bokman."

"Why see the judge?"

"Because being in jail is a legal matter."

"All right, Papa. I'll tell the men to come pick up their chairs out in front of the Shoo-Fly, too."

"Yes, yes, of course." But he hadn't really heard me.

I ran as fast as I could down the boardwalk, wondering all the while about bail.

Reverend Gardiner was home, working on his sermon for next Sunday. He looked at me standing on his front stoop with bulging eyes, as I told the story; then he nodded. "I'll go get Dilsey's rocker and bring it home. You say your father's seeing Mayor Ottenberg and Judge Bokman?"

"Yes, sir. I've got to leave now and go to see Mr. Prescott. Will you please tell the other men?" I gave him their names.

I was off again running. Miners going up and down the boardwalk stared after me, as if they'd never seen a girl running on a worthwhile mission before.

The Prescott house was different from the others. It had pale gray paint on it, while the other places still hadn't even been whitewashed, except for the chicken coop and the Ottenberg home. There didn't seem to be any sense in whitewashing a house when winter was coming closer, minute by minute.

Mr. Prescott, not being a minister, didn't take the news as calmly as Reverend Gardiner, who must have learned by now that the Lord works in some mysterious ways. Either that or reverends in Montana Territory ran into the law more often than people would think. Mr. Prescott let out a yell, *"What? Annabelle in jail?"* He was a tallish man with brown hair that was fast disappearing on two sides of his head, showing long white grooves of skin. Because he was a member of the school board and in a way, I supposed, involved with his wife's collecting for a new building, I told him a bit more than I'd told the preacher. Still all he could say was, "Annabelle in jail?"

"Yes, sir, and your parlor chair with the purple plush seat is out in front of the Shoo-Fly Saloon. Papa's gone to see the mayor and Judge Bokman. I'm going to go find Papa. You're a lawyer, aren't you, Mr. Prescott? You'll know what to do, I suppose."

Having made him feel better by my saying that, I was off once more—this time to the Ottenberg homestead, which was a sort of log building. I had to go through some pine trees, over a little wooden bridge that crossed a brook, and through a meadow past the chicken coop to get to the front door.

Colonel Ottenberg finally came to the door after I'd beaten on it three times. I could see my father standing in the parlor behind him. I thought they both looked dazed, as if somebody had hit them over the head with something, and at the same time plenty put out. Colonel Ottenberg barked at me, "Who in the devil are you, little girl?"

Annoyed by his greeting, I told him, "I'm Hope Foster. My father's standing there right behind you. I was with your daughter, Miss Emily, when she was put in jail."

"Oh, you're *that* girl. Yes, yes," I heard him mumbling, as he left the doorway.

Papa came to stand in his place. He looked down at me. "Did you do what I told you to, Hope?"

"I surely did." I told him where I'd been and what I said. Then I saw Colonel Ottenberg going through a door behind the parlor. He hadn't asked me inside, but I got a look at his parlor by staring on both sides of my father. It was crammed full of horsehair, leather chairs, and other things, like crossed swords over the mantel, bearskin rugs, and deer and elk antlers on the walls. It didn't look as if a lady lived there at all. I was sorrier than ever for Miss Emily.

I gathered that Colonel Ottenberg had gone off to get dressed to visit his daughter in jail, so I asked Papa, "Are you still going to see Judge Bokman or are you going to visit Mama?"

"The mayor and I are going to see the judge together."

I came closer to him and said, "You know we were there outside of the saloon for a couple of reasons, Papa. Mama and the other ladies were mostly there because of the way Mr. O'Hare treated us over the school. But that wasn't the reason Miss Ottenberg joined Mama and me."

"Yes, I know. Your mother told me last night."

This got my goat a little. Grown-ups always told secrets to each other before children could get to tell them. It took a lot of the fun out of life. Well, I had another secret. "Papa, I know that Doctor Marah's a lady, because she doesn't shave. I learned about her all by myself. Mama didn't tell me, but she told me that you knew."

Aha! This took him by surprise all right. He didn't know that I knew that, too. What a look he gave me. I hurried on before Colonel Ottenberg could come back. "Papa, is that why you wanted Doctor Marah to leave town when O'Hare put that notice in the *Oracle*? Because Doctor Marah is a lady?"

"Yes, who could expect a lady to fight?"

"That's right, of course, but we're doing the fighting for her." Then I asked him, "Should we ask Doctor Marah to come to see the judge with us?"

"No, leave Doctor Marah out of this as much as possible, Hope. And for the Lord's sake, keep her secret. She was quite disturbed when she heard from your mother that Miss Emily has taken it upon herself to punish Mr. O'Hare on her behalf. She scarcely knows the Ottenbergs."

Because I thought I had it figured out, I whispered to him, "It really isn't so much because of Doctor Marah, Papa. I think it's because somebody Miss Emily was in love with got killed in a duel."

"Ah!" I think he would have gone on to say more, but just at that moment Colonel Ottenberg came out dressed in his hat and soldier's cape.

So off we went together down into Ottenberg. I felt important because I was walking with the mayor, but I was worried, too. With Mama in jail, what would we do about dinner? Papa couldn't cook worth a dang. Could Doctor Marah? Could a woman doctor cook? Even if she could, it wouldn't be right to ask a boarder to take over in the kitchen.

I got to go inside the judge's parlor. Mrs. Bokman, who answered our knock on the door, invited all three of us in. She even had a smile for me as she showed us to chairs in the parlor room. My, but it was nice: green-brown velvet portieres, gold-plush seats on the gilded-leg chairs, bisque vases with cupids and Dresden shepherdesses on the mantel. They had a stereopticon viewer, too, next to a large box of pictures. I was very curious about them. What did judges like to look at? I wondered.

But I didn't get a chance to find out that day. Neither of the Bokmans asked me to look at the pictures, and nobody asked me to talk either. Colonel Ottenberg and Judge Bokman did it all. While they were talking, Mrs.

Bokman kept opening the door time after time to let in the menfolks of the other ladies in jail. I wound up finally sitting between Reverend Gardiner and Mr. Prescott.

The judge sounded quite calm—a lot more so than Colonel Ottenberg—when he told Mr. Prescott, who was a lawyer also, "I haven't been here long enough to get a court properly set up, so I suppose the best thing to do is hold a hearing here and now."

"We can go across the street to the courthouse," came from the mayor.

"No, my chambers aren't finished yet. There isn't any west wall. The courtroom is even less finished, mayor. We'll hold the hearing right here."

Mrs. Bokman made a small noise that I recognized as a giggle. It sounded odd after what her husband had just said. Colonel Ottenberg must have thought so, too, for he looked put out.

Mr. Prescott ignored her, though. "We'd better send for Mr. O'Hare now," he said.

"Yes, one of you please go fetch him," ordered the judge.

One of the other husbands went to the Shoo-Fly and was back in a little while with the "enemy," who was looking very pleased with himself and took no notice at all of my powerful glare.

Judge Bokman saw it, though. He remarked, "What a horrible expression on that child's face. Is she ill?" I supposed he thought if I was sick he didn't want me around his wife, who was going to have a baby.

I answered, "I'm not sick, sir."

"No," said Papa. "She's my daughter, Hope. She was out on the sidewalk with the women."

Then Mr. O'Hare spoke up for the first time. "You bet she was. Being a pest along with the rest of them, obstructing my business, Your Honor."

The judge cleared his throat before I could get out a word about not being a pest. There was something in the way he cleared his throat that made everyone in the room stop talking. He asked O'Hare to tell the story of what had happened today and the day before that. When he was finished telling how bad Mama and the other ladies were, the judge did a surprising thing. He turned his head to look at me and said, "All right, Miss Foster, I want you to tell me exactly what you were doing there with those other ladies. Afterward I will ask each of them what they were trying to do. I am perfectly aware that this is a ridiculous way to conduct matters and it would never do at all back in the East, but this is Montana Territory and things don't ever seem to operate in an ordinary fashion out here." He sighed.

I got the feeling from the look on his face and the sigh that being a judge in the West wasn't as easy as people might think. All the same, it annoyed me that he wasn't sure of my story not being a lie. That was what he'd hinted at, anyhow. I said, "You won't have to go over to the jail and ask my mother and Miss Ottenberg if I am a liar or not. I do not tell lies."

Mrs. Bokman giggled some more, though I couldn't figure out why, but nobody seemed to notice. All eyes were fixed on me. So I told the judge about how I took the chair to the Shoo-Fly and why, saying that I thought Mr. O'Hare had been very mean about not letting us collect in his saloon. I mentioned the *Oracle* notice, but I kept Doctor Marah's secret. Then I told about meeting Miss Emily and how Mama and the other ladies had come too. I finished with, "We never even stuck out a foot when the miners walked past us into that saloon."

"Hmmm." Bokman turned back to Mr. O'Hare. "And you sent for the sheriff and got him to come over?"

"Yes, Your Honor, but not before I warned them women to go home and leave me and my customers alone." Oh, but O'Hare looked tickled with himself, grinning from ear to ear.

Bokman asked him, "Were the ladies at all obstreperous?"

Obstreperous was one of the very words I'd planned to look up in Doctor Marah's dictionary. I could tell by the look on his face that Mr. O'Hare didn't know its meaning either. He was lots older than I was and should have.

"What does that mean, Your Honor?" he asked the judge.

"Were they unruly? Were they loud?"

I had the meaning now. So did Mr. O'Hare, who shook his head and scowled. He seemed disappointed that the ladies hadn't been.

I watched the judge heave himself up and out of his deep leather chair. He said, "All right, I'm going over to the jail."

"We'll all go," came from Colonel Ottenberg, who was the next most important man present and knew it.

And so off we went, me included, everybody but Mrs. Bokman, who stayed home. Before I left she gave me—the last person to leave—a piece of vanilla fudge from a glass-topped candy dish on a table by the front door. She smiled at me at the same time. But I didn't know whether it was because she approved of what I'd been doing outside the Shoo-Fly or because she just liked my looks. I liked hers. And I thought she made mighty good fudge. I wondered what it was like being married to a judge. Even nasty old Mr. O'Hare had seemed respectful of her husband.

The four-cell jail was so new it still smelled of fresh-sawed lumber on the inside. I could see right into the cells. Three were full of ladies. The other one had two men in it, horse thieves, Friday's *Oracle* had said. No, the judge told the sheriff, there wasn't any cause to bring Mama and Miss Emily and the others from behind the bars out into the sheriff's office. Judge Bokman would stand at one end of the office and ask the questions he had in mind. He didn't even have to raise his voice.

Standing between Papa and Reverend Gardiner, with Mr. O'Hare all too close to me, I listened to Mrs. Prescott talk to the judge about Mr. O'Hare's "hard attitude." I thought she put it very well, but after all she was married to a lawyer and it was their job to be good talkers.

The judge listened with his head cocked to one side. Then he cocked it to the other when Mama spoke next. I thought she did well, too, probably because she'd been in drama societies back in Oregon.

She looked well, too, considering she was behind bars. The ladies waved at the men and at me. There was a sort of glow about their faces, which I imagined came from doing a good deed or maybe from fermenting. I was sure that they'd been doing a lot of talking, trying to cheer each other up until we got there. We'd heard singing before we came inside. Even Miss Ottenberg was smiling and nodded at the other ladies—not at her frowning father.

I stole a quick glance at the men, while Mama was talking to the judge. They didn't look at all happy. They were chomping on their mustaches, chewing tobacco nervously, spitting into cuspidors, digging in their beards with their fingernails, looking at the ceiling, and shifting their weight from foot to foot. They all looked uncomfortable, Sheriff Sherman most of all.

After Mama was through, Judge Bokman turned to face the men. I heard him say, sounding angry, "This sounds to me like a tempest in a teapot, gentlemen. These women were not threatening anyone with bodily harm, but they were making a public nuisance out of themselves. I want to make quick work of this business, because it doesn't deserve a lot of anyone's valuable time. So I am fining each of the ladies the sum of two dollars. Your family members may pay the sheriff, and he will hold the fines until I've got the proper legal machinery set up here in town. Then you can take your wives and daughters home in time for them to get dinner."

Mr. O'Hare let out a snort. I figured he'd wanted a heavier fine than just two dollars. He threw Judge Bokman a disgusted look and shouldered his way outside through the other men.

"Albert?" my mother called. I looked toward her cell and saw her reach for her cape on the bunk. "Albert, please pay the sheriff now. And Hope, you run on home, dear, stir up the fire, and pound some flour into the venison steaks that are in the pantry."

I watched Mama sweep her arms out as widely as she could in her crowded cell. "Ladies, we shall meet at the same time tonight to collect for the new school building."

"Not Emily!" thundered Colonel Ottenberg, who stood next to Sheriff Sherman.

Mama smiled sweetly at him, but she didn't say anything. Instead she reached through the bars of the next cell to grip Miss Ottenberg's shoulder as if to comfort her or give her courage. I didn't know which, but Miss Ottenberg seemed to.

She looked up at Mama and said, "Yes, Nora, yes. I certainly will."

As the ladies got up and the men were hauling silver dollars out of their pockets, looking very annoyed for the most part, the judge said to the women, "Ladies, I want you to remember why you are being fined."

"We shall not forget, Your Honor." Mrs. Gardiner favored the judge with her nicest smile as Sheriff Sherman unlocked the door of her cell. "Your Honor, please give my compliments to your wife," she told him, as she took her husband's arm and pushed through the crowd of men.

Obeying Mama, I went out right behind the Gardiners. I was just as glad to run ahead of all the ladies and their menfolk to start our supper. I didn't really care to hear what Papa would have to say to Mama and she to him. What she did say would be filled with a lot of "my loves," I was sure. And I certainly didn't want to be within earshot of what Colonel Ottenberg might say to Miss Emily once she'd been let out of the third cell, which would be the last one unlocked.

It appeared to me that there were really three ringleaders of the Ottenberg fermenters, which is what I called them now. Mrs. Prescott, Miss Emily, and my own mother.

I decided that it was rather hard to think of your own mother as something other than a woman who kept house and took care of you and your family.

I found Davey sitting alone in the parlor, head in his hands and elbows resting on his knees. Sulking for sure, he said, "Hope, Silas says he won't play with me anymore because of what you and Mama did. He says his pa won't let me. My mother's a jailbird; that's what his pa says."

I told Davey, "No, Mama's not a jailbird. She's out now and on her way home." I couldn't help but add, "That sounds just like old Mr. O'Hare. You can tell Silas for me that this is the very first time I've ever heard his father take any interest in him at all. It might be a good sign at that." I took off my shawl, hung it on a peg, and put on an apron.

"What about dinner, Hope?"

"I'm starting it now. You can help me. How about going and getting the venison out of the pantry for me?" We had a big pantry, one with a wide grating open to the air on one side. Food left near that end stayed fresh and no flies could get in. The only thing wrong with it was that food froze solid at night.

While Davey was in there, I got a cup of flour out of the roll-top bin. Then, because I hadn't seen hide nor hair of Doctor Marah, I went to his room and rapped on the door.

"Come in, Hope," answered the doctor.

"How did you know it was me?" I asked, as I opened it.

"Oh, I know your knock from everyone else's."

I tried not to stare, but I just couldn't help it. Now that I knew she wasn't a he, I couldn't keep my eyes off Doctor Marah. She certainly could be taken for a man, all right.

Keeping up the appearance must be quite a strain, though. Men didn't walk like ladies, and their voices were deeper. My, but she was something to be admired.

I said, "I learned a new word today. Judge Bokman used it. *Obstreperous*—it means unruly and things like that."

Doctor Marah nodded. "I know the word. It's seldom heard in these parts, though it seems to fit quite a lot of people's behavior. How did the judge use it?"

"He asked Mr. O'Hare if Mama and Miss Emily and the other women were obstreperous out in front of the Shoo-Fly, before they were arrested and thrown into jail."

"Good Lord in Heaven! *What are you saying?*" This got Doctor Marah up out of her chair. "When did this happen?"

"Oh, just a little while ago. Doctor Haverford knows."

"*I* certainly didn't know. I came back home only about twenty minutes ago from seeing a woman with an acute stomachache. What happened to your mother and the others?"

Because I had heard our side door open, which meant Papa and Mama were back, I said, "Mama will tell you all about it during dinner before the sisters go out collecting tonight. It's all right now, Doctor. We're having deer steaks and beans. Mama is going to cook the food. Papa paid her fine and got her out in time to cook for us. Judge Bokman is a fast worker, even if I don't think he likes the way things get done in his line of work here in the Territory. I have to go now and pound flour into the venison. Good-bye."

At the table Mama did all of the talking, while Papa and Davey kept their eyes on their plates, letting everybody know that they were in a pout. Between bites Mama told Doctor Marah all about the women being arrested and then let out. "Let me tell you it was quite an experience, Doctor. We sang a great deal to keep our mutual spirits up."

"I'm certain that it was an ordeal. I'm happy that you've let Mr. O'Hare and the whole town know what you think of him, and perhaps he has learned his lesson because you got out with such ease. Perhaps he will even contribute to the new-school fund now." Marah sounded hopeful.

"No, Doctor Marah." I saw Mama shaking her head strongly from side to side. "O'Hare will not get the chance to even things by contributing to the school fund. We are not through with the keeper of the Shoo-Fly Saloon—not by a long shot."

"Oh, my Lord, Nora," Papa burst out. "Haven't you created enough of an uproar in town?"

"Albert, my love, we have yet to roar."

"What are you going to do?" Davey wanted to know, as he put down his napkin. He looked interested.

"Mama, don't you tell him. He might tell Silas," I warned.

"No, I won't. He says he's off of me, so I'm off of him."

Papa put his napkin down, too, without putting it into the ring. "I don't want to hear what the ladies of Ottenberg are planning to do next. I'm afraid that I already know." He got up, pushed back his chair, and went out into the shebang.

Mama leaned over the table toward Doctor Marah. "Tonight we collect as always, and tomorrow we'll be back with chairs in front of the Shoo-Fly."

"Me, too, Mama?" I wasn't so sure that I wanted to do that again.

"Yes, Hope. We need you there in case Mr. O'Hare sends for the sheriff again. We think that he will. When he does, we want you to do just what you did today."

"Oh, Mama." It had been exciting today but nerve-wracking, too. I was weary. "Are you sure that this is what you want to do?" I asked.

"We are set on it." Mama nodded over her coffee cup. "As a matter of fact, we made a pact while we were in jail. We will never be satisfied until Mr. O'Hare takes out a notice in the newspaper apologizing publicly for what he said about Doctor Marah and for how he treated us."

I said, "Mama, you're asking a lot of a man as stubborn as he is."

Mama said grimly, "Mr. O'Hare is going to find out that he is dealing with some very determined women."

I said nothing. I'd seen Mother like this before, mostly when she wanted Papa to stock some merchandise in the shebang he didn't want to stock. I looked at Doctor Marah sitting there in a white shirt, string necktie, and man's waistcoat, and I wondered what was going on in her mind.

The doctor said softly and slowly, "Nora, I do appreciate what you're trying to do in my behalf, but perhaps it would ease matters for everyone if I leave town the way your husband suggested before."

"No, it would not, Doctor. You'd disappoint a lot of good people—men as well as women. Doctor Haverford needs you here."

"That is true enough." Doctor Marah's face seemed to me to have grown weary all at once, and now she looked older, too.

"And you will keep out of our saloon business, promise me, Doctor?" Mama was grinning.

The doctor smiled at her. "All right, I promise. If necessary, I'll even cook supper for the Fosters, though I can't make anything but crab soufflé, Welsh rarebit, and pecan pie."

For a girl, Jeanette Marah must have had a very strange upbringing back in Maryland, but I imagined there'd been a cook in her house.

"If I have to, I'll help, too. I can fry just about anything that you can put into a pan." I said this, but in my heart I hoped I wouldn't have to. I didn't dote on house tasks much.

I was late getting out of school the next day. Miss Willis had caught Margaret and me whispering about the ladies in jail and kept us one-half hour after school. I thought this wasn't fair of Miss Willis, but then she kept Silas in, too, for doing the same thing. What he had said to one of the smaller girls about my mother and Mrs. Prescott and the others hadn't been nice at all.

I ran straight home from the chicken coop, got a chair, and headed down the boardwalk toward the Shoo-Fly.

But there weren't any ladies there! Only two rows of empty chairs. Silas was there, though. He always got home first, because he splashed through the brook instead of taking the time to cross it on the little wooden bridge from school to town. He leaned against the saloon with his hands in his pockets, looking pleased with himself. I stiffened all over at the sight of him.

He told me, "If you're looking for your ma, nanny goat, Sheriff Sherman's got her and the rest of them old hens. They're right back where they was yesterday." He grinned an awful grin, like a mean dog showing all his lower teeth ready to take a bite out of somebody. "Remember a while back, nanny goat, when you said I'd wind up in jail? Well, it seems to be your ma who's there instead. And your doctor friend'd better get out of Ottenberg, too, before my pa's done with the lot of you."

The kitchen chair was still in my hands. I lifted it up by the back and seat, ready to ram Silas in the midriff with the legs. But before I could jab him, he jumped sideways and backed through the swinging doors, yelling, "Pa, Pa!"

I ran for the shebang once more to get Papa, who'd get the colonel, who'd get the judge again.

So for the second night in a row we went through the same business. This time, though, the judge scolded the ladies and fined them each five dollars because he said it was a "second offense." I still didn't know what bail was. When I asked Papa if it was the same as a fine, all he said was, "No, it isn't. And I don't want to talk about it, Hope. I don't even want to think about jails."

After Mama was let out tonight, I walked home with her and Papa. All the other ladies and men were trailing behind us, except for Colonel Ottenberg and Miss Emily, who were up ahead. Emily and her father were walking a distance apart, although she wasn't walking behind the way she used to. They were both looking straight ahead, and I saw that they weren't talking to each other.

The rest of the people seemed to be wrangling not so much about the two fines but about being in jail a second time. The men seemed to think it was a very disgraceful place to be. But from what I could overhear the ladies didn't agree. They were saying that their reason for being there blotted out the disgrace. It was plain to me at least that they'd agreed in jail on what they were going to say outside of it.

They were right, but where was it going to end? Margaret had told me during the afternoon recess, "My papa claims he's never seen such a pigheaded bunch of females in all his life as we've got here in Ottenberg. The next thing that's going to happen is that these silly women will want to vote and be on juries the way they do in Wyoming Territory."

It was on the tip of my tongue to tell Margaret that I'd like to vote someday and to ask her if she wouldn't like to vote, too. But I didn't say that. It would only have led to a fight.

I'd heard Doctor Marah and Mama talking at breakfast that morning about what had gone on in Wyoming Territory. Seven years back the legislature had passed a law to permit ladies to vote in the hope that a lot of unmarried women would move out there and the bachelors could get wives. Then, two years later, the legislature tried to get rid of the law. *Repeal* was the word Doctor Marah had used. The vote was close and had been defeated by a margin of only one in the state legislature. But women there had kept the right and could still vote now.

CHAPTER EIGHT

BENIGHTED

I certainly had mixed thoughts when I went to bed that night. Whatever I'd started when I got my chair and sat down in front of Mr. O'Hare's saloon seemed to be getting out of hand. Anyhow, it was all certainly exciting. Having your own mother in jail two afternoons in a row was even more of an adventure than gathering cash for a new school.

Maybe it would go on as long as the collecting, though I doubted if I'd like that. Certainly Papa wouldn't. He hadn't been happy at all when he took that five-dollar gold piece out of his waistcoat pocket to pay Sheriff Sherman. He'd muttered at the time, "This thing's getting out of hand."

Colonel Ottenberg had behaved badly. He'd paid to free Miss Emily with the remark, "And to think I was proud of this building, because it was the first brick one in my town."

Mrs. Prescott had overheard him and said so everyone could hear, "It serves you right, Mr. Mayor. If the first municipal building had been a decent school, none of this would ever have happened."

All of the ladies had cheered while their menfolks looked glum, except for Reverend Gardiner. As for Mr.

O'Hare, he'd gone back grinning to the Shoo-Fly the minute Judge Bokman upped the fine to five dollars. O'Hare had seemed to think that his lady troubles were over, but I knew better because I'd heard Mama and Doctor Marah just after I'd gone to bed. There were a lot of useful knotholes in my door that made for good hearing.

Mama had said, "I do believe that Mr. O'Hare thinks he's seen the last of us. Well, he certainly has not. You should have seen how he smirked at the judge in the jail today. Even Albert noticed it and became angry, and you know how much Albert dislikes what we are doing."

I noticed that Doctor Marah's voice wasn't any higher when she talked woman to woman than it ever was. She was naturally a low-voiced lady. She answered, "I wish I could take a hand in this matter, Nora."

"You can't, Jeanette," my mother said. "If you do, O'Hare will surely pick a fight with you that would lead to some sort of violence. He'd either hit you or shoot you. He'd do his best to provoke you into being in the wrong."

"I suppose you're right, Nora, but I can't help but feel that I'm hiding behind your skirts because I can't wear mine!"

Then I heard both of them laughing. Doctor Marah's laugh didn't sound one bit like a man's. If any other Ottenberger had heard it, he or she would have suspected the truth right off.

After that they said good-night to each other, and I heard both their doors close squeakingly. Most doors in town squeaked, because the houses were built so fast.

In spite of my wonderings about the future, I slept like a log that night. In fact, I even overslept and didn't hear

Doctor Marah's door squeak open. Davey was the one who told me at breakfast, "Doc Marah's gone. He didn't leave us any note on his door either."

"What?" I almost added, *She's* gone? but remembered just in the nick of time that Davey didn't know the secret.

"Uh-huh, Mama called him for breakfast, but he'd gone. She's looking for him now, I guess. He didn't even say good-bye. Maybe he's run away because of Mr. O'Hare."

Just then Mama came in the side door. I asked her anxiously, "Is it true that the doctor's not here and he didn't leave a note?" I was too upset to fix myself my breakfast pancake, though the frying pan was ready and the batter mixed in the bowl on the kitchen table.

"Yes, it's true, and there weren't any emergency calls for him last night. Your father and I went out separately early this morning asking about him. The owner of the Big Bend Hotel says that he took the six-o'clock stage out of town this morning."

I asked, "Do you know where Doctor Marah went?"

"Helena, it seems. The hotel owner took note that Doctor Marah had a folded Helena newspaper sticking out of his coat pocket when he boarded the stage."

All this made me wonder. Was the Helena newspaper advertising for a doctor to come there? Could this be why Doctor Marah had gone away? Was she trying to keep Mama and the other ladies out of jail by leaving temporarily? Had she run away for good?

Because I was worried, I asked, "Mama, did Doctor Marah take everything in his room?"

She gave me a smile as she took off her shawl. "No, Hope. Not even his razor."

Davey said softly, as if he missed the doctor, "Maybe he'll grow a beard in Helena and never come back here."

"No, I doubt that, Davey."

The look on her face was sad. I suspected that she wasn't sure of what she was saying. I asked as I turned over part of the breakfast pancake I'd poured onto the skillet, prying it loose from where it was sticking, "Mama, what are you going to do about Mr. O'Hare now that Doctor Marah's left town?"

She told me as she poured a cup of coffee boiled black as molasses, "Have a council of war with the ladies and abide by what all of us decide to do."

"How are you doing with the collecting, Mama?"

"We have over eight hundred dollars now, and we still take in a nice amount every evening. The men of Ottenberg have been very good about this. Miners have generous souls sometimes. We were afraid that they'd stop giving to the new school when we were jailed now and then. But they seem to understand about the schoolhouse, and though sometimes they josh us they continue to contribute just the same."

As I put my messed-up pancake on a plate, I asked, "But they don't like Doctor Marah, do they?"

"No, they don't. We never bring Doctor Marah into any of our conversations when we go out collecting in the saloons."

"You don't say whose idea it was to get the money?" came from Davey, as I heard the shebang door open, which meant Papa had come back.

"No, we don't. Hurry up with your pancake, Davey, and you, too, Hope. Don't be late to school."

Late? I wished I wasn't going at all—not when I had Margaret Libby pitying me because my mother had been in jail and Silas telling me that she was a jailbird when he wasn't calling me nanny goat.

While I was polishing off my breakfast, Papa came in, with both cats following him mewing for their breakfasts, too. He was chewing on his mustache again. "Doc Marah's gone," he announced, telling us what we already knew. "The doc bought a ticket to the capital. Some folks in town are already saying good riddance to the coward and are hoping for no return." He sat down at the table, then held out his coffee cup for Mama to refill from the pot on the stove. "Nora, he's supposed to have said something to the stagecoach ticket agent about making overtures to some woman in Helena."

Mama exclaimed, *"A woman? Overtures?* Albert, did Doctor Marah buy a return-trip fare to Ottenberg?"

"No, Nora, the agent said that he didn't." Papa filled his mouth with so much hot coffee that his mustache lifted at the corners. "What will you fermenting females do now, Nora?"

"Have a meeting and decide our course of action, my love."

Because of school I wasn't at the council of war. I had to sit at my desk being elbowed by Davey while I tried to do long-division problems with my mind really on Doctor Marah's leaving town. By noontime the news was all over Ottenberg. A lady bringing lunch to her little girl told Miss Willis, and at afternoon recess Miss Willis asked me about it after the others had gone out to play.

"Is it true that Doctor Marah has left Ottenberg, Hope?"

"Yes, ma'am, it seems to be, but he left his dictionary behind."

This made her look more puzzled than upset. So I added, "Maybe it means he hasn't gone for good."

"Maybe not, Hope. It does seem strange, doesn't it, that he'd leave when it was his idea to collect for the new schoolhouse and it isn't even here yet. Has your father heard about when it might be arriving?"

"I don't think that he has. May I go outside now, please?"

"Yes, go on out and play."

I left her looking at the blackboard and frowning. I wished I knew, too, when the schoolhouse was going to show up. Papa had sent for it, but there'd been no word from Chicago that it was on its way—not yet at least. He said that this wasn't anything to worry about, though. He'd sent for things before, and they had simply showed up without any warning. "Albert Foster has mighty good credit," he'd told us, which meant that he was trusted as far away as Oregon and the prairie country.

Once I got outside I never did get to play on the seesaw with Margaret. Instead I argued with Silas, who'd been lying in wait for me under a yellow pine. He sneered at me as he said, "I hear tell that your doctor friend has been run out of town."

"Not one bit of truth in it, Silas O'Hare. Doctor Marah wasn't run out. He went because he wanted to. Your father didn't have one single thing to do with it, so you go tell him not to get any more bigheaded about this than he already is."

"What about them women who've been pesterin' us at the Shoo-Fly?"

"They are deciding what they plan to do." I gave him my most wicked grin. "After all, Doctor Marah was never with them in your father's nasty old saloon, was he?"

"No, nanny goat." He grinned back at me in a blood-curdling manner. "But my pa knows that Marah was behind them women all the same. If he ever shows his face in the Shoo-Fly, my pa's gonna get him. You tell Doc Marah that for us."

I said, "You bet I will. When I see him again, I'll tell him that you're the most ornery, spiteful, mean-natured, dirty little boy in the United States of America—and a nincompoop, besides." I tried to think of another big word that he wouldn't know. He'd know nincompoop, because that's what his father had called Doctor Marah. I said, "And you are benighted to boot." This was the second word I hadn't looked up yet in the dictionary. It had a bad sound to it, but who could be sure what it meant? What if I'd complimented Silas? Heaven forbid!

I whirled around and ran back to Miss Willis to ask, "Please tell me quick so I can change it if it isn't right. What does *benighted* mean?"

Her eyebrows shot up a little higher. "To be dim. To be left out."

"Is that all? Nothing worse than that?"

"Pretty much all, Hope. It isn't a word you use every-day, you know."

"Well, I used it just now on Silas." I felt a little disappointed but brightened up as I added, "He *is* a dimwit, I guess. Is Ottenberg benighted, too?"

"Some of its citizens definitely are, yes," she answered.

Mama and the other ladies didn't carry chairs to the Shoo-Fly that afternoon. They'd decided at their council of war, on the advice of Miss Emily, to postpone any further action until they heard something from Doctor Marah.

I told Mama, "Mr. O'Hare's going to think he's licked you because Judge Bokman fined you five dollars last time you were in jail."

"She who laughs last has the best laugh, Hope."

Papa, who was trying to read Wednesday's *Oracle,* said from behind the paper, "I heard the old saying that 'he who laughs last, laughs best,' Nora."

"Oh, my love, it works just as well both ways."

"My love," he told her, "I am tired of ransoming you from jail. I'm looking forward to peace and quiet. It would suit me just fine if Doc Marah asked us to ship everything she owns in this house to Helena."

"Papa!" Because we were out in the shebang, I looked wildly all around me. He'd said *she* straight out. What if someone had heard him—even Davey. Davey was too young to keep secrets.

But it was all right. There wasn't anybody there this afternoon, except for Essex asleep on a bolt of warm serge on the yard-goods counter and Manchester curled up on one of the chairs next to the stove. It was a chilly afternoon—clear but chilly.

I asked, "Papa, have you heard anything new about the schoolhouse yet? Miss Willis asked me about it today."

He had some good news for me. "Yep, this very day. It's on its way C.O.D., which, as you know, means cash on delivery. If the good ladies don't come up with the last twenty dollars, I might even donate it out of the goodness of my heart."

Mama said very seriously, "The ladies will mention you in their prayers for that, Albert."

He laughed. "I heard the other day from Reverend Gardiner that they're praying for Tom O'Hare all the time now. O'Hare hasn't given a nickel to the school fund. Does he know about their praying?"

I said, "Oh, yes, Papa. He knows. I was there when he was told. He didn't seem to take to the idea. He acted almost as if he'd been insulted."

"In a way he has. Think about it for a while, Hope."

Yes, Papa was correct. Next time Silas called me nanny goat, I'd tell him that I was praying for his soul. But if I did that, I would truly have to do it. That idea went down crosswise with me.

Four days of peace and quiet went by with the sisters collecting more and more cash to put into the shebang safe. I went out with them on two nights. Rather than walk past the Shoo-Fly, they took the trouble to go down off the walk into the street and come back up again. That wasn't so easy either. The boardwalk had been built quite a ways off the ground. Men got up it all right, but the ladies had to lift their long skirts and huff and puff a bit if they were at all overweight. It hadn't rained for so long that all of the puddles had dried up. Yes, it took careful walking to get around some of the bigger dry holes. Avoiding Mr. O'Hare had caused us some work.

* * *

On the morning of the fifth day of October, a Sunday, Doctor Marah came back to Ottenberg. Oh, how folks stared to see Marah get down off the stagecoach from Helena. Most of them kept quiet, but two miners made impolite noises to insult the doctor. While Mama and I started forward down off the porch of the shebang to greet Marah, the lady with Doctor Marah came down the folding steps.

At the sight of her I heard Papa draw in his breath and so did Doctor Haverford. So did the ladies standing near Mama. The men made a sort of "ah" sound, but it seemed to me that the sound the ladies made was different.

The stranger Doctor Marah was holding a hand up to steady was a beauty. She was slender and tallish for a lady and had wonderful red-yellow curls all over her head. Perched on top of them was a small black bonnet with gold- and garnet-colored feathers. Her traveling costume was black, which showed off her gold skin and greenish eyes perfectly.

"Who is that?" I heard Mrs. Prescott ask Mama.

Nobody could tell her, but we weren't in suspense for long. Doctor Marah brought the strange lady, who didn't hang on the doctor's arm, but walked alone, straight up to us.

I heard the doctor say, "Ladies, this is Miss Agnes Carruthers from Helena. She's come to stay for a time. I hope you can put her up, Mrs. Prescott."

Eying Miss Carruthers, who was smiling at her, Mrs. Prescott said, "Well, Doctor, I don't know about that. Miss Willis is slated to take my spare room in November when she rotates again."

The tall stranger from Helena, who was even more

handsome up close, had a velvety voice. "I do not expect to stay here any longer than the end of the month, and, if possible, I may even leave sooner than that." She gave Doctor Marah a little smile.

I didn't know what to think, but I'll bet I knew what other people were thinking—that Doctor Marah had brought a wife or fiancée to Ottenberg.

Mrs. Prescott was silent for a time, then she said, "All right, until the first of November then."

Miss Carruthers said, "Thank you," then turned to Marah. "Can you have my baggage brought to the proper place?"

"Of course." And Marah went back to the stagecoach, leaving us with Miss Carruthers.

She asked, "How is Mrs. Bokman these days?"

"Just fine," replied Mama. "Do you know her?"

"Yes, but I haven't seen her in some time, though I understand from Doctor Marah that Mrs. Bokman has discussed me with him."

I didn't understand this at all. I went on staring at Miss Carruthers until she walked off with Mrs. Prescott, following the man Doctor Marah had paid to carry Miss Carruthers's satchel and two carpetbags.

This left Doctor Marah with Mama, me, and Dr. Haverford, and then Papa came to join us. I heard Haverford ask Marah very softly, but sounding furious, "Why did you run off the way you did without telling anyone you were going? You gave me a scare, let me tell you."

Marah chuckled. "Well, I guess I did leave suddenly, didn't I? I did it on an impulse. I decided all at once to act on what I'd been thinking about for quite a while, before we get snowed in up here and before I thought better of my idea. I took off for Helena, did my business there, and came back bringing Miss Carruthers with me."

Doctor Haverford demanded, "Who is this woman? Everyone in town is going to say you've brought your future bride here."

Jeanette Marah smiled. "That's what I thought they'd say. Let them. I spotted Miss Carruthers's notice in the Helena paper and then went to talk to Mrs. Bokman, who hails from Helena, about her. Mrs. Bokman highly recommended her services. She says Miss Carruthers hung out her shingle there last year."

"She's a doctor, too?" Haverford exclaimed.

"No, not a doctor—a lawyer."

Doctor Marah looked down at me. "Hope, you're looking bewildered. Lawyers have their names painted on boards and hung out, too, to let the public know they're available for work."

Then Marah turned back to the older doctor. "Well, sir, when I got to Helena, I knocked on Miss Carruthers's office door, told her the whole tale about what was going on here, and asked if she could help the ladies of Ottenberg in their hour of trouble. I promised to pay her fees, and I think I should because the women of Ottenberg are trying to help me. Miss Carruthers thinks that there should be some sort of showdown with Mr. O'Hare. So she has written and telegraphed some of her friends from all over the country about the school here being held in a chicken coop and about O'Hare's behavior. Miss Carruthers claims it's an extremely newsworthy town where decent, law-abiding ladies go so often and willingly to jail for what they believe in."

"Newsworthy? If that means what I think it means, Ottenberg is going to have a very bad name. God forbid that my Nora's going to jail will put the town on the map nationwide." Papa spoke gloomily. "The mayor is going to hate this bit of news."

"Anyhow, Mr. Foster, Agnes believes Ottenberg will be the scene of her first important legal case. She has a great dislike of Judge Bokman. She says that in her estimation he is a 'whiskey judge.' He always favors men in his decisions."

"Oh, Lord." Haverford gave Doctor Marah a sour look. "I hope you know what you're doing."

"So do I!" said Papa and went back into the shebang while the old doctor walked off toward the Big Bend Hotel.

As for myself, I stood with one arm wound around the post of the porch while Mama and Doctor Marah talked about the amount of money that had been collected while Marah was gone. I was thinking.

I'd thought of becoming a schoolteacher someday like Mama because I liked words so much. But the truth of the matter was that I didn't like arithmetic and had a terrible time with multiplication and long division, so perhaps I'd better consider something else. Since I'd come to Ottenberg I'd met a lady doctor and now a lady lawyer. Apparently there were choices other than being a schoolteacher.

I'd noticed for years that everybody who came to our house asked Davey what he was going to be when he grew up, but they never asked me. When Davey was finished saying that he wanted to be a cavalry trooper, I'd generally put in that I'd like to be a teacher, but nobody seemed very thrilled about that. I'd only said it because it showed I had ambition, too.

That night Miss Carruthers met in the shebang with the sisters before they went out collecting. Perched on a counter top beside my brother, because all of the chairs were taken, I heard what she had to say.

"Ladies of Ottenberg, I admire your enterprise and spirit, and I sympathize on all counts with what you are trying to do. I am told by Mrs. Prescott here that a mere slip of a girl showed you the way. You had the deep wisdom to be led by a simple child. I refer to Hope Foster."

Me—a simple child? I gagged at this, but Miss Carruthers went on before I could say I wasn't a child anymore and I certainly had never been simple. Lawyers could surely talk. "Ladies of Ottenberg, I have good reason to believe that the attention of the entire nation could become focused on this small city as a result of your spirited actions as you strive to bring light to some of the benighted men hereabouts."

Benighted. There it was again and she'd used it right, too. This told me that lawyers weren't afraid of dictionaries either, the way some folks were.

She went on. "What I suggest is this—that you refrain from sitting out in front of the Shoo-Fly Saloon until the time is fully ripe."

"Yes, yes," muttered one of the ladies whose husband had really kicked up a fuss about her being in jail.

"What about the schoolhouse and collecting for it? It's supposed to be on it's way here," Mama asked.

I noticed she didn't add that it might be snowbound

someplace in the Dakotas and not arrive until May, but I kept quiet. There wasn't any reason to disappoint people with such dark ideas. Papa knew, though. It was coming by wagon. He'd had another message from the Chicago place that sold houses and churches and just about everything else that could be nailed together.

Doctor Marah, who was sitting on top of the pickle barrel close by Davey and me, answered, "Naturally you will go on collecting. The miners haven't turned against you, have they?"

"No, they seem to find it amusing that we are angry with Mr. O'Hare and have gone to jail because of it. They tease us," answered Mrs. Gardiner.

"Then the men don't take you very seriously?" Miss Carruthers was onto this like a coyote on to a lame duck.

"Not particularly, it seems. Some of them consider O'Hare a sort of hero," said Mrs. Prescott.

"They shall take you seriously, but it may take time." The lady lawyer could put on a grim expression when she wanted to. "When the time is ripe, you should take turns sitting out in front of the Shoo-Fly Saloon day and night. That will provoke Mr. O'Hare and smoke him out. You should be as silent as ever, but you could take signs with you—signs that will tell the entire town what O'Hare has said and done. There could also be signs saying that the city fathers should have put city money into the building of a proper schoolhouse."

Mrs. Gardiner popped up and said excitedly, "Such as 'Get our poor little children out of Colonel Ottenberg's chicken coop.'"

"Excellent. That's right to the point," said the lady lawyer.

Miss Emily said all at once, "Be sure you make the colonel's chicken coop *his* coop—not the Ottenberg coop. He's my father, you know, but that does not mean that he and I see eye to eye on everything. As a matter of fact, we definitely no longer do."

The lady lawyer beamed at her. "And you are on the side of the ladies who want a new school even though the chicken coop belongs to your family? That is admirable."

Miss Emily nodded. "It's uncomfortable for me at home now. Papa and I don't speak to each other much anymore unless it's to say 'Pass the butter.' "

"But Emily, he never did talk much to you," said Mrs. Prescott.

"That's true enough, Annabelle. He never talked much to my mother either. So I suppose I haven't lost a lot, have I?"

"No, you haven't. And you've gained many good friends," added Mama.

I wanted to say, Miss Emily, if it wasn't for you, the kids in the coop would be calling the town Rottenberg instead of Ottenberg. But I only thought it.

I was beginning to understand Miss Emily more and more all the time. Probably she talked when other people talked, because she thought they might be like the colonel and wouldn't be interested in anything she had to say, so she rattled on and on. And she ended up annoying them because she wasn't listening to them. She was very nervous but because of her size, it was something that didn't occur to most folks who met her. It seemed to me that she was more her father's errand girl and servant than his daughter.

Mrs. Gardiner took my attention away from thinking

about Miss Emily when she waved her handkerchief to get Miss Carruthers's attention. "When will the time be ripe?" she asked. "It should snow quite soon now, and it won't be pleasant at all to sit out in front of the Shoo-Fly. We're shivering already, and you think we ought to sit out there night and day when we begin again. We trust Doctor Marah when he tells us he brought you here to help us and we know that you are trying. But we can't help being confused."

Down went Mrs. Gardiner and up came my mother. "Yes, Miss Carruthers, Mrs. Gardiner has said what most of us are thinking. We will go on collecting, of course, but what do you mean about the time being ripe?"

Miss Carruthers lifted her arm to the ceiling of the shebang as if she was pointing to the row of hams hanging up there. "All should be in good order in Ottenberg before the first flakes fall."

I repeated that sentence in my brain. It was flowery, but easy to remember. I'd tell it to Miss Willis tomorrow at morning recess. She hadn't come to the meeting tonight.

Mama asked again, "That still doesn't tell us when, Miss Carruthers."

The lady lawyer replied, "As soon as my friend comes up here from San Francisco. She is on her way now. I know because she has kept in touch with me by telegraph. I believe I can assure you that every one of you will find her very interesting, as well as very interested in Ottenberg events. Until then, ladies, please hold your fire."

Another lady? She must be important if we were all supposed to hold our fire until she arrived. I wondered what on earth she would be doing in Ottenberg that had anything to do with Mr. O'Hare and a new schoolhouse.

CHAPTER NINE

A CHAIR, A TOOTHBRUSH, AND A NIGHTGOWN

Mama confessed to me that she wasn't only waiting for the ripe time, she was holding her breath to boot. Miss Carruthers had come to Ottenberg as a lady of mystery, and she kept right on being one. All I learned about her was that she hailed from Cleveland, Ohio. That made me say "Aha" to myself.

I didn't set eyes on the lady lawyer again until the stagecoach came jerking into Ottenberg three days later. It seemed to me that I had met every stage that had come to town for months, though of course I hadn't because I'd been going to school.

This stagecoach arrival was important, too. Miss Carruthers had sent a message around town that she wanted as many ladies as possible to meet it and give moral support to a certain passenger who would be aboard it. That afternoon Miss Carruthers didn't wait up on the boardwalk or porch of the shebang with the other people when it came rolling in about four thirty. She was right down in the street waiting. Without her plumed bonnet, her curly red-gold hair was easy to spot all right.

I'd heard some people in our store telling Mama that the Prescott boarder seemed to them a mighty brazen-looking female who dyed her hair. But I didn't agree.

You could tell it was real, because the little freckles on her nose just matched the color of her head. I was pretty sure such things as powdering and painting didn't matter a hoot to Miss Carruthers.

I kept my eyes fixed on the lady lawyer as she flung out her arms crying, "Ruth!" I figured that Ruth had to be the person we were all waiting for, the-time-is-fully-ripe lady.

I'd seen Miss Willis, Doctor Marah, the Bokmans, and Miss Carruthers arrive, and each of them had interested me, but Ruth-whoever-she-was put them all to shame. She was more small than tall with pinkish cheeks and chestnut-brown hair, but oh, my, her traveling costume! Ottenberg had never seen anything like it. I heard Mama gasping and Mrs. Prescott, too. No lady in Ottenberg owned a burgundy-red bonnet like that, with white waterlilies and scarlet poppies on top and black ribbons hanging down behind. The newcomer's coat was red, black, and green plaid with three little capelets of black cloth over the shoulders to keep off the rain. She didn't carry a reticule but a black-leather satchel that looked stuffed full.

Mrs. Prescott knew her name. She said to Mama, "Nora, it looks as if Miss Dalrymple of San Francisco has come ready to go to work, doesn't it?"

While Miss Carruthers and Miss Dalrymple embraced, I turned around to ask Mrs. Prescott, "What kind of work does she do?" I wondered if she was another lady lawyer.

"She is a newspaper reporter, Hope. A lady writer."

Aha! I knew what they were because the *Oracle* had a news gatherer and writer. But he was a man. I hadn't known that women did that kind of work, too.

The lady lawyer and lady reporter were fast walkers.

Not paying a bit of attention to the men who were staring at them admiringly, they came right up to us. "Here she is," announced Miss Carruthers to Mama and Mrs. Prescott and to the other schoolhouse collectors. "This is Ruth Dalrymple of San Francisco, originally from Steubenville, Ohio."

And then Miss Carruthers introduced us each and every one—even me.

Miss Dalrymple didn't greet the ladies the way most ladies did—with just a nod and a pleasant smile. Instead, she shook everyone's hand, starting with Mama's, just like the men did.

When she got around to my hand, Miss Carruthers told her, "This is Hope Foster. She is responsible for starting this remarkable enterprise I've told you about."

I said, "I got the idea from my teacher, Miss Willis, who said that some ladies did the same thing to a man in Cincinnati who beat his wife."

Miss Dalrymple nodded. "Yes, I have been told of that good work. I keep in touch with friends back in Ohio and also with Ohio friends out here in the West. News slowly works its way West, chiefly by letters from woman to woman, but soon I believe these events shall make headlines." As she shook my hand Miss Dalrymple said very loudly, "I think Hope Foster should be commended for her courage. I'll be sure and say that the brave ladies of Ottenberg have daughters equally as noblehearted. Where is the saloon in question?" She let go of my hand and looked up and down the street.

I pointed. "It's the Shoo-Fly, up there a ways, the one with the green-and-black painted sign."

"So that's the place. What is the name of the saloon-keeper in question?"

"Thomas O'Hare," answered Mrs. Prescott.

Miss Dalrymple turned to her friend, Miss Carruthers. "Agnes, has he thrown you out yet?"

"No, I haven't given him the opportunity, Ruth."

"Ah." I saw the woman reporter look around at the crowd of ladies assembled to meet her. She asked, "Will one of you please hold my satchel for me while someone else goes to find the doctor?"

Mama took the satchel and asked, "What doctor? Which one?" Mama looked puzzled.

I was, too. Why did Miss Dalrymple want a doctor? She looked very healthy to me.

"The young doctor who has been so badly abused here in Ottenberg."

I said, "Oh, you mean Doctor Marah?"

"That's the one. Agnes, let's get it over with as quickly as possible."

Miss Carruthers nodded, looking very serious. "Yes, Ruth. I do believe that the time is now ripe."

I watched the two women link arms and start down the boardwalk matching each other's stride, though Miss Dalrymple had to run a bit to keep up with the taller lady lawyer. They marched past some men, who grinned and politely lifted their hats. Smiling and nodding at them, the two handsome-looking ladies sailed along, then suddenly went right through the doors of the Shoo-Fly Saloon.

"Merciful Heavens!" exclaimed Mrs. Gardiner, who'd come closer to me.

"Hope, go find Doctor Marah right away," Mama ordered. "He's at Doctor Haverford's office. He may be needed."

Mrs. Prescott said under her breath, "Lord, I hope there won't be any bloodshed."

Bloodshed? I was off like the shot out of a pistol, running down past the Shoo-Fly.

Just as I got abreast of the swinging doors, they opened outwards and swiftly, too. Out came Miss Dalrymple clutching at her remarkable hat, then Miss Carruthers skidding. All I saw of Mr. O'Hare was his big red hands as he gave the ladies a final push right into me. Somehow they managed to stay on their feet—but not me! Down I went into a heap, getting boardwalk splinters in both hands. My left palm was bleeding onto the boards.

While I was still on all fours, I heard O'Hare shouting, "I know why you females came in here just now—to make trouble for me. Even if I never saw one of you before and don't know the other by name, I know who sent you here —that new doctor and that shebangkeeper's wife, Mrs. Foster. You women are cuttin' into my business already. I won't have no more of your interferin'. Get out and stay out, or I'll see to it that you go to the lockup again!"

Miss Carruthers, once she'd got her balance back, was ready with a reply. She shouted back, "You have wounded a poor innocent child."

That was me, of course. There had been blood shed. Mine!

O'Hare stuck his head out over the tops of the swinging doors. From where I was on the walk I could see Silas looking out from under them with his tongue stuck out at me. O'Hare gave me a withering look and then said,

"Yes, by God, that's the Foster hellion. She's at the bottom of this, too."

As Miss Dalrymple helped me up, I called out to both of the O'Hares, "I didn't come inside your den of sin at all. I was only passing by on my way to get Doctor Marah."

O'Hare roared at me, "Hasn't that man packed up and got out of town for good yet, damn him?"

"No, he hasn't!" I called back at him.

With Miss Carruthers on one side and Miss Dalrymple on the other, I faced both O'Hares down. "No, Doctor Marah hasn't gone. He's not scared of the likes of you. He won't *ever* leave Ottenberg!" That was true enough in a way. After all, the *he* O'Hare was objecting to was a *she*, even if he didn't know it.

O'Hare came through the double doors onto the boardwalk. He said, "You tell them female pests and that horse doctor for me that I think he's the biggest coward in all of Montana Territory, and most of the men hereabouts would be pleased if he got out of town while the gettin' is still good."

Some miners on the boardwalk and on the street let out a cheer. O'Hare bowed to them while Silas did a little dance on the walk, making me long to kick him.

Miss Carruthers stood right up to O'Hare. "That is a threat if ever I heard one!" she cried.

"Yes, indeed!" said Miss Dalrymple, adjusting her hat where a water lily had drooped. Once she'd propped it up among the poppies, she went on to me, "That man is a bully of the worst stripe. I predict he will live to regret his actions and words. Go get Doctor Marah, please. We shall be waiting with your mother."

So I started on my way once more, though the splinters burned and my palm was still bleeding and my dress was torn at the hem. I could hear a cheer going up behind me. It wasn't a deep-sounding one. It came from Mama and the other ladies, who had seen what happened.

When the cheer faded away, I could hear laughing, which wasn't coming from the ladies. Some of the men who'd gathered to see the stagecoach arrive had been amused by what Mr. O'Hare had done. They'd approved of it. That must mean that they agreed with what he'd said about Doctor Marah. It wasn't only that they wouldn't go to Marah as a doctor; they'd like to see him leave town, too. If only they knew. . . .

Just as I made my quick running turn to head up the outside steps of the building where Doctor Haverford had his second-floor office, I heard somebody calling my name. Margaret was running across the street, leaping the big holes.

"Hope, Hope," she was crying out. "Come see. Justice has come!"

What was she talking about? I called out, "I'm busy now," but she reached me, grabbed my arm, and pulled me off the boardwalk.

I struggled with her, telling her, "Margaret, didn't you see what happened just now out in front of the Shoo-Fly? I've been wounded." I showed her my scratched-up hands. "Miss Carruthers, the lady lawyer, sent me to get Doctor Marah."

Margaret shook her head. "You won't find him or Doctor Haverford up there now. They're over across the way with Mayor Ottenberg and Judge Bokman. The wagon's come. It finally brought Justice to town."

There she went again, talking about justice. I knew what that word meant. I'd heard it used often enough by people who said there didn't seem to be much of it in the world.

Margaret noticed the bewildered look on my face. She laughed and told me, "Miss Emily's *statue* of Justice is here."

Oh! I remembered now. That very expensive statue. I nodded. Sure, I wanted to see what a $900 statue looked like, and at the same time I could round up Doctor Marah.

The shipping wagon that had come from California was in the street outside the courthouse alongside some other taller and bigger wagons that had blocked the view of the Shoo-Fly's doors. There stood the statue all right in the middle of the boardwalk, just the way it had been taken out of the wooden packing case and straw.

Justice was a white stone lady about Mama's height and width. She certainly wasn't dressed for October in Montana Territory, though. She was wearing sandals and her long gown didn't have any sleeves. I couldn't make out her face very well, because her eyes were covered with a blindfold. But I could see what she had in her hands. One held a sword. The other had a set of scales, made not of marble but of metal, probably because chains couldn't be made out of rock.

Colonel Ottenberg was standing on one side of her and Judge Bokman on the other. The town's only picture taker was nearby with his head stuck under a black cloth. I stood with Margaret while he took a picture of the three of them: the mayor, the judge, and Justice. When the bright flash ended and the photographer was finished, I looked around for the two doctors.

Dr. Haverford was talking with Mrs. Bokman, who was out today wrapped to the ears in a big purple shawl and fur jacket. Doctor Marah was standing all alone a distance away as if everybody was avoiding him.

This gave me an idea. I told Margaret, "All right, I've seen what Justice looks like, and I suppose she'll be set up right away somewhere in the courthouse. Will you tell Doctor Marah that he's wanted at our store right away?"

"Hope, my father doesn't want me to associate with Doctor Marah."

"Fiddlesticks! You aren't associating. You're just giving him a message. I want to talk with Mrs. Bokman. Please, Margaret."

"Oh, all right." And off she went.

I waited awhile pretending to admire Justice until Doctor Haverford moved away to talk with the judge. Then I threaded my way through the people to Mrs. Bokman. "Hello," I told her. "I'm Hope Foster. Remember me? You gave me a piece of vanilla fudge at your house one time."

"Yes, I recall you. You're the girl whose mother was—" All of a sudden she stopped talking and pulled the shawl closer about her. She smelled of violets.

"—who was in jail." I finished for her. "Isn't it wonderful? She's been there two times now."

I saw her nod but not exactly smile. Then I told her what was really on my mind. "The lawyer who's come to town, Miss Carruthers, says she knows you. She says that your husband isn't her friend, but you are."

Mrs. Bokman looked a bit startled, it seemed to me, but all the same she nodded.

I went on. "I guess Miss Carruthers hasn't come calling on you."

"No, she hasn't. Do give her my best wishes, though."

"I'll be glad to. Miss Carruthers tells us that she's come to help us in the battle against Mr. O'Hare. She's got a friend of hers here too, a reporter from San Francisco. I suppose she's going to write newspaper pieces about Ottenberg and us and Mr. O'Hare. Won't that be exciting?"

"It will be interesting in any event, Hope. It's getting quite bitterly cold these days, isn't it?"

"Yes, ma'am, it is. Miss Carruthers wants to leave before the snow starts and she gets trapped here, and we want to get a new schoolhouse and put it up, and I suppose you want to have your baby before Ottenberg gets snowed in, too."

She smiled a sort of little smile. "I don't so much care about being snowed in, but I would like to have my baby and be up and around for Thanksgiving Day."

"Oh, I bet you will be. We can make tunnels through the drifts if the snow gets really deep, so you can carry the baby anywhere in town and show it off. It's going to be the first baby born here. Maybe you should call it Ottenberg Bokman. Have you thought about that name?"

What a strange look she gave me. "No, I haven't."

I guessed she didn't like my name, but I didn't bear her any grudge. I said good-bye, and as she went to join her husband and Colonel Ottenberg, I hurried after Doctor Marah, who'd started away right after Margaret had delivered my message to her.

I looked down at my hands. The bleeding had stopped but they were still sore. Once Marah finished talking with

Miss Carruthers and Miss Dalrymple and had been brought up to date on what had happened at the Shoo-Fly, I was going to ask her to pluck the splinters out of my palms.

The Ottenberg ladies began to move faster after Justice arrived in town. Miss Dalrymple, who was staying with the Prescotts, too, talked privately with Doctor Marah out in the yard-goods part of the shebang with Miss Carruthers listening in. Then the lady lawyer and lady reporter went to the Prescotts', saying that they'd be back to our store after we'd all had dinner. The other ladies who'd watched what had gone on outside the Shoo-Fly were to gather together at a meeting in the shebang at eight o'clock that night.

But, while Doctor Marah and we Fosters were hurrying through a dinner of black-bear stew, we had visitors.

They were very unexpected visitors and danged unwelcome, too! First we heard some pistol shots out in front of our store. Since that wasn't so unusual in Ottenberg, we went on with our dessert of strawberry-preserve pie. But after the shooting came a crash that we knew was the sound of glass breaking—and a lot of it, too.

Papa got up so quickly that he nearly knocked the table over. He grabbed the kerosene lamp on our roll-top kitchen cabinet and ran out into the shebang. Davey was at his heels with both cats streaking scared in front of him.

Mama and Doctor Marah and I looked at one another. Then Mama said, "Come on. If this is what I think it is, it concerns the three of us more than Albert."

So we went out, with Mama in the lead, carrying the lamp that had been on the dining table.

We saw a large crowd on the store porch and spilling

out into the street. The men had come with pine-knot torches—fifty or more of them, it seemed to me. I couldn't tell for sure, though, because of the darkness of the night. Those I could see close up had pistols in their belts and at their sides. In front in a derby hat was Mr. O'Hare, with Silas beside him, carrying a torch that flickered and sent sparks upward. O'Hare was shaking his fist at Papa, who was standing in the shebang behind the big window he'd been so proud of. We'd displayed our finest goods in that window for people to admire, and now it was smashed, mostly on the floor in big triangle-shaped pieces of glass.

"What the hell do you want here, O'Hare?" Papa called out, angrier than I'd ever seen him before in my whole life.

"We want Doc Marah. That's what we want!" O'Hare shouted in return. "Well, Foster, are you goin' to get him for us or not? We plan to ride him out of town tonight."

"No, I'm not going to get him," Papa bellowed, while Davey shook his little fist at the men.

I heard Doctor Marah, who was beside me, draw in a deep breath. She said to Mama, "I'm going to go out to them."

"No, Jeanette, don't do that." Mama put her hand on Doctor Marah's arm. I watched Marah reach out and lift it off.

"I have to go, Nora. You can't shield me forever."

Mama turned to me and caught me by the shoulders. "Hope, duck out the side door and get Sheriff Sherman over here right away."

I went out of the store as fast as I could, feeling my way in the dark to the side door. Once I was outside, the light of the torches made it bright enough for me to see. I stopped just long enough for a swift look at O'Hare's mob of men. Two of them were holding a long pole, one at each end. Yes, they were going to make Doctor Marah ride the rail out of Ottenberg. The men with the pole would jerk it up and down while they carried it so the person riding it got as many bruises and lacerations as possible. It would be as bad as a horsewhipping.

Somebody at the back of the crowd spotted me and let out a yell, "Catch that kid there before she gets away!"

Somebody else, a man with a yellow beard, made a grab for my hair and got hold of one pigtail. But I twisted around and bit him on his other hand. In all the yelling and shouting that was going on up front near O'Hare, nobody paid any heed to the man's howling, as he jumped up and down shaking the hand I'd taken a little chunk out of.

Loose again, I went thudding across the street, leaping potholes, into the sheriff's office. "Come, save the doctor!" I called out.

Sheriff Sherman, who'd been sitting in a chair with his feet on the jailhouse stove fender, got up right away. "What's that you're saying, Hope?"

"Mr. O'Hare's come to the shebang with a crowd of men and a rail to run Doctor Marah out of town on. Come quick, please. Run!"

And with these words I was gone again. No matter how fast he traveled, the sheriff, who was big as a barn, wasn't as fleet of foot as I was. I won all the races at school for girls of my age, which meant that I beat Margaret Libby every single time. The only person who might be faster than I was would be Davey, who was long legged for his age.

A CHAIR, A TOOTHBRUSH, AND A NIGHTGOWN 173

I stopped in the shadows at the side door of our place. Before I went inside I was going to get the lay of the land and wait for the Sheriff to catch up to me in case I had more explaining to do.

Where was Doctor Marah? Where was my father?

Then I saw Doctor Marah. Mama hadn't been able to stop Marah's going out to face the mob. There she stood, pale as snow, on the porch of the shebang with her hands in her pockets and her coat open to show there was no gun. The miners had moved back into the street, so only Jeanette and Mr. O'Hare were on the porch facing one another.

The saloonkeeper, who was armed with a pistol like the men he'd brought with him, was shouting at Marah, "You did this. I been told it was your smart idea to collect for the school in the first place, and you think you're too all-fired fine and fancy to drink with good honest miners."

"That's right, Tom!" shouted a miner in the center of the mob.

"Yep, too good for the likes of us working stiffs!" another miner cried to Marah.

Afterward there was a moment of quiet, except for the muttering of the crowd. I looked across the street toward the jail and saw the sheriff lumbering along.

But before he arrived, Doctor Marah lifted her hands. Her voice rang out, "Please be quiet a minute and hear me, gentlemen."

"Gentlemen?" There was a burst of laughing. I thought Doctor Marah had used the wrong word, too, and so did the crowd.

"Yes, gentlemen. Will you hear me out?"

"All right, speak your piece and then we'll fetch the rail," said Mr. O'Hara. He called over his shoulder to some men just behind him. "Let the pup spit out what he wants to say. We'll be gents enough to do that for him."

There was cheering and a waving of torches.

"Thank you," Doctor Marah shouted in order to be heard. "I do not think that I am better than any man here. I do not drink whiskey, that is all. It is true that I had the idea to collect in saloons for the new school building, but I don't see that as a crime. Other saloonkeepers have welcomed the ladies of Ottenberg who came collecting."

Calm as a head of cabbage, that was the doctor. Oh, but I was proud of Jeanette Marah. Twice as proud because it was a woman facing down a mean crowd of men who thought she was a man.

All at once O'Hare took a step forward and pushed his face right into hers. At the same moment Papa came up to stand shoulder to shoulder with Doctor Marah. Then the owner of the Shoo-Fly said loud enough for everyone to hear, "Don't you try to deny that you think you're too good to fight me. I ought to fire my pistol at your boots and make you do a jig until you say you'll fight me. Maybe if I shoot off some of your toes, you'll change your mind, little Doc."

Before Doctor Marah could say anything, Papa growled out at the crowd, "Doctor Marah don't have to fight you or any other man in town if he doesn't want to, Tom O'Hare! This is a free country, remember?"

I watched O'Hare reach out as if to grab Doctor Marah by the shoulder, but before he could Sheriff Sherman came panting up onto the porch. He caught O'Hare by the arm and held it. "Go on home, Tom. And don't you try to get your pistol out. I've got my eye on you. Go on back to the Shoo-Fly now, and take all your friends, too."

"No, not yet, please!" Doctor Marah spoke up once more, holding up her hands for silence. "I want to say that I do not believe in violence. I think anyone who has to settle his differences with guns or fists just to prove his manhood isn't any different from any other male animal that fights to show it's boss of the herd. Fighting makes a person more beast than man."

"Hurrah!" That was a lady's high voice. I looked out over the throng, and there stood the Prescotts and Miss Carruthers and Miss Dalrymple. The reporter was the one who'd called out. The three women started to clap for Doctor Marah. So did I and Mama, too, standing inside the broken window.

"Don't be a beast anymore, Mr. O'Hare," the lady lawyer called out.

All at once things changed for O'Hare. One of the men he'd brought with him started to laugh, then another and a third and finally most of them were laughing. One man even hooted, "Don't you be a beast no more, Tommy."

"Oh, go on home, boys," Sheriff Sherman called out to them.

They went. Miss Carruthers had changed their mood for them with one sentence. I stayed where I was beside the side entrance to our place, watching as the miners went away. Two of them took off their hats to Mrs. Prescott and the lawyer and reporter and bowed drunkenly. I figured that O'Hare had been handing out free whiskey to the men who'd come with him. Probably he'd been doing that ever since he'd thrown the lady lawyer and reporter out of the Shoo-Fly. He'd talked the men in the crowd into coming to get Doctor Marah, but he couldn't keep hold of them long enough to get them to use the rail.

As far as I could see what he'd done and said tonight hadn't done O'Hare much good. It looked as if every saloon in Ottenberg had emptied out onto the boardwalk to watch O'Hare, who was red-faced with anger or embarrassment. As he and some of his mob went back mumbling to his saloon, the watchers didn't say anything. They just looked, and a few of them were laughing or smiling. Others were staring from O'Hare to Doctor Marah and Papa and the sheriff on the porch as if they were doing some thinking. I hoped that those who'd heard what Doctor Marah had said would tell those who hadn't. I thought those had been good short speeches, all right. They wouldn't do Mr. O'Hare's name any good or his business either, I suspected.

Silas was the last one of all to leave. He stood with his torch blazing away, glowering at Doctor Marah and the others. Finally he backed away, and as he left his eyes fell on me. He lowered the torch to stick it out in front of me. Then he opened his mouth to insult me.

Suddenly a funny thing happened. The torch went out. All it was doing was smoking.

I bent over laughing at the look on his face as he stared at his torch. I was still laughing after he'd thrown the pine knot down and walked away disgusted.

A couple of minutes later I didn't have the time or spirit to laugh at Silas anymore. I saw Miss Carruthers and Miss Dalrymple and Mrs. Prescott talking to Mama out on the boardwalk while Papa and Doctor Marah spoke with the sheriff, who was examining the store's broken window. The ladies were still talking when Mama called out to me, "Hope, come here at once." She was beckoning with her arm.

The other women were speaking and nodding at each other in some sort of agreement as Mama told me, "Hope, get your brother, please, and go to Miss Emily's house and the Gardiner's and the house of every lady who has ever helped collect for the schoolhouse. Tell them to come to Fosters' store right away. You take the east side of Ottenberg while Davey takes the west. Tell him to be sure to ask each lady to bring a chair with her."

Miss Carruthers had overheard Mama. She broke away from Miss Dalrymple, who was writing with a pencil on a pad of paper, to tell me, "Please tell the ladies that they should bring a nightgown, too—and a toothbrush."

"*What?*"

I'd figured that they meant to sit outside the Shoo-Fly tonight, but not in their nightgowns.

Miss Carruthers went on, "That's correct, my dear. Now hurry along with you."

I could see my brother on our porch now, stepping in and out of the broken window. But before I got him, I asked the lady lawyer, "But if the ladies are going to sit out in front of the Shoo-Fly tonight, who's going to collect in the other saloons?" We didn't have the whole $1250 yet.

"You are, child. You and your little brother and any other school children you can get to help you. You children should take a hand in this noble and splendid enterprise, too."

"Yes, indeed!" exclaimed Miss Dalrymple, with her pencil up in the air. "I'll put this on the telegraph to San Francisco first thing in the morning, 'In Ottenberg even the children visit saloons when they are ordered to by their parents.' "

I hoped that wasn't exactly what would be in her newspaper. Nobody in town would like that. But I guessed she was excited, too. She would put it differently over the telegraph.

As I went after Davey, I rehearsed in my head what we were supposed to tell the ladies to bring with them. I didn't understand one bit why they'd need a nightgown and toothbrush. We Fosters couldn't begin to put all of them up overnight at our place—not even if they slept on the floor of the shebang. Counting Mama, there were twenty ladies by now who'd either collected for the school or had sat down in front of the Shoo-Fly. The number had grown since we'd begun what the lady lawyer had called our "noble and splendid enterprise."

If all of them showed up tonight, they would make two long aisles of sitters.

CHAPTER TEN

IRREVERENT

Nineteen of them came, and each and everyone of them carried a chair and a small valise or satchel. They looked plenty bewildered, too, just as bewildered as I was. I guessed Miss Carruthers would explain once they were all seated in the shebang. But before she got around to it, she sent Davey and me out with Papa's collar box.

"Go on, you two," she told us. "Put some variety into the lives of the men hereabouts. Show them some new faces in the grog shops."

"The Shoo-Fly, too?" asked Davey.

"Absolutely not, child. Now be off with you."

When I looked at Mama, she told me, "Yes, it's all right, children. Do your collecting and come straight back here and give the money to your father. He'll be waiting for you."

"Of course, he'll be here! How can he leave when his front window's broken? Thieves could walk in whenever they wanted," said an angry Emily. Tonight she was bundled up to the eyes in crocheted scarves. One of them was a green wool and the other a bluish violet. Aha! She wasn't dressed all in black anymore. That seemed to be a good sign. So was her standing up to her father. No, Miss Emily would never be pretty, but at least she could be colorful.

She was right about the thieves, of course. Papa could sit out front ready to meet them with a shotgun, but that would be very uncomfortable for him. It promised to be a chill October night, and after all it was already past the middle of the month.

Papa and Doctor Marah had retreated to the parlor to play cribbage. I stopped on my way to the side door to say, "Doctor Marah, I thought you were noble and splendid tonight."

"Thank you, Hope." She wasn't smiling. "Thank you, too, for getting the sheriff so swiftly."

"That was easy. I don't think you really needed him, though."

She shook her head. "I don't know. There's no way of telling how a mob is going to behave from moment to moment. If O'Hare had held the men in his mental grip, they might have carried out his threat about the rail."

"Well, it didn't happen, and you certainly showed him up."

"Yes, until the next time," said Papa glumly. "Who's going to buy me a new window?"

"Mr. O'Hare will, I'm sure," said Doctor Marah. "Give him a bill, and if he doesn't pay up, ask Mr. Prescott to help you collect. Prescott's a lawyer. He'll make his services available to you, even if he won't work for me."

I asked, "Why won't Mr. Prescott work for you?" This was interesting.

Marah told me, "In spite of his wife's beliefs, most of which he shares, Mr. Prescott has told me that he is afraid to be associated with me. I am not popular in Ottenberg among some men, thanks to Mr. O'Hare's notice in the

Oracle and my answering notice to it. Prescott has to rely on the men of Ottenberg for his legal business, and quite a number of them wouldn't like it if he took me on as a client."

"That's stupid," I told her and Papa. Davey nodded beside me.

"That's the way it is, Hope. There's another reason, too, why he stays out of things. As a lawyer, he should not defend a member of his own family in court. I refer to his wife."

"I think that's stupid, too."

"But that's the way it is, Hope."

"Is this why you went to Helena to get Miss Carruthers to come up here?"

The doctor grinned at me. "Let us say that Miss Carruthers wanted to come and look the situation over once I'd told her about it."

I had another question. "Do you know what Miss Carruthers is planning to do tonight?"

She nodded. "Yes, I do. She has asked me to remain inside here and not show myself outside again. I'm not to take any part in the events to come."

That didn't tell me much. I asked Papa the same question.

"Yep, I know, and because of what happened to my window, I'm all for it. I know the folks involved, and I'm pretty sure that what the ladies have in mind will work. Go on, get on with the collecting. Get wiggling. You'll find out what the fermenting ladies are up to soon enough." I heard him sigh, then saw him lift his head and wink at Davey and me.

Whatever was about to happen, it seemed to me that Papa had come over to Mama's side all the way. He was done with his complaining and his wavering.

Davey and I went in and out of saloons together, taking turns holding the collar box and asking for donations. Everybody treated us all right, and most folks gave us something, though one man at the Oro Fino Saloon did ask me, "Say, when are you folks goin' to stop askin' me to empty out my pockets for a schoolhouse nobody's set eyes on yet?"

I could understand how he felt, so I told him, "We don't like it any more than you do, mister. We're supposed to be done by the time snow comes to stay."

He laughed as he dropped a fifty-cent piece into the collar box. "I'm prayin' for an early blizzard this year."

Afterward we went on to saloon number twenty-one before we crossed to the other side of the street. As we went over to number twenty-two, the friendly Dolly Varden, we saw Mama and Miss Emily and the other ladies coming out of the shebang in a long line with their kitchen chairs under one arm and their satchels under the other. They were marching along with their chins stuck straight out in front of them. What a brave and splendid sight! I stopped to admire them.

Behind the long file of ladies came Miss Carruthers and Miss Dalrymple, but they didn't have chairs and no satchels. It didn't seem that they were about to sit down with the others.

Mama spied Davey and me standing out on the boardwalk in front of the Dolly Varden and called out, "Go on, children, do your duty, also!"

So in we went and collected $5.25 and came back out onto the boardwalk. Naturally we looked at the Shoo-Fly the moment we came out. The nineteen ladies had sat down making a packed-together but sort of crooked aisle that blocked the whole boardwalk. In front of the swinging doors sat Miss Ottenberg, the largest and heaviest of them all. Miss Carruthers and Miss Dalrymple took their places against the wall of the dressmaker's shop next door to the Shoo-Fly.

I watched a miner come out of the Dolly Varden behind Davey and me and start toward O'Hare's place, but all at once he stopped in his tracks, wheeled around, and went back inside the Dolly Varden. Another man went down into the street, stood for a minute in the ruts looking at the aisle of glaring ladies he'd have to walk through, shook his head, and went into a saloon two doors away from the Shoo-Fly.

Mama spotted Davey and me again and waved us on into the saloon next to the Dolly Varden, where we were given $7.32. One of the miners had just won a big poker pot and was feeling generous.

Davey went out the swinging doors ahead of me while I thanked the miner. When I came out, I found my brother rooted to the spot. "There goes old Silas," he told me, pointing at the figure sprinting across the street to the jailhouse.

Davey and I waited before we went into the saloon next door. We stood together in front of the town barber shop and watched while Sheriff Sherman came out, crossed the street, and stood over the ladies, who were sitting with their hands folded in their laps. Miss Carruthers and Miss Dalrymple came forward to talk with the sheriff.

All at once I saw Miss Ottenberg get up, raise her satchel up over her head, and walk away from her chair. It seemed to be a signal. One by one, Mama last of all, the sisters arose and lifted up their baggage. Then, led by Miss Emily, they stepped down off the boardwalk and in a long file trailed Sheriff Sherman over to the jail.

Naturally, because I'd done it twice, I knew exactly what to do. I let Davey go on alone with the collar box now that I'd shown him how to collect and what to say. Picking up Mama's chair, I ran to Papa and burst in on him and Doctor Marah through the side door. "Mama's gone to jail again," I called, and I set down the chair.

My father nodded. "It happened faster than I'd expected."

I said, "Davey's busy collecting. I'll go see the mayor and Mrs. Prescott and Reverend Gardiner and the judge. I know what to say."

"All right, Hope, you do the chores tonight. You tell all the menfolks of all the ladies you know." Papa looked up from the cribbage board to me. "And you'd better tell the gents at the same time that they can expect to fix their own breakfasts. On the advice of Lady Lawyer Carruthers, your mother and the other ladies are going to refuse to let themselves be ransomed by fines tonight. They are dead set on spending the night in jail!"

"*All night long,* Papa?" That explained the toothbrushes and nightgowns then.

"And perhaps all day tomorrow and the next day and the next."

This was too much, even for me. "But why?" All those dinners and lunches and breakfasts. And no Mama!

Doctor Marah explained, "The ladies and Miss Carruthers want to force a trial before Judge Bokman. If he tries to fine them again, they will refuse to pay. Ottenberg will be put on the map because of their actions, or so swears Miss Dalrymple. Miss Carruthers has advised the ladies that if the judge orders Sheriff Sherman to throw them out of jail, they are to resist."

Because I felt so stunned at this queer news, I sat down on the chair Mama had used. I'd heard of people being thrown *into* jail but not of people being thrown *out*. The idea took some getting used to.

While I was collecting myself, Doctor Marah said, "Well, this has been quite a day, hasn't it?"

"Yes, very exciting, too." I felt like frowning and did. "Maybe too exciting."

Doctor Marah smiled. "Your father has told me just now that I am obliged to you for a secret you've kept for me. So thank you once again, Hope."

I glanced swiftly at Papa, who was nodding at my unspoken question. He'd told the doctor that I knew all right.

I said, "Yes, I figured it out. I noticed that you didn't have sideburns and didn't seem to own a razor." I paused. "Yes, ma'am, I know you're a Jeanette, and I think that trying to be a female doctor is noble and splendid." There. I'd said those words twice to Doctor Marah in one day. I added, "Cross my heart and hope to die, I'll keep your secret just as long as you want me to."

Doctor Marah gave me a sort of twisted smile. "The time may be ripe for Miss Carruthers now that her reporter friend is here, but it isn't ripe for me yet. I told

Miss Carruthers that I'm a woman, but please keep thinking of me as a man." Leaning back in the chair, Marah told me, "I'll tell you another secret while I'm about it. Doctor Haverford is ill, very ill. He's been suffering from spells of dizziness lately."

I thought of how I'd seen the old doctor staggering once or twice in the past couple of weeks. And I'd even seen him grab porch posts to steady himself. Silas, and not just Silas either, but some grown-up Ottenbergers, had said Haverford was drunk. I felt sorry for the old doctor.

Marah went on, "I came out here not only to study under him but to take on some of his work load. He tries to do too much. He doesn't want it known he's not well. People would lose confidence in him then."

I couldn't help saying, "Ottenberg *men,* you mean?"

"Yes, mostly the men. However, things may change in time. I received word this morning by mail that I've passed my examinations for my medical degree. So I'm now a full-fledged doctor of medicine and can practice in a number of states and territories."

"Congratulations!" Papa exclaimed, which told me that he was hearing the good news for the first time, too.

"Hope," Doctor Marah said, smiling at me again, "I think now that I'm telling all my dark secrets I should let you in on yet another one. Not even my relative Doctor Haverford knows this one. When I was your age, my father taught my two brothers and me how to use a rifle and pistol. All of us became expert marksmen before he was satisfied with us."

"Then you could kill Mr. O'Hare in a duel?" This was most interesting, but I knew it would have to be kept secret, too. What a burden carrying all these secrets was getting to be!

"Probably I could, if I chose to. But I do not choose to and don't tempt me regarding O'Hare. I'm human, too, you know. I don't feel either noble or splendid. At times, when some of the men make loud comments about my lily liveredness, I think it might be a good idea to shoot a hole in Mr. O'Hare to shut everyone up for good. That would get men patients to come to me, but I can't say that I'd approve of the manner in which I got them. It would be very peculiar for a doctor to start a medical practice by shooting someone, wouldn't it?"

Papa laughed. "You might say that medicine is a queer trade. The patient can't live without the doctor, and the doctor can't live without the patient."

I said, "But that's like running our shebang, too, isn't it, Papa? You can't get along without customers, and they can't get along without what you sell very well."

Papa jerked his thumb at me. "Hope has a good head on her shoulders, Doc."

"She has, indeed," said Marah. Then the doctor asked me, "What are you going to be when you grow up entirely, Hope?" She wasn't smiling at all now.

At last! Somebody had asked me *the* question. I said, "I don't know yet. I used to think that I'd be a schoolteacher for a while, because that seemed to be all that a lady could do, except become a seamstress or a store clerk, but now I've seen that I could be a doctor or a lawyer or reporter and maybe even more things." I shook my head.

"Hope, you can think about that later," Papa interrupted me. "Now you'd better get a real wiggle on. Take a lantern and your brother, who ought to be done by now, and make the calls on the poor husbands. While you're about it, one of you might stop in at the jail and find out the visiting hours."

I got up and looked around our familiar parlor at the golden-oak table and horsehair sofa, the carpet with rose and cream flowers on it, and the cottage organ with vases full of pine boughs, for fragance, on top of it. But Mama was gone. She should have been here. She'd never been away from Davey and me overnight before in our whole lives.

I asked Doctor Marah, "What else can you cook besides fancy stuff?"

"We'll survive, Hope. Don't you worry," answered the doctor, who hadn't really replied to my question.

Papa told her, "You know, it's an ill wind that doesn't blow some good."

A motto? That sounded like Mrs. Prescott. Papa didn't use them often. I listened carefully as he went on. "I imagine I'm going to sell canned goods hand over fist as long as the good ladies of Ottenberg are in the calaboose. I might even make a profit on account of all this."

Afterward I went out in search of Davey, so we could tell husbands and fathers and brothers that they might be missing meals for a while. It wouldn't be welcome news, I knew for sure.

The usual thing went on that night, with the men and Judge Bokman going over to the jail, accompanied by me, of course. But the routine was a bit different this time. Miss Carruthers was sitting in a chair outside the cells while the lady reporter sat on a bench behind the sheriff's desk with a note pad on her lap. It seemed to me that both Ohio ladies looked bright-eyed and alert.

The minute the judge and the husbands and fathers and brothers and Colonel Ottenberg came in, all of the imprisoned ladies—all nineteen of them—got up off the stools and bunks in their cells. They were surely packed tightly in there. Miss Ottenberg was first to speak up.

Oh, she had her courage up now. She called out, "Judge Bokman, sirrah, I want you to know at once that we demand to be brought to trial. If you impose a fine and if our menfolk dare to pay it, we shall not budge one inch or iota from this place. If you set bail for us to set us at liberty until we come to trial, we shall still refuse to budge from here."

Aha! Now I knew a bit about what bail was. Not a fine exactly but something that let people out of jail. I would ask Papa more about it later.

Colonel Ottenberg let out a string of strangling sounds while Miss Emily went on calling out to the judge, who was looking like a thundercloud by now. "I want you to know that we have legal counsel here, in the person of Miss Agnes Carruthers of Helena."

Mrs. Prescott added in a high voice, "Formerly and originally from Ohio, however."

Judge Bokman only grunted. It didn't seem to me that he'd even heard about the Ohio fermenters or perhaps he didn't care or maybe he didn't even approve of them. I'd expected a fancy speech from a judge, but all I got was, "Ladies, there are a number of things I can do. I can have you ejected from here, you know."

Mama spoke up next. "Then, sir, we shall take up stations on the boardwalk just outside. We shall stay there, a number of us, night and day."

Mrs. Gardiner said, "Yes, we shall."

The judge told her, "Your menfolks can carry you off bodily."

I heard Miss Dalrymple laughing and saw how fast she was scribbling on her pad. I supposed that whatever she was writing was going out by telegraph the first thing in the morning.

Mama spoke again. "If we are dragged home by the hair on our heads, as you seem to be suggesting, Judge Bokman, we have promised each other that we will take at once to our beds and not do a lick of cooking or housekeeping."

The husband of one of the ladies I didn't know by name said quietly, "You better let them stay in the lockup then, Your Honor."

Reverend Gardiner touched the judge's arm. "Bring them to trial speedily, Your Honor, and get this over with. We don't want to be the scandal of the nation for the way we treat our womenfolk."

"I think we already are going to be." Judge Bokman had turned around to give Miss Dalrymple a sharp look. Obviously he knew who she was, and why she'd come to town. From her he turned his gaze onto Miss Carruthers.

With his hands in his pockets so deep that the tails of his black frock coat stood out behind him, he leaned forward over the lady lawyer to ask her, "Do you represent these accused women?"

"Yes, I do." She was on her feet, too. "Doctor Marah brought me from Helena. He felt that if the ladies got into deeper difficulties, they might need an attorney. He was sure that no lawyer here in Ottenberg would help them."

"He was quite right," put in Mr. Prescott.

"All right." Judge Bokman blew out his breath in annoyance. "This is a very ridiculous business. It is all highly irregular. But then everything seems to be irregular about this whole affair. It appears to me that to keep the peace speed is of the essence. We shall have a trial tomorrow."

"Yes, sir, that's the spirit. Get 'em home and tendin' to women's bus'ness," said a husband. Just looking at him made me sorry for some lady behind bars. He was a whiskery, red-eyed, tobacco-chewing type of man.

"That would suit us just fine," Miss Carruthers told the judge, giving him a look that said, "Let's fight."

"Ridiculous, utterly ridiculous," were Bokman's last words, as he turned on his heel and went out, shaking his head.

The lady lawyer took charge after he'd gone. "You may as well go home, gentlemen. The ladies are staying the night here. You needn't worry about their whereabouts or their welfare. They are perfectly safe, and they won't lack for company or comfort."

It didn't seem to me that the crowding in the cells would make for much comfort, but I supposed the sheriff would arrange sleeping places for everyone somehow. Some of the women waved good-bye to their men. Two of them blew kisses, which the men didn't return because they were too embarrassed.

After the men had left, the ladies began to sing a hymn we sang at church now and then. It was "Blessed Are Thy Courts Above." It seemed to be a nice hopeful choice. I noticed that Miss Carruthers and Miss Dalrymple, from their seats outside the cells, sang along with the ladies on the inside.

So then I started for home. Thinking ahead, I was pretty sure I wouldn't sleep well that night. I'd have a lot on my mind wondering what was going to happen tomorrow. It seemed to me that Mr. O'Hare should be in the jail, too, for threatening Doctor Marah and window breaking. But he wasn't. In fact, the Shoo-Fly was going full toot across the street. Even over the loud piano playing I could hear lots of laughter. I figured O'Hare was giving out more free whiskey. He'd probably got over his pout because Doctor Marah had thwarted him, and now he was celebrating the ladies' being in the jail again. News traveled fast in little Ottenberg. Somebody must have told him too that the satchels they had carried held what they would need to spend the night away from home—in jail.

Because of the trial, Miss Willis let out those of us who showed up at school the next day at eleven o'clock. We were fidgeting so much with excitement we couldn't keep our minds on our lessons. She was just as excited. I noticed once that she was holding her teacher's copy of the sixth-grade reader upside down, as she followed me while I was reading out loud.

At noon I took Mama and the other ladies some elk-meat broth Papa had boiled, but I found out that they really didn't need it. The sheriff had got their meals from a Chinese chophouse that did the jail cooking. They also had all sorts of good eats brought by the Ottenberg ladies who weren't in jail. I saw plates of cakes, crullers, and cookies in every cell. Mama told me through the bars that they had sung the night away. They'd spent the morning eating and receiving a stream of lady visitors, which hadn't stopped coming for a minute. I thought that was very nice.

Sheriff Sherman spoke glumly to me when Mama was through. "I didn't get a minute's shut-eye all night in here, and I didn't even try to enforce visiting time. If a visitor had brought in a cake with an iron file baked inside of it, I'd have let any lady file her way through the bars and crawl outside. As it was, I moved my men prisoners to the Big Bend Hotel, where they could get some peace and quiet. I locked my deputy officer in with the claim jumpers and horse thieves over there, the lucky stiff. I wish to heaven I could've gone over to the hotel with him instead of listening to those singin' ladies all night." He did appear to be blearyeyed as he went on mumbling, "It's always busy inside here, but I'd take men who are wicked as sin over ladies who are good women any day of the week, believe you me. Them women don't never sleep." He shook his head.

I looked past him at Mama and the others, who were talking to Miss Carruthers and Miss Dalrymple in low tones. The reporter had been very busy. That morning she'd made six trips to the telegraph office before ten thirty. Papa had kept count.

My mother's was the very first trial held in the new courthouse in a courtroom that wasn't quite finished yet. The carpenters had to quit work at one thirty when people started coming in to sit on the brand-new benches. With hammers stuck into the back pockets of their overalls, the carpenters took seats on the right side of the room, where they were only half done with nailing up a partition. The benches were in place and a big desk for the judge but no chairs. They'd been rounded up from all over Ottenberg. I'd brought one of the nicest parlor chairs for Mama to sit on.

The statue of Justice was in the courtroom, too, standing in one corner. There hadn't been time yet to set her out front of the courthouse where she belonged. There was a cuspidor right beside her. I surely hoped someone wouldn't miss when he spat tobacco juice in her direction.

I sat with Davey, Papa, Doctor Haverford, and Doctor Marah. Actually I sat between Papa and the old doctor, who wasn't looking one bit chipper that afternoon. His cheeks were sort of swollen, it seemed to me, and were rusty pink in color. He seemed to have trouble breathing too. I'd never noticed that about him before, but then I'd never sat next to him before either.

I couldn't truthfully say that I understood the trial Mama and Miss Emily and the others had, though I listened as carefully as I could.

Mr. O'Hare was in the courtroom along with Silas and some of the Shoo-Fly's customers. He was called up front to sit in a special chair that faced everybody. Miss Carruthers and the judge asked him some questions that everybody already knew the answers to.

First of all, they asked him what his name was and what line of work he was in. Then, while Miss Dalrymple sat on the first bench writing and writing away, Miss Carruthers asked him a different question. "Mr. O'Hare, did you lay violent hands on any one of these accused ladies present in this room?"

"Not violent. I only removed them from my place of

business. They came in to beg money from my customers, who shouldn't be disturbed."

A miner somewhere behind me called out loudly, "Hey, Tom, nobody oughta be disturbed while he's busy drinkin' whiskey anywheres."

O'Hare grinned and Judge Bokman hit his desk with a wooden hammer. I learned later on from Doctor Marah that it was called a gavel. A gavel was supposed to shut everybody up except the person the judge wanted to hear from at the moment. It wasn't so different from Miss Willis's ruler that she slapped on her desk to get everyone quiet.

Then Miss Carruthers asked O'Hare about the notice he'd put in the *Oracle*, wanting to know if he'd truly done it. After he said that he had, she read it out loud to the courtroom. Next she read Doctor Marah's notice out loud, too.

Everybody began to talk to his neighbor, so the judge banged on his desk some more with the wooden hammer. He told Miss Carruthers that as far as he could see this didn't have anything to do with the ladies sitting out in front of the Shoo-Fly Saloon, blocking the way so men had to walk through an aisle of them.

"Oh, yes, it does." Miss Emily popped up out of the front row of borrowed chairs where the ladies had been told to sit by the sheriff. "The chief reason I am here, Your Honor, is that I hate the very thought of dueling. It leaves widows and orphans in its wake and pining maidens who never marry."

Aha, she had finally put her sorrow into words. I thought that was very noble of her to tell her sad secret in front of the whole town. "That dreadful notice of Mr.

O'Hare's"—Miss Emily turned around and pointed a black-sleeved arm at the saloonkeeper—"was an open invitation to Doctor Marah to challenge him."

"Please sit down, Miss Ottenberg," ordered the judge.

"All right, sirrah, I shall. I have spoken my piece." So down she went, glaring at O'Hare and Silas.

After O'Hare, Mama was called to sit in the chair that had been brought over from the jail. I watched her flick off the seat with her handkerchief first. The judge asked her why she had come to the doors of the Shoo-Fly Saloon with her chair. She told him that she wanted everyone in Ottenberg to know what she thought of Mr. Thomas O'Hare's action. She objected to his throwing her and the other ladies out of the Shoo-Fly and to his placing an insulting and threatening notice about Doctor Marah in the *Oracle*.

One after another the ladies came up to sit in the jailhouse chair and say the same thing in their own words.

Finally Judge Bokman spoke directly to Miss Carruthers. "I hope you are pleased with yourself. I have never seen such goings-on in my entire legal career. These women don't even pretend to be innocent of obstructing business and being public nuisances. I realized that the practice of law could be rather unusual in the territories, but this case surpasses anything I anticipated. Mr. O'Hare publicly insulted Doctor Marah in his newspaper notice, but I fail to see that he challenged him to a duel. The word *duel* does not appear in the notice at all. Mr. O'Hare has a perfect right to refuse entry to his establishment to anyone he chooses to. It is a free country in that respect. I cannot say that I approve of Mr. O'Hare's laying hands on some of the ladies of Ottenberg, but not one of them has claimed that he hurt her."

This brought me to my feet in one bound before either Papa or Doctor Haverford could pull me down. I hadn't liked Judge Bokman's tone just now or anything he'd said. I called out, "It isn't so! He hurt *me*! Mr. O'Hare threw Miss Carruthers and Miss Dalrymple out, and when he did they hit me and I fell and got slivers in my hands. I was only passing by the saloon, too."

The judge looked straight at me. "Yes, you're the Foster girl, aren't you? You were the first one to sit down outside the Shoo-Fly Saloon." He was frowning at me. He went on sharply, "Somehow I do not see you as an innocent victim in this matter at all, Miss Foster. How old are you?"

"I turned thirteen the first part of last month."

"That is old enough to know better. Sit down at once, Miss Foster. You don't seem badly wounded to me at all."

And so down I sat, fuming inside.

The next moment I was blushing. Miss Carruthers was telling everyone there about me—how brave and noble and splendid I was and about how miserable the chicken-coop school was. I could see Miss Willis, who was sitting on a bench in front of me, nodding and nodding, though I doubted if it was because she agreed about my nobility and splendidness. Miss Carruthers was a golden talker, and she looked mighty handsome indeed in her black-velvet gown as she flung her arms around gracefully, praising first me, then Mama and Miss Emily and the others. When she finished she bowed her head. Quite a few people, me among them, applauded her.

I whispered to Papa, "Mr. O'Hare ought to be on trial for breaking our window, not Mama."

"Well, he isn't. He sent his boy to tell me he'd pay me when I gave him the bill and I know the proper sum. Now be quiet, Hope, and let us hear what the judge has to say."

Judge Bokman didn't say much after Miss Carruthers was through. He hit his desk with the gavel and said very loudly, "I am weary of this folly. I hereby fine each defendant the sum of ten dollars. And if any lady takes it into her mind to stay in jail rather than pay the ten dollars, I will have her transported to the jail in Helena in spite of the lateness of the season and the threat of snow."

There was a lot of hubbub and noise, and down came the hammer once more. Over all of it rose Miss Carruthers's voice. I saw her pointing at the statue of Justice. "Justice is not only blind but deaf and dumb as well in Ottenberg. Ottenberg builds a fine courthouse, jail, and town hall, but puts its most precious treasures—its children —into a chicken coop!"

Banging that little wooden hammer once more, Judge Bokman thundered at the lady lawyer. "You have been threatened with contempt of court by me before, Miss Carruthers. In Helena you called me a whiskey judge to my face. You said then that I favored saloonkeepers over one of your clients. You spent a night in the Helena jail for that and for your irreverent attitude toward the law. Do you want to go to the Ottenberg jail, too?"

Irreverent? That was the third word I'd expected to look up in Doctor Marah's dictionary and never got around to. Well, I'd learned what *obstreperous, benighted,* and *irreverent* meant just by keeping my ears open. That was interesting.

Miss Carruthers was talking again. "I have been in Ottenberg's jail all night as it is, Judge Bokman. Sheriff Sherman is a fine gentleman, which is more than I can say for most other men in this town. He is also a generous man. Last night he donated five dollars to the school fund when the ladies promised him that they would not sing 'Blessed Are Thy Courts Above' once more that night."

"I am happy that Sheriff Sherman saw fit to give money to the school building, Miss Carruthers. But that is not important here. I hereby fine you, Miss Carruthers, the sum of ten dollars for your attitude toward me and my court."

He got up and went out the little door behind his desk so fast that his coattails flew out behind him. He'd had the final word. I supposed that was something judges often got.

Well, it seemed to me that Miss Carruthers wasn't going to have to go to jail. I wondered if she would have used an iron file to saw her way out if it had been baked into a cake for her.

CHAPTER ELEVEN

WHAT LOT?

Papa muttered beside me, "Bokman left just in time to save himself from having to send Miss Carruthers to the hoosegow."

"But not before he fined her ten dollars," put in Doctor Marah dryly.

I watched Doctor Haverford pat Doctor Marah on the shoulder as Papa got up and reached into his vest pocket where he kept the money for Mama's fines. I heard the old doctor say very softly, "Well, you certainly were discussed plenty this afternoon."

"Yes, but I doubt if this will bring men patients to me. It stirred the whole thing up all over again."

I had to agree with Doctor Marah. More than one man who was going up along with my father to plunk down his cash to get a lady back home was giving Doctor Marah a hard look as he passed by. One thing Miss Carruthers had done was make it clearer than ever that their sitting outside the Shoo-Fly wasn't only because of the new schoolhouse. So in the minds of some of the men, Doctor Marah was costing them money.

I was asking myself after the trial the same question Margaret Libby was asking me. She'd been there with her father and mother and had heard everything that was said, too. She hadn't understood any more of it than I had. "Hope, what good did the trial do? Why did the ladies want a trial anyhow? And where was the jury?"

I said, "I guess this wasn't a jury trial. The judge was supposed to be enough. I don't know what good it did, but I suspect Mama can tell me when I ask her. And if she can't, Miss Carruthers surely can."

As it turned out I didn't have to put the question to either one of them. Miss Carruthers and Miss Dalrymple came to our parlor that same night to say good-bye, because they both were leaving for their homes the next day.

It seemed to me that Mama and the other two looked mighty tired from lack of sleep, but even so they were in good spirits. I listened to them and heard Miss Carruthers say to Mama, "I'd hoped to win the case, of course, but a great deal of good came out of our defeat, believe me."

Miss Dalrymple nodded her head. "Yes, indeed. I've sent story after story over the telegraph to my newspaper about the stirring events here. By the end of the month a great many people will have read of the gallant ladies of Ottenberg and of their mighty efforts to fight greedy and brutal men in getting a decent school for the town's children. The names of Colonel Ottenberg and Mr. Thomas O'Hare of the Shoo-Fly Saloon will be mud from California to Maine. You fought a good fight, Mrs. Foster, once your delightful and clever daughter showed you the way."

She meant *me*! I was to be in newspapers from California to Maine. I said, being truthful and modest, "But all I did was go out and sit down."

"Yes," said Miss Carruthers, "but you sat down in the right place at the right time."

I wanted to ask her if she'd told Miss Dalrymple Doctor

Marah's secret but couldn't. I was pretty sure that she hadn't, for fear the lady reporter would put it in her stories. It would certainly be interesting reading but wouldn't be a secret any longer then.

The lady reporter grinned at Mama. "You know, I wouldn't be one bit surprised if people all over the country send you contributions toward the new school."

Mama said in what seemed to me a proud voice, "I am sure that would be very kind of them, but we don't need their money. My husband made a count of the cash last evening, while I was behind bars across the street. We are only $100 short of our goal of $1250."

"Mrs. Foster, will you be going out collecting again tonight?" asked Miss Dalrymple.

"Yes, and for one of the very last times, we hope."

"Then I shall go with you. My readers will be interested in what it's like to collect money for a worthy cause in a Montana Territory den of sin and alcohol amid drunken sots."

"No, ma'am, you won't be going there with my wife."

We all turned around in surprise and saw Papa standing between the curtains that separated our shebang from our parlor. Essex pushed past him, making a beeline for Mama's lap. The cats had missed her the night before and had kept running from my bed to Doctor Marah's, jumping up and then down again. They knew somebody important was missing.

Miss Carruthers hadn't liked what Papa had said. She was on her feet ready to do battle again. "Why are we not to go, Mr. Foster?" she demanded. "Are you turning against the idea of the schoolhouse at this last minute?" Her voice was crackling with fury.

Mama was up, too, not red in the face but looking startled. "What is it, Albert?"

He laughed at the two of them. "Simmer down, ladies. I've been pretty much won over for quite a while, though I can't say I like the idea of my wife in jail or paying jail fines. Sit down. To keep the peace in Ottenberg or rather to get some peace in my own household, I'm going to donate that last hundred dollars, myself, as a gift from the Whole Shebang. It will be a token of admiration for your grit and determination."

Sounding alarmed, Mama asked him, "Albert, can we afford that much money?"

"I think we can, Nora. I asked myself while you were occupied across the way last night whether we should have a fat Christmas or a slender one this year. And I decided that paying for the new school building—inasmuch as I had two kids in it—was more important than a fancy holiday season."

Mama and the other two women beamed at Papa, but not me. I couldn't help but say, "Does that mean no oranges and walnuts and no toys for Davey?" I thought it would be wiser to complain for Davey about a slender Christmas. Not only was he younger than I, he wasn't here to get scolded for sounding selfish.

I didn't fool my father much, though. He said, "Davey won't feel left out by Saint Nicholas, Hope."

"And you'll have a new schoolhouse," added Miss Carruthers.

"All right," I told her, "if it's bigger than the old one was, so I won't have to sit close to Silas, that ought to be a dandy Christmas present."

Mama had already sat down. She let out a sigh as she

picked up the jersey she'd been too busy to knit on for quite a spell. "Thank you, Albert. I have to confess that I am weary and I know that the other sisters are equally worn out. All this evening collecting has been something of a strain on our time and energy."

Then she spoke to Miss Carruthers and Miss Dalrymple. "I've heard from Doctor Marah, Miss Carruthers, that Mrs. Bokman spoke with him about you. If Mrs. Bokman is a friend of yours, why isn't her husband?"

The lady lawyer smiled as she sank into her chair again. "You heard what her husband said to me in the courtroom about putting me in jail. He became very angry with me about my views, some of which he'd already heard about before we got into the courtroom. As for Mrs. Bokman, why don't you get to know her and ask her yourself? I think you would like her."

"Well, I hope to have the chance," Mama said in melancholy tones, "if Judge Bokman will permit his wife to associate with women who have been in jail."

"I suppose that could be a problem," Miss Carruthers agreed, not smiling now.

I added, because I was mad at the judge, "If that's the case, Mrs. Bokman isn't going to have much in the way of lady friends, because an awful lot of the nicest ladies in Ottenberg were across the street last night with my mother."

Miss Carruthers laughed and said, "Well said, Hope. I'm very sure that Mrs. Bokman is well aware of this, too. Emerald is nobody's fool."

"Emerald, is that her name?" I wanted to know.

"Yes, it is."

This interested me. I'd heard of ladies called Ruby and Pearl but never Emerald.

"The Bokman baby's due quite soon now," said Mama. "It would be nice if by then Mrs. Bokman had some women friends to help her out. But perhaps her own mother's on the way to the Territory to be with her."

I saw Miss Carruthers shake her head. "I doubt that. It's so late in the year now that her mother wouldn't dare travel and risk the snows. She is quite elderly and lives a long way away—in Ohio."

I asked right away, "Is she a fermenter, too?"

Miss Dalrymple, who'd been playing with Essex, looked up and asked me quickly, "What is a fermenter?"

So I had to explain myself, and everyone, including my own mother, laughed at my way of putting things. Once I'd explained that this is what I called ladies who had advanced views about things and, in particular, ladies who came out of Ohio, they understood me. They agreed with me that they were indeed fermenters and that being a fermenter anywhere was very interesting and exciting.

Before she said her final farewell to us, Miss Dalrymple promised Mama to mail her some snipped-out newspaper stories on the events in Ottenberg we'd been involved in. She warned us, though, that it could be some time before we got any because of being snowed in. Still, she was certain there would be articles about Ottenberg and the Shoo-Fly in papers other than the one she worked for in San Francisco.

"Yes, that will give us all something to look forward to in the springtime," Mama told her in turn.

Finally after another cup of coffee, the two out-of-town,

Ohio-born ladies went back to the Prescotts to spend the night.

I wouldn't be around to say good-bye to them at the stagecoach, because I had to go to school the next day. I felt bad about that, but I'd surely remember them and their courage for a long time—if not for my whole life.

First thing of all the next morning at school, I made an announcement that, thanks to my father's gift of the whole $100, we could now pay off the new school building in full the minute it arrived in Ottenberg. I tacked onto my announcement the fact that the sisters wouldn't be going out to saloons at night anymore.

Some of the kids cheered, and Miss Willis acted as pleased as Davey and I expected her to be. She didn't let us out of school early, though, to celebrate reaching our goal as he and I had hoped. This disappointed us.

More than that it peeved me. I was even angrier when she asked me to stay inside the coop at recess time, because she wanted to talk to me. I didn't get up out of my seat to go to her desk. I sat where I was, and she came over to me.

She started by saying, "Hope, I want you to tell your father and your mother how very much I appreciate all the effort they've put into getting a new school building."

"All right, Miss Willis, I will." And that was all I said. I was itching to get outside to talk to Margaret.

She didn't say anything for a long time, then finally she added, "I know that you and Davey went out collecting, too, and, of course, I know about your picking up the first chair and sitting down in front of that saloon. I know how much courage that takes."

I wondered if she was only flattering me.

She smiled a little mournfully. "You think I don't know, but I do. If I hadn't been teaching school here, I would have been out there with you and the other ladies in a flash."

Aha! She had called me a "lady." That was the nicest thing she'd ever said to me.

I kept quiet, wondering if she would say more nice things. She went on, "Do you recall my telling you about women sitting down out in front of the store of the man who beat his wife in Ohio?"

"Yes, Miss Willis, I do."

"Well, I brought the first chair there. The others joined me. I didn't say anything about this the first night at your store when the ladies gathered, because I was afraid they might think I was boasting or they might get the idea that I was a troublemaker. Teachers must be very careful, you know."

I stared at her. "So you were the *first* one? Your story was what gave me the idea to sit down outside the Shoo-Fly!"

Miss Leota laughed. "See, Hope, you can learn more from teachers sometimes than your ABCs and the multiplication tables." She leaned over my desk with both hands on it. "Tell me, Hope, did you do what you did just for the sake of the new schoolhouse?"

"No, ma'am, it was for Doctor Marah, too."

Then she said something that made me jerk all the way down to my toes. "For Jeanette's sake?" she asked me very softly.

Miss Willis knew, too! I gasped and asked, "How did you find out?"

"Doctor Marah told me herself, just before she went off to Helena."

I wondered how many other Ottenberg people knew the secret. "You haven't told anyone else, have you?"

"Not a soul. Have you, Hope?"

I shook my head. "No, not even Margaret, and I won't say a word until Doctor Marah tells me that I can, but may I tell Mama and Papa that you know?"

"Of course, if you wish. How did you find out?"

I told her about not finding a razor in Doctor Marah's room and about Essex and Manchester's being so fond of the doctor and about Mama's telling me that what I guessed was true.

"You have a rather sharp mind at times, Hope Foster."

With those very kindly words she went back to her desk to correct some papers. After a while she got up to ring the handbell from the top step of the chicken coop to call everybody back inside. As for me, I sat where I was, with my head in my cupped hands and elbows on the desk, admiring Miss Willis. I'd never noticed before how handsome she was—and clever too.

When everybody had come in and squeezed into their desks, she said, "I want to make an announcement. I am going to write a thank-you letter to Mr. and Mrs. Foster, Doctor Marah, and the church ladies on behalf of all of us, for working so hard to get us a new schoolhouse. I want all of you to sign your names, so these good people will know that we appreciate their efforts."

Instantly Silas got up from his seat so fast he nearly knocked another smaller kid into the next bench. Oh, he was surely big for his britches this morning. As a matter of fact, he was hanging out of them, top and bottom. Without asking Miss Willis's permission, he said, "I ain't signin' my name to that paper. All I got to say is that I'm glad them ladies are through pesterin' the town. Maybe now they'll quit bein' so bothersome to my pa and me. I say hurray for that!"

I flared at him, "They're sick and tired of your old pa!"

Davey added straight out, too, "Your pa owes my papa plenty for a busted window. If he don't pay up, maybe he'll go to jail, too."

"My pa ain't never been in jail, Davey Foster!"

"He ought to be and all those men who came to our shebang with him to get Doctor Marah. If your pa doesn't pay up, sure as God made little green apples, he'll go to jail." Those were my words, and I was proud of them.

Then Miss Willis banged on her desk with her ruler. After she'd got us quieted down and back to studying, she went to the coop's window to push the curtain aside and look out. I watched her. She stood there for a while, then, sighing, came back to the stove to hold her hands over it. It had certainly been a nippy morning, though the skies were clear.

It was the very end of the third week in October now, and where was our new schoolhouse? I wondered. We needed it right away. It was getting more and more impossible every day in the chicken coop. When the stove wasn't lit, we were bundled up in our coats and jackets so tightly we could hardly move. Once the stove got going, we got so warm and perspired so much that Miss Willis was afraid to let us go out and run around at recess, for fear we'd all catch galloping pneumonia.

* * *

On the thirtieth of the month, a Saturday, it finally came. I was just about the first one in Ottenberg to know.

Papa came into the parlor with a grin spread so wide over his face that the ends of his mustache were turned up. "Well, folks, it's here. The schoolhouse made it!"

Mama and I were setting the table for lunch, while Davey teased Manchester with a ball of yarn. I laid down the fork and knife in my hand next to a plate, threw off my apron, and ran outside to see what I could see. How wonderful that it had arrived on a Saturday when Davey and I were home from school.

But what did I see? Nothing much. Nothing but three mule-drawn wagons standing out in front of our shebang. The skin on the mules was steaming, because they'd been pulling the wagons up a grade into town. The morning was so chilly that their breath was steaming, too. I looked from the porch down into the wagons. What was there was covered with gray canvas. But I'd heard from Papa's lips that the schoolhouse was here. If I hadn't heard him, I would have thought the delivery wasn't anything more important than some goods for the store. I couldn't tell which wagon had the school bell in it. All the same, I just knew there was a bell in one of the wagons. The folder from Chicago had said so.

Without getting my jacket, I ran down the boardwalk to tell the good news to everyone I passed who might be interested. I told Mrs. Prescott and Mrs. Gardiner, who were out shopping, "The school finally got here." Then I went to find Doctor Marah, who I knew was with Doctor Haverford in his office. I pounded up Haverford's steps, opened the door, and yelled, "It's here. The schoolhouse is here. Come see it in front of the store."

From there I went to the Libby house and told Margaret to tell everybody she knew. Afterward I went to jail and told Sheriff Sherman, who was a good friend of mine by now. After telling him, I told everyone I met on the boardwalk and from there ran all the way out to the Ottenberg house to let Miss Emily know.

She came to the door chewing a part of her lunch. I could see her father beyond her sitting at the table eating, too. Before she could swallow what was in her mouth, I told her the news and was on my way home again. I didn't wait to hear what she would have to say. All I'd had time to notice was that she was wearing a pretty, lacy, rose-colored knitted shoulder covering.

There was quite a crowd out in front of the shebang when I got home. Men were peeping under the canvas, nodding, and talking to each other. Doctor Marah, Mr. Prescott, Papa, Reverend Gardiner, and Doctor Haverford were standing together on the porch in front of the boarded-up window looking quite pleased about everything, it seemed to me.

"By the Great Lord Harry, it did get here!" Mr. Prescott was saying. He sounded as if he didn't believe it.

"Yes, it did, glory be to God," agreed the minister. "And there isn't any snow in sight yet."

That was true. In spite of the fact that my hands had turned red and I thought my nose would drop off with cold, the sun was shining brightly. But there wasn't one bit of warmth in it.

I called out to Papa, before I ran inside for my coat and mittens, "When are you going to nail the boards together?"

"Right away, Hope. Fast as we can. After all, Halloween's tomorrow. The directions came along with it." He laughed. "With all the volunteer help we've been offered, it ought to go up fast."

In the shebang doorway, I asked, "Where are you going to put it, Papa?"

"Here in town, of course. On a lot."

"What lot, Papa?"

I heard Reverend Gardiner ask the next question. "What lot, Mr. Foster? Where?"

"Oh, my Lord!" My father looked as if a bolt of lightning had hit him.

Mr. Prescott asked, "Yes, Albert, what lot?"

I stared at my father. His face was changing in front of my eyes. It seemed to be crumpling. He said very slowly, "We haven't got a lot."

"No lot, Albert?" asked Doctor Haverford sharply.

"No, sir. No lot."

Haverford let out a great bellow. "You mean to say, nobody thought of getting land to put the schoolhouse on?"

"Yes, sir, it sort of looks that way," answered Papa. "In all the excitement of collecting the cash, nobody thought of buying a place to put the building on." I thought he looked very sheepish and was suddenly sorry for him. I hadn't thought about a lot either.

Doctor Marah put in quietly, "Don't feel so guilty about it, Mr. Foster. We're all as responsible for the oversight as you are. We'll just have to buy a piece of property to put the school on right away."

"There are a number of vacant lots," said Reverend Gardiner, trying to sound hopeful.

"Yes, that's so." Mr. Prescott was digging the toe of

one of his boots into the boardwalk where there was a knothole. After a bit he went on to say, "And they are all owned by your very good friend, Mayor Ottenberg."

Papa groaned. "My Lord, I'm sure going to hate to have to tell the ladies this news." His sorrowful gaze was fixed on Mama, Mrs. Gardiner, Mrs. Prescott, and Miss Willis, who were down by the wagons excitedly peeking under the canvas. "We can't erect a building on thin air. I say we're licked at the last moment. O'Hare's going to have the last laugh after all, it seems. I've paid for the building now. Every cent we collected went for it."

"Hmm," came from Doctor Haverford, who hadn't said much yet. I didn't think his hmm was very helpful. What else he said wasn't either. "Well, we certainly can't ask Miss Ottenberg to donate a lot to us or to buy one for us. She really doesn't have any money of her own; she told me that. She and her father aren't speaking at all these days. He's dead set against any women in town who have collected for the schoolhouse. He calls them sneaky scheming female varmints and backstabbers, and to his way of thinking she's one of them. There's a second Civil War going on in that house."

Mr. Prescott nodded. "I suppose we men could go see Colonel Ottenberg all together."

Not replying to him, Doctor Haverford asked me, "Hope, does the colonel know yet that the new school's arrived yet?"

"I don't know. I went to the Ottenberg house to tell the news."

Haverford nodded. "Yes, that's what your father told us. But did you speak personally with Colonel Ottenberg?"

"Oh, no, he never speaks to anybody as unimportant as kids. I told Miss Emily—not him. He was eating lunch when she came to the door."

I noticed that the old doctor was staring rather strangely at me, as if I was coming down with some interesting and unusual sickness. "Hope, how about you and me visiting the colonel right now?"

"Me?" I squeaked.

"Yes, you. With you along he won't suspect anything." Suspect? What did he mean?

"What do you have in mind, Doctor?" Papa's voice sounded anxious and hopeful at the same moment.

"I am going to buy a piece of property. Two pieces, as a matter of fact. I will say that one is for me to build a small hospital on in due course, and the other is for the home I plan to build later."

I think I understood him faster than the men did. I asked, "But one of them will *really* be for the school."

"That's correct."

"It's trickery," said Reverend Gardiner.

"So it is, but I don't see any other way, do you?"

"No, as a matter of fact, I don't," agreed the minister.

I couldn't see for the life of me why Doctor Haverford wanted me along, but when Papa said, "Go with him, Hope," I went inside after my best jacket, mittens, and bonnet. I figured I should dress up for the mayor.

Later, on the way to the Ottenberg house, Doctor Haverford asked me, "I hear that you know about Doctor Marah's little masquerade?"

"Yes, sir, I do."

"She's a very brave woman, Hope."

"I think so, too. So does Mama. We've kept the secret.

Papa, too. And Miss Carruthers, the lady lawyer, she knew."

He sighed, then wheezed. "Jeanette can't keep up the masquerade the rest of her life, you know."

"I guess not." I couldn't think of anything else to say, so I was quiet the rest of the way as we crossed the bridge and meadow, passing the chicken coop.

Certainly I didn't say anything of any importance inside the Ottenberg parlor. Miss Emily showed me an album of old daguerrotypes while Doctor Haverford talked to her father. I asked her once under my breath if she'd told the colonel about the schoolhouse arriving, and she shook her head. That was good even if it was trickery.

Sometimes, over what she and I said about the pictures of Ottenberg relatives and pictures of her father taken during the Civil War, I could hear Doctor Haverford and Colonel Ottenberg rumbling at each other. Both of them had deep voices. Over a glass of wine I heard the doctor say once, "Now, Mr. Mayor, is that your final price? It's a pretty steep one, you know."

Colonel Ottenberg spoke quite clearly. "That's my price. Two hundred and fifty dollars per lot. Take it or leave it, Doctor."

Two hundred and fifty dollars a lot! That was a lot too much in my estimation. Papa had only paid fifty dollars for the ground we put the shebang on last summer.

I cocked my head to one side to hear better just as Miss Ottenberg showed me the picture of a young man with long, fair sideburns and a lock of hair over his forehead. She sniffed as she touched it, and I knew who it was by the sad sniff. It was her young man, who had been killed in a duel.

While I stared at the picture, feeling sorry for her, I heard Doctor Haverford saying, "All right, I'll pay you the full five hundred dollars this very day."

Colonel Ottenberg let out a sound that might have been a chuckle. "Oh, I trust you, Doctor. I can wait for the money. You can pay me Monday."

"No, sir, when I do a thing I do it *now*. You can draw up bills of sale for the two lots while the young girl who came here with me gets the money and fetches it out here."

"What girl?" I tore my eyes from the young man's picture Miss Ottenberg was still looking at to see Colonel Ottenberg pointing at me with his cane. "Her? The Foster minx. That girl?"

"Yes, sir, she's a trustworthy child and fast on her feet. Come here, Hope."

Miss Emily had turned a page now and was showing me some pictures of captured Confederate cannons. I said, "I have to go," to her and went over to the doctor, who'd taken some little keys strung on a piece of strong twine out of his vest pocket.

"You go along to my office, Hope, and unlock the bottom drawer of the instrument cabinet with the second biggest key. The big one is for the door to the outside. In the drawer you'll find a metal strong box. The smallest key will open it. Take out five hundred dollars in twenty-dollar gold pieces and bring them here."

I did some quick arithmetic in my head. That would be twenty-five gold pieces, a lot of money.

"I'm sending you, Hope," said Doctor Haverford, "because no one out to rob anybody would ever suspect that you, a child, would be carrying so much money on you."

That's why he'd wanted me along. Nobody would try to rob a poor, innocent child. He was right. Sometimes being a child had its good uses after all. So I took the keys and out I went, running as fast as I could.

It seemed a wise idea not to let Papa or Mama catch sight of me, so I came up behind the doctor's office between some buildings. From the top of his steps I leaned over and saw that there was still a crowd around the wagons. Yes, it wouldn't be long before somebody brought the news of the schoolhouse to Colonel Ottenberg.

It was easy getting the office and cabinet drawer open and then the strong box. There were a lot of gold pieces it it. I counted out twenty-five of them. They were very heavy—much too heavy to carry in my jacket pockets.

And then I saw the cuspidor in the corner. Thank Heaven, Doctor Haverford was a cigar smoker, not a tobacco chewer. I dumped the dry cigar butts out into his wastebasket and put the money into the cuspidor. Then I locked everything up again, threw the keys into the cuspidor, too, and, with the cuspidor rattling and jingling under my arm, ran for the Ottenberg place once more. I figured that no one would ever try to take a cuspidor from anybody by force, for fear of getting nasty tobacco spit all over him. I tried to run so the coins wouldn't jingle so much. Tobacco juice never did that. It sloshed.

I got to the Ottenbergs without anybody saying a single word to me. As a matter of fact, nobody even saw me. Once I was inside I handed the cuspidor to Doctor Haverford.

"It's an odd container the girl's brought back," the colonel complained.

"It's clean. It's only used for cigars," I told him.

"Well, for my part, I think Hope's found a pretty smart way to carry cash." Doctor Haverford reached in and hauled out the coins until he had a pile of them stacked up before him.

"Here you are, Haverford." I watched Colonel Ottenberg hand over two pieces of paper to the doctor, who pocketed them along with the keys he'd also fished out of his cuspidor.

We left after the two men had shaken hands.

On the way back I asked, "Doctor Haverford, why didn't you go get the money?"

"Because I don't do any more rushing around than I have to nowadays. And I didn't want to take the chance of Colonel Ottenberg finding out that the schoolhouse was here with no land for us to put it on, while I was away getting the cash for him." The doctor laughed. "It seems that Colonel Ottenberg also forgot that the school building would need a lot. He's had his mind on other matters, too."

I said, "That's lucky. What will you do now?"

"Oh, I'll sign over one of these papers to the town of Ottenberg Monday, deeding them the land for the new school building. The schoolhouse can start going up this very afternoon."

"Oh!"

"My gift of land is going to come as quite a shock, Hope, but it will be accepted. I'll tell the city fathers Monday. They can hardly refuse my present, though some of them aren't going to like it much."

I told him, "I think it's splendid of you."

He smiled down at me through his whiskers. In spite

of the rumpled way he looked, he was certainly a nice man in my estimation. "Well, Ottenberg can't ever say when I'm no longer around that I didn't do anything for its welfare."

"I think that what you're doing is very noble. And it will annoy Mr. O'Hare, to boot," I said.

"I'm not doing what I'm doing to spite O'Hare. Thank Heavens, I can say I'm doing it for a better reason than that."

"Yes, sir."

All at once he did a thing he'd never done before. He took my hand in his and squeezed it through my mitten. We came back to town, Doctor Haverford and I, hand in hand. After what he'd just done, I was very proud to walk with him.

He'd saved our new school!

There was a to-do, of course, when Colonel Ottenberg found out he'd been hoodwinked by the doctor. It turned out that nobody went to his house to tell him the news. On his afternoon stroll through his town he naturally saw the wagons being unloaded on one of the just-sold lots. When he asked what kind of building was going up, one of the volunteer carpenters told him that it was the new schoolhouse.

In a furious huff, he came stomping up to Doctor Haverford's office. Doctor Marah, who was there in the office too, told us that the mayor called the doctor just about everything bad and wicked he could lay tongue to, including some words Doctor Marah said weren't in her dictionary.

But it hadn't done the colonel one bit of good. The

lots were legally sold, both of them. To add insult to injury, right on the spot Doctor Haverford had signed over the larger of the two lots to the colonel as a gift to the town. He didn't even wait until Monday. That went down so crossways with Colonel Ottenberg that he became speechless. All he could do was open and close his mouth and stomp out.

"What about Miss Emily?" I said to Mama later. I was worried about her. I was sure that her father would have plenty to say to her now. He'd told Doctor Haverford up in his office that this was all the work of those "conniving females who had weasled their way into Haverford's affections and made him as crooked as they were."

Mama sighed and told me, "Hope, we must take comfort from the fact that Miss Emily has already stood up to most of the men in the town. Perhaps now she will find the courage and strength to assert her independence and stand up to her father. If she needs help or shelter, we shall stand ready to give it to her. She knows that. If her father gives her a great deal of trouble, we shall deal with him."

I grinned. "You'll take chairs and go sit down in front of the town hall where his office is?"

She laughed. "We might do just that! And I suspect Mayor Ottenberg knows it. All Emily has to do is let us know if she is being treated badly."

I told her, "I bet he knows that, too, Mama."

I had planned to congratulate Doctor Haverford for standing up to the colonel after church the next day, which happened to be Halloween as well as Sunday. If he didn't get to church, I'd call on him after our Sunday dinner at the Big Bend Hotel. We were good friends now.

Sunday morning just as I was starting out to Sunday school with Davey, Reverend Gardiner, who should have been in the church tent, came hurrying along the boardwalk toward our shebang. He stopped me to ask, "Where's Doctor Marah, Hope?"

I pointed to our place. "Inside. Getting ready for church."

When he hurried on, I told Davey, "Something's wrong. He looks sort of grim. You go on ahead to Sunday school. I'll come after I find out what the matter is."

Papa was out front measuring the boarded-up window to see how big a piece of glass he was going to have to order from Portland, so he could give a bill to Mr. O'Hare. We found out Silas was the one who had thrown the rock through the window. He'd even bragged about it at school.

I heard Papa call out to the minister, "Hey, why aren't you in church?" Then he laughed.

"It's Doctor Haverford, Mr. Foster. Haverford's dead. I have to tell Doctor Marah." The preacher didn't mince words.

"Oh, my God, how did it happen?" I saw my father pocket his folding rule, as my knees felt suddenly weak and wobbly.

"The manager of the Big Bend Hotel came to me just now with the news. The old doctor was called out last night to an emergency some miles away on Bear Creek. A miner had stuck a pickax through his foot. Haverford got his horse from the livery stable and rode out there.

Only the mare came back to the stable early this morning, and she was lame. The livery-stable people sent some men after the doctor. They found him lying in the Bear Creek trail—dead."

I felt like crying. After yesterday's talk with Doctor Haverford, I'd really grown to like him. And now he was gone.

Papa demanded, "How did he die? Did somebody shoot him for his money?" That was common enough around mining camps. I'd surely like to see anybody who killed Doctor Haverford put into our new jail.

"No, Mr. Foster. Nothing of the sort. There wasn't a mark on his body. It seems he was thrown from the mare, and when he tried to catch her, he had a stroke and died. I was told not long past by Doctor Marah that he was a mighty sick man."

"That he was." Papa stood with his hands in his pockets, staring at his boots as if he'd never seen them before. He looked up. "That seems to leave young Marah as the only doctor in town, doesn't it?"

"It seems so." I watched Reverend Gardiner looking up at the sky in a worried way. "Winter should be on us very soon now. There won't be time to get another medical man to come here. Do you think the men of Ottenberg will reconsider and go to Doctor Marah after all?"

"No, not most of them in any event. If somebody important went first and they got the notion that Marah knows his business, that might help. But nine out of ten men here—and they aren't all O'Hare's friends either—swear up and down that they'd go to a horse doctor before they'd go to a coward."

"But, Mr. Foster, some of them saw how courageously Marah behaved when O'Hare came with that mob and a rail."

"Not enough, I'm afraid. Now I'll step aside, so you can tell Doctor Marah and my wife. Afterward we'll put our heads together about a funeral and a memorial."

Memorial? I knew that word. Something that somebody did to remember somebody who had died. I came forward then and said, "I heard you talking just now. Doctor Haverford bought the lot for the school. Why don't we get the school named after him once it's nailed together?"

Neither one of them said anything. They looked at me, then stared at one another, and finally Papa and the preacher nodded. At last Papa said, "That ought to do it, Hope." With a lump in my throat, I thought of how Doctor Haverford had held my hand that day. It was a memory I'd always keep with me.

CHAPTER TWELVE

SOME OTHER THINGS TO SHOUT ABOUT

Because it was what Doctor Marah, who was Doctor Haverford's secret relative as well as his partner, figured the old doctor would have fancied, the funeral was a plain one. It was held two mornings later in the town cemetery, which was new, of course, because Ottenberg was. Yet already the cemetery had eleven graves—mostly for men who had died in mining accidents or been shot for one reason or another.

Reverend Gardiner talked for a while beside Doctor Haverford's grave about what a good man the old doctor had been and how he'd gone on serving the sick and injured though very ill himself. I stood shivering in the heaviest clothing I owned while he talked. The wind blew ice-cold off the mountains whose snowcaps were so white that in the sparkling sunshine they made my eyes ache to look at them. They were beautiful all right, under the bright blue sky, but they certainly didn't comfort me because I knew that the snow would be coming down to the lower parts of the country any day now. Oh, this had to be one of the coldest days I'd ever lived through.

To try to keep my mind off how frozen I was, I looked around to see who else was there besides my family. Doctor Marah and the Gardiners and the Prescotts, of course.

And there stood Miss Willis grabbing her bonnet when the gusts of wind got strong, and Miss Emily beside her, towering over her. The colonel was a good distance away from them, with his hat off in respect and his white beard blowing in the breeze. Most of the sisters from the church, along with the husbands who weren't working on the schoolhouse at the moment, were also present. Doctor Marah had decided that the nailing and hammering shouldn't stop for one minute, because Doctor Haverford would not have wanted any precious time lost.

Another unhappy thing had happened in Ottenberg, and it was holding up the building of the school. Some of the instructions from Chicago on how to put up the building hadn't agreed with the numbers painted on the boards. It had taken some refiguring by a town carpenter who really knew his onions to get things straightened out. We weren't done yet with the school, and here it was the second of November, which meant that the snow was overdue.

While I was thinking about this problem I counted the men in the cemetery—seventy-four of them. Most of them were miners, but I also saw the barber and some storeowners and twenty saloonkeepers, too. Mr. O'Hare wasn't one of them, though I knew Doctor Haverford had been a steady customer at the Shoo-Fly before the ladies started their collecting. Silas wasn't there either, but the other school kids were.

Standing over to one side, probably to keep as far away as possible from us Fosters, stood Judge Bokman. He was alone and with his hat off, too, like Colonel Ottenberg. Judge Bokman was getting bald on top of his head. I thought it must be very painful standing there with what hair he had blowing in the gusts. The sun shone down on the top of his head and made it glisten, but there wasn't any warmth at all in the sunshine at this time of the year.

Seeing him shivering there alone made me think of his wife. I was curious about her and about what Miss Carruthers had told Mama and me about knowing her in Helena. The fact that she was named Emerald was also something that interested me.

After Reverend Gardiner had finished the funeral service, and some miners with shovels were filling in the grave, Reverend Gardiner and his wife walked home with us and Doctor Marah. Mama asked the Gardiners inside for coffee or tea. Something hot was what we all needed to revive us, for two reasons: the sadness of paying our last respects, and the cold afternoon that had turned our feet and hands to cakes of blue ice.

When she was halfway through her first cup of tea and able to talk again without her teeth chattering, Dilsey Gardiner suddenly said, "Hope, I have a message for you, dear. I've already discussed it with your parents."

"Oh?" I came over from looking at stereopticon slides of waterfalls in the Swiss Alps to sit beside her on the sofa next to Essex.

Without disturbing our cat, she put her cup down on the table next to her and said, "Mrs. Bokman has asked me whether you would come help her with her housework for a time. She says it's become too much for her in her condition."

I could understand that all right. Ladies who were so near to having babies shouldn't be beating rugs and scrubbing floors and lifting galvanized-metal laundry tubs off the stove. I looked at Mama rocking in her chair and saw her nodding. Then I looked at Papa, who was eating a gingersnap and saw him nodding, too. Finally, because I thought Doctor Marah was part of the family, I looked in that direction and got one more nod. Then I said, "Well, I suppose I could go over there right after school and do my homework later."

Still, I really didn't like housework much, so I asked, "Is Mrs. Bokman going to pay me?"

"Oh, yes," answered Mrs. Gardiner. "She told me she's willing to pay you a whole ten cents an hour."

Ten cents! That was pretty good pay for somebody my age. "I'll go over there this very afternoon, right after lunch."

Mrs. Bokman, herself, opened the front door to me, after I knocked and waited for a while. I was glad she'd come to the door instead of the judge. I didn't want to have to talk to him. He probably wouldn't bother me while I was working, I had decided, because it would be beneath him to notice a child.

Mrs. Bokman wasn't even dressed in a bodice and skirt —only a long pale-blue wool dressing gown and carpet slippers of blue-and-silver cloth. Her long yellow hair hung down over her shoulders. "Oh, you did come, my dear?" were her first words.

"Yes'm, where do you want me to begin?" I had an apron with me and was ready to make the dust fly as soon as she told me where.

She put her hand to her forehead. "You might tidy up the kitchen, sweep the parlor out, put some more wood in the stoves, and then come to my bedroom. Because my husband is over at the courthouse, I'd like you to read to me afterwards."

Read? That didn't sound like work to me. I wondered what judges' wives who were named Emerald read, while I hurried through the housework.

Because it got dark so early, now that it was November, I read to her by lamplight. What she wanted to hear were poems by Henry Wadsworth Longfellow and an English poet called Tennyson. I looked up each poem she wanted in an index by the first line she gave me. Then I found the page of the poem and read it aloud to her. I figured she must know a lot of poetry and really dote on it to remember so many first lines by heart. Sometimes she'd even recite lines under her breath as I read aloud and she lay back on her pillows.

When I'd finished the last line of the last poem, she said to me, "Wesley usually reads to me. He likes to, but he's too busy now." That explained the reading then. And the judge's name was Wesley.

She smiled at me, such a nice smile, and asked, "What do you think of my husband?"

Because I worked for her, I didn't think I ought to tell her the truth. So I said what ladies said about people, "I think he's a lovely person."

She had a soft laugh. Reaching behind her, she pounded one of her pillows into a more comfortable shape. "You got to know my old friend Agnes Carruthers quite well while she was here, didn't you, Hope?"

"Not too well, ma'am, but I did talk to her."

"Tell me, please. What did she have to say about me?"

My, but Emerald Bokman asked a lot of hard questions. I answered, "She said that you were a lovely person."

This set Mrs. Bokman off into a long fit of laughter. "Oh, please, don't say that again because I know Agnes, and she never said anything as feeble as that in her whole life."

I felt my face getting red and hot. "No, ma'am." Mrs. Bokman was grinning at me from among her pillows now. "Well, to tell you the truth, I know that you were the one to tell Doctor Marah all about Miss Carruthers being a helpful lady lawyer and that Miss Carruthers says your husband is a whiskey judge and he claims that he put her into jail once."

"So he did." She nodded.

"Why?" I moved my chair closer to the bed.

"She defended a lady in Helena who went into a saloon and threw a brick into a big, expensive mirror, because the saloonkeeper had said in the Helena papers that he hoped to die of shame the day women got the right to vote in the United States."

I asked, "Was that lady from Ohio, too?"

"No, as I recall, she was originally from Indiana. That's just next door to Ohio, you know. Well, to make a longish story short, the woman who smashed the mirror refused to pay for it and demanded to be brought to trial. My husband had to sentence her to three days in the Helena jail. Because Agnes Carruthers raised so much trouble in the courtroom, he sent her there overnight, too. She and her client shared a cell."

I said, "But your husband didn't send her to jail here."

"Well, he did there! It almost led to my not marrying him. After all, Agnes is my first cousin, the oldest daughter of my father's brother. I used to be Emerald Carruthers. Agnes came to Montana Territory after she finished studying law. She and Wesley failed to hit it off from the very beginning when I introduced them. She didn't think I should marry him, but I loved him. He told her to her face that he thought she was a silly female who said everything that popped into her head without thinking first of the consequences."

Knowing Miss Carruthers, I doubted she had taken that calmly. So I asked, "What did she say to him?"

"That he was a stuffy, old, cantankerous crank of a man and much behind the times."

"Oh, my!" What else could I say? He *was* sort of old.

She went on, "So you could say that Wesley and Agnes could have showed more sense, but I loved him and in spite of the fact that he put my cousin into jail I married him. After I'd thought about that trial for a while, I could understand his position. Hope, Agnes is a lawyer. She knows the law. Lawyers have to obey the law as much as anyone else, you know. Agnes was not obeying it in his courtroom in Helena when she publicly insulted him. So he sent her to jail briefly to teach her a lesson he thought she needed to learn."

"It didn't work, Mrs. Bokman."

"No, it didn't seem to, did it?"

I asked, "Is Judge Bokman a whiskey judge who favors men over ladies?"

She was silent for a while, making a tent out of her fingers. "No, dear, I wouldn't say that he is more than any other judge in the country." She paused and added, "I do wish Agnes had come to call on me. But she certainly wasn't here long, was she?"

Truly trying to comfort her, I said, "No, she wasn't. But she did ask about you and wants you to have lots of lady friends here. She was in a hurry to get back to Helena before the snow came."

Then I asked, "Does your husband want ladies here to vote someday the way they do in Wyoming Territory?"

"No, he hasn't quite come around to that way of thinking yet."

"What about you?"

Mrs. Bokman raised her arms and told me, "Oh, I'd like to vote someday. Wouldn't you?"

"Yes, I would. Ladies should vote, too." Next I asked, "Does the judge believe in dueling?"

"Certainly not!" She looked shocked.

"That's good to hear. We Fosters don't either, and neither does Doctor Marah."

While Mrs. Bokman rubbed some salve on one of her elbows, she said softly, "One would scarcely expect such a thing of a woman, would one?"

"Huh?" What did she mean?

"Oh, Hope, Doctor Haverford told me the secret last week when he came to see me. He told me that if anything ever happened to him, I would be perfectly safe under the care of Doctor Marah—Doctor Jeanette Marah."

"My!" The wind had been knocked out of me for a moment. Then I thought to ask, "Does the judge know about Doctor Marah being a woman?"

"I haven't breathed a word of it to Wesley. When our baby comes, though, Doctor Jeanette will bring it into the world."

"But Judge Bokman might not like the idea one bit."

She laughed, and then she yawned. "It seems to me

that Wesley has very little choice in the matter. I think it might do him some good not to get his way in absolutely everything. Judges are inclined to decide things, you know."

"It seems that way, ma'am."

"Hope, you had better go home now. I get weary very quickly these days, and I want to nap for a while. Do tell your mother that I think you are a fine clever girl and a good little reader. I have heard that you're the one who took the first chair to the front of the Shoo-Fly Saloon. I approved of that, you know. The town needs a new school, and Mr. O'Hare needs a lesson in manners. Several people have said nice things about you to me. I hope you will come back tomorrow. Help yourself to some peppermints from the candy dish in the parlor on the way out."

I got up and said, "Yes, ma'am." Then because she'd asked me a few questions, I decided to ask her one I was simply dying to know the answer to. "Is your name really Emerald?"

Mrs. Bokman nodded gravely. "Yes, my name is Emerald. My mother named me that because she used names of precious gems for all her daughters. Her own name was Jewel."

"Oh." That explained that. I'd surely remember to ask her someday what were the names of her other sisters.

As I opened the front door of the Bokman house to leave, I ran smack into the judge on the middle step. He looked me up and down and said, "So you decided to come, did you?"

"Yes, sir, I'm working for your wife."

Aha! That would fix him. I went home congratulating myself that I'd had the last word in a conversation with a judge. And I'd let him know that I was working for his wife—not for him. I wondered as I went down the boardwalk toward the shebang what the judge's thoughts were about Doctor Marah now that Doctor Haverford was gone. I wondered, too, if those Ottenberg men who had been standing around Doctor Haverford's grave were thinking of what they were going to do this winter if they got sick. Winter was a wicked time for all kinds of ailments.

A lot of folks who fell ill in the autumn never made it through to spring in the cold-winter territories. Everybody who had ever lived in a northern territory knew that.

It turned out to be quite a night, all right, just as it had been quite a morning and an afternoon.

That night Mr. O'Hare got his comeuppance, though nobody who'd taken part in getting a new schoolhouse for Ottenberg was responsible. No, Mr. O'Hare got into a shooting scrape with a pure stranger, a man who had ridden in from Idaho Territory that same day. He'd made the rounds of the saloons drinking whiskey, and about nine o'clock staggered into the Shoo-Fly. He picked a fight with Mr. O'Hare's bartender first, because he refused to give him any more whiskey. The bartender called for O'Hare. I guessed the Idaho man never turned around to give Mr. O'Hare the chance to surprise him with his bung starter. Instead, Mr. O'Hare tried to throw him out, and it wasn't as easy as it had been with us ladies. The stranger grabbed his pistol from under his sheepskin jacket and shot Mr. O'Hare once through the shoulder and a second time through his left elbow.

Silas came to our side door right after it happened, so

we Fosters learned about it fast. I opened the door after he called out and was the first to see him. There was blood on the front of his shirt and sleeves.

I gasped out, "What happened?"

"My pa's been shot!" Silas's big freckles stood out in his dirty face like copper pennies. "Didn't you hear the shootin', Hope?"

That was a silly question to ask anybody in Ottenberg, where there was so much shooting after dark. "No, I never can tell where the sounds are coming from."

By now Mama was out of her rocker and peering over my shoulder. She caught me by one arm and pushed me out of the way. "Come in, child," she said to Silas. "Can we help you?"

"I hope so, ma'am." I saw him gulp.

"Well, what can we do?"

"You can ask that doctor to come see my pa."

I couldn't resist saying, "Do you mean Doctor Marah?"

"That's him. Yes."

Mama turned to me. "Hope, Doctor Marah's in his room. Please go get him at once." She added to Silas, "Sit down, boy. You look to me as if you're about to keel over in a faint at any minute."

"Thank you, ma'am." And he sat down.

I went to Doctor Marah's room and rapped on the door.

"Silas O'Hare's here. He says his father's been shot. He wants you to come right away. Are you going to go?" I asked.

"Yes, I have to. It's my duty, Hope. If the man's been shot, he needs my help."

"I think you're being noble and splendid again."

"Thank you, Hope, but somehow I don't think your heart's in what you're saying."

"It isn't, Doctor Jeanette."

I didn't go to the Shoo-Fly with Silas and Doctor Marah, of course, but Mama did. She'd done some nursing in both Oregon and Idaho Territory and helped doctors there. Ottenberg needed another doctor, but it also needed ladies who were real nurses. Yes, that was one other thing I could do someday besides teach school, I supposed, if I wanted to.

When Mama returned alone an hour later, she told us little by little what had gone on at the Shoo-Fly. Some men had carried Mr. O'Hare into the saloon from the boardwalk and laid him down on top of the bar. That was where she and Doctor Marah had found him.

I interrupted. "Why was there blood on Silas then?"

"Because he'd been out on the boardwalk when the shooting took place, and he tried, poor little tyke, to hold his father up in a sitting posture. Some men shooed him off and took O'Hare inside out of the cold."

Well, that explained the gore on Silas. I'd been thinking about some things, too, while Mama was away. "Whose idea was it to come get Doctor Marah?" I asked her. "Silas's or his pa's or one of the saloon customer's?" This seemed very important to know.

"It surely wasn't that poor child's. He was too upset to think clearly, and it wasn't Mr. O'Hare's, because he was half-unconscious. Some miners sent the boy over here for the doctor."

That was good. They would have preferred Doctor Haverford, but they did call Doctor Marah when it came down to a life-or-death matter. If she did well by Mr. O'Hare, they'd call Jeanette again to be their doctor. I just knew it.

So I asked Mama, "How did Doctor Marah do?"

She gave me a queer look, then told me, shaking her head, "How in the world would I know for certain, Hope? I'm not a medical doctor. But it seemed to me that Doctor Marah knew what to do."

Davey understood what I had in mind. "Did Mr. O'Hare die?"

"Good Heavens, no!"

"But Mama," I asked, "what did Doctor Marah do for him?"

"I saw him look at Mr. O'Hare's face, then watched him listen to his heart and lungs. Then he had miners carry him upstairs to his bedroom over the saloon."

"What was that like?" I asked.

"Hope, what difference does a bedroom make? It was just a bedroom with a bed and a chest of drawers and the usual other things. Some miners got Mr. O'Hare's coat and shirt off, and Doctor Marah looked at his wounds. Then he took out one of the bullets."

I asked, "Only one of them? Why only one?"

"The doctor left the second bullet in Mr. O'Hare's elbow because he was afraid he might shatter the bone if he tried to get it out. He doesn't want the elbow harmed any more than it is now."

"How did O'Hare get shot in the first place?" Papa asked. He'd just come in from locking up the shebang for the night.

Mama didn't tell us right away. She handed me a hank of blue yarn. "Hope, help me with this, please. While you do that, I'll tell you what one of the miners who took Mr. O'Hare up to the bedroom told Doctor Marah and me."

I put the yarn around my held-apart hands, so she could pull it over and around them to wind it into a ball. Like half the ladies in Ottenberg, she was making something for the Bokman baby. They were sewing, knitting, tatting lace, crocheting, and embroidering all over the place.

So while Mama rolled the ball she told us about the stranger who'd shot Mr. O'Hare and who was now in jail. She finished by saying that Doctor Marah was going to stay over at the Shoo-Fly to talk to Mr. O'Hare when he became conscious.

"Were the miners nice to Doctor Marah?" I asked.

"Oh, yes, they were pleasant and very cooperative."

"Hmmn."

I waited up that night until eleven o'clock, as late as Papa would permit, for Doctor Marah to return. But she didn't come back by then. Jeanette still wasn't back the next morning when Davey and I went off to the chicken coop. On the way, we walked by the new school building. It was nearly finished by now. Some men were up on the roof, nailing on the part that would hold the school bell. The bell, itself, was down on the ground with a rope tied to it so it could be hoisted up and put into place. Then all the men had to do was move our benches and desks and stove and Miss Willis's desk and chair and the blackboard out of the chicken coop into the new place.

Naturally Davey and I stopped to admire the schoolhouse that so many people had worked hard for. Margaret Libby joined us there. She said from inside the depths of the long, green-plaid muffler over her face, "It looks like a real schoolhouse, doesn't it?"

"What did you expect—a railroad station?" asked Davey.

I was tempted to add that the Libbys hadn't done anything to help get it for the town but didn't. It wasn't Margaret's fault that her parents had acted the way they had. Instead, while walking together to school, I told her about Mr. O'Hare and Doctor Marah.

She was very interested. When I was through, she said, "Maybe the other men will go to him now, too. I'll tell everybody I know, and my father and mother besides."

"That'll be good, Margaret. We'll both tell Miss Willis at recess." And then I told her, too, about my job at the Bokmans' and being paid a whole ten cents an hour.

Her eyes bulged at my good luck. "Hope, you'll be rich by Christmas!"

"Oh, I don't know about that," I said modestly.

I ran home from school for lunch to see if Doctor Marah had come back yet and found that she had. She was eating a bacon sandwich with Papa.

While I started one for myself, because Mama was waiting on customers out in the shebang, I asked Doctor Marah, "How's Mr. O'Hare?"

"Not in very good shape, Hope. I was just telling your father. Mr. O'Hare is leaving Ottenberg this afternoon on the westbound stage."

"Leaving?" I was so surprised that grease dripped from the fork I still was holding up in the air.

"Yes, on my advice Mr. O'Hare is going to a hospital in Portland where a doctor will remove the bullet from his elbow. I'd do it myself if it weren't winter. I just don't like the idea of tackling it when he'd have to stay here in below-zero weather. I'm afraid that arthritis would settle in his arm permanently, and he'd be miserable for the rest of his life. He's getting out while the getting's good, I suspect. This could be the last stagecoach in or out of here for months. It's a wonder to me that any driver or company will take the chance with snow on its way."

I took the hot bacon out of the pan and asked, "What's he going to do with the Shoo-Fly?"

"He's already sold it."

"That was fast," said my father.

"Yes, it was, but he'd had offers for it before."

"What about Silas, Doctor Marah?" He wasn't at school this morning—not that anyone had expected him to show up.

"Silas will go to Portland with his father. I think it will be good for him."

"Why?" I asked, as I put the bacon between two slices of bread.

"The boy has female relatives there."

"His mother?" Oh, I had wondered plenty about her, and so had Margaret Libby.

"No, two aunts. They are nuns, teachers at a Portland school for boys. He will go to their school."

Aha! Nuns and Silas O'Hare. That would be very interesting, indeed. They'd have their work cut out for them, all right.

Doctor Marah spoke to Papa. "It's a sad situation, Mr. Foster. O'Hare's bedroom was filled with camera portraits and even an oil painting of a beautiful woman. He told me she was his wife. A year after Silas was born she ran away with another man, and she's never been heard from since." Papa said, as he ate the last bite of his sandwich, "Well, I suppose that could explain O'Hare's powerful views on womenfolks."

"I imagine that it could." Doctor Marah let out a long sigh, like one that Mama came out with when she was exasperated with Davey. I had noticed that ladies sighed a lot more than men did. I supposed it was because they weren't allowed to cuss.

I couldn't resist saying, "Mr. O'Hare seems to think you're just dandy now, Doctor Marah, but what would he say if he knew you were Dr. Jeanette?"

Both Papa and Doctor Marah laughed. Papa said, "If O'Hare leaves today as scheduled, he won't find out."

"No, *he* won't, Mr. Foster, but I can't keep this masquerade going forever, you know."

"Oh, we know that, Doc, we know."

I added my penny's worth. "It won't be forever." Then I asked Papa, "Did you get paid for the window Silas broke?"

"Yep, a whole seven dollars, which is what I estimated it to be. One thing you can say about O'Hare; he pays his debts before he clears out of town."

"That's good, Papa." Then I asked Doctor Marah, "Did Mr. O'Hare say he was sorry now about the way he treated you?"

"No," she shook her head, "but he paid me, too. He asked me my fee and gave it to me right away."

I said, "You have to give the devil his due, I guess."

Back at the chicken coop that afternoon, I had some more surprises.

Silas was the cause of them. He came into the coop

looking sunken about the eyes and pale, because he'd been up all night and because he was worried about his pa. His shirt had been changed, though. There wasn't any blood on it now, and I was grateful for that. I imagined getting him cleaned up was Doctor Marah's doing.

We were all surprised to see Silas. He'd walked to school when he hadn't needed to, which was strange. His reasons for coming were even stranger.

He said he was sorry for the way he'd acted all year. He even apologized to Miss Willis. Then he said, "Good-bye, I'm off to Oregon." But what he did next just about made me faint on the spot. He took a silver dollar out of his pocket, squeezed past Miss Willis's desk and the stove, and came over to where I was sitting with Davey and Margaret. He put the dollar down on the desk in front of me. "Hope, that's money I earned puttin' down new sawdust every week on the floor of the Shoo-Fly. I know it's too late to help pay for the new schoolhouse, but maybe your pa can order some colored chalk for the blackboard. I'm givin' the dollar to you, because that doctor who lives with you was nicer to us than we ever was to him. My pa wants you to know he's sorry, too."

Before I could pick up the money, he'd wiggled past desks and pupils and was outside running toward Ottenberg. We never got over our surprise fast enough to say good-bye to him.

I held up the dollar, and Miss Willis inclined her head toward the money gleaming between my fingers. "I shall write the name Silas O'Hare on the very top of the blackboard at the new schoolhouse. I shall keep it there all year in his memory. Woe betide any pupil in my school who dares to erase it. He may never be a scholar, but in the end Silas proved to us that he has the makings of a gentleman."

On the next day, the afternoon after the O'Hares had left, an eastbound stage brought us a letter marked "The Fosters of the Whole Shebang." It had three newspaper clippings inside, two from California newspapers and one from Oregon. They were about "Wicked Ottenberg, the chicken-coop-school town" and what went on there. My, but the colonel and city fathers and Judge Bokman would hate to read what Miss Dalrymple had written about Ottenberg. Everybody else would enjoy it, though. So, once we were finished reading what Miss Dalrymple had sent us, we took the envelope over to the Prescotts to pass on to the Gardiners, who would pass it on to somebody else. There'd been a brief note from the lady reporter too. She said that later on she'd send any whole papers that had her stories about Ottenberg events in them.
There had been quite a bit about me—Hope Foster, "the remarkable Western girl, who arranged the downfall of a corrupt saloonkeeper and might in time drive him out of town." That wasn't actually true. I hadn't shot Mr. O'Hare. It had never even entered my mind to do so. I wasn't even so sure about the downfall of Mr. O'Hare or his corruptness, but he had been embarrassed by me and by the ladies who got the schoolhouse for Ottenberg, so I supposed in a way Miss Dalrymple was right. And as Mama said, "Waiting for more outside newspapers telling about Ottenberg events will make for an interesting period from November till May."
The second afternoon after the O'Hares cleared out,

Miss Emily called unexpectedly on Mama and she had plenty to say. I wasn't there, so Mama told me all about it later. Miss Emily had said that her father was so furious about being hoodwinked by Ohio-controlled females and Doctor Haverford that he felt the need to blow off steam to somebody. Because she lived with him and he didn't want the men who voted in Ottenberg to know what a bad temper he was in, he was blowing off steam talking to her. Mama had suggested to Miss Emily that she blow off some steam herself at him. She'd promised Mama that she'd holler right back every time he hollered at her. She told Mama that she wasn't only going to turn over a new leaf, but a whole danged chapter.

Hearing this made me happier than ever that we were going to move into the new school building on Saturday. Once we were there, in town, we wouldn't have to hear the Ottenbergs carrying on at one another.

Naturally I didn't have it in mind to tell Emerald Bokman about the clippings criticizing her husband, but I did plan to tell her about Miss Emily and the colonel that second afternoon. I was going to tell her that the colonel was fighting a second Civil War. That would make Mrs. Bokman laugh.

But she never gave me a chance to open my mouth that day. She didn't seem to be in a lazy enough mood to lie down and have me read out loud to her. I liked that job much better than the housework.

No, today she wanted to get the house cleaned up spic-and-span, as if she expected mighty important company. She was terribly spry, telling me to "clean this" and "clean that" while she polished silverware and furniture and the cookstove, swept out the corners, dusted the ceilings, and even moved the heavy cottage organ, which I had never heard her play.

I came home at six o'clock so weary I practically fell onto the sofa. My plopping myself down annoyed both cats, so they leaped up from the pillows and headed for the shebang to sleep somewhere else. We'd closed early that night.

"What's the matter with you, Hope?" Mama asked me.

"Are you feverish?" Papa wanted to know.

I told them, "No, I'm fine. Just worn out. Mrs. Bokman didn't let me sit down for a minute, and neither did she. We turned that house upside down, let me tell you."

"Oh!" came from Mama. I saw her smile as she looked down at the baby hat she was knitting.

Doctor Marah came in at suppertime from clearing out Doctor Haverford's office and his room at the Big Bend Hotel. Marah planned to go on boarding with us, though she'd inherited the other lot Doctor Haverford had bought from Colonel Ottenberg. If she wanted to, she could build a house on it in the spring.

As Doctor Marah took off the warm wolfskin coat she'd just bought from Papa and her old black hat, I noticed something interesting.

White speckles on the hat brim! I saw Marah shake the speckles off onto the kitchen floor and heard the words, "It's finally come. It's snowing."

"Snowing?" Papa repeated softly.

"It appears to be," Mama said, without dropping a stitch. "The sky was the right color late this afternoon for snow by nightfall. Or perhaps you would rather I'd said the wrong color?"

"Snow!" snorted Davey, who, young as he was, had already seen enough of it in Idaho Territory to last a lifetime.

They'd said it all. I didn't say a word about the snow. It was here. It couldn't be stopped by man or beast, but it surely could stop both creatures from doing a lot of things they might want to.

That night, just as I was getting ready for bed, I heard a rapping at the side door again. Since I slept closest to it, I got up, put on my wrapper, and went with the lamp to open it. "Who is it?" I called out.

"It's Bokman. Judge Bokman."

I knew his voice by now and let him inside without calling Papa. There was snow on the judge's shoulders, and his hat brim was filled with it.

"I'd like to have a word with Doctor Marah, Hope." He used my first name now.

"Is it the baby?" I asked. He looked worried.

"Maybe. I'm not a doctor."

"I'll go get Doctor Marah. Please sit down." I turned up the kerosene lamp on the parlor table for him, so he could look at our stereopticon slides if he wanted to.

As I had when Silas came to us, I knocked on Marah's door. Doctor Jeanette came out at once, still dressed in shirt sleeves and a vest. I told her who was in the parlor. Mama came out of her bedroom in her wrapper and nightgown a minute afterward. She nabbed me in the little hallway before I got back to the parlor.

"Is it the baby, Hope?" she asked me, while Doctor Marah and the judge talked together out of our hearing.

I said, "Maybe, Mama."

"I think it is, Hope. When a baby's about to be born, the mother often gets a burst of energy and cleans the house like a crazy woman."

I hadn't known this. It was quite interesting. I'd be sure to remember to tell Margaret Libby tomorrow.

Then Doctor Marah came back smiling. She told Mama, "Nora, will you please go over to the Bokman house right away and keep Mrs. Bokman company until I'm ready to accompany the judge?"

"Yes, of course." Mama went back into her room and shut the door while Doctor Marah went into her room. I was left alone outside.

So I went back to the judge. "Would you like a cup of tea? I can stir up the stove and put the kettle on."

"No, I would not." He was drumming on our parlor table with the fingers of one hand.

"Would you like to look at our stereopticon slides of waterfalls in the Swiss Alps?"

"No, I would not." He looked up at me. "What I would like is a drink of whiskey."

I told him, "Miss Agnes Carruthers said that you were a whiskey judge."

"I am not. That is not what she meant at all."

I knew from his wife's telling me what the lady lawyer had really meant, but I wasn't going to let him know. I also knew how he felt about ladies voting.

I supposed Papa would expect me to do the proper thing by a guest in our house and give him whatever he wanted. So I got our whiskey bottle down out of the cupboard and set it and a glass next to the stereopticon viewer. I was letting the judge pour himself the size of drink he wanted. That way nobody could blame me for the consequences!

Then while he was pouring, I went over to the sofa, sat down, and watched him. My, he certainly looked unhappy.

I didn't get to watch him for long. Mama must have dressed very quickly—certainly without her corsets. She got down her coat and big scarf and bonnet and said, "I'll get over to Mrs. Bokman first. Please wait here, Judge, for Doctor Marah. Is Hope keeping you company?" I saw how her eye fell on the bottle and the glass. She didn't chide me, though.

He told her, "Your daughter is a variety of company. What I mean to say is that in a manner of speaking, she is."

"Good." I doubted if Mama understood him either, but out she went, letting in a breath of icy air down off a mountain peak.

The judge finished his whiskey swiftly and was drumming his fingers again when he said all at once, "Where in the name of Heaven is that doctor?"

"Right here, Your Honor, and ready!" came Marah's voice.

And out of the hall Doctor Marah stepped. Doctor Jeanette Marah.

At last I found out what had been in the mysterious locked horsehair trunk that had been shipped to her. She had on a black-and-white-checked, bustled gown with a white collar and cuffs and a black polonaise draped across the front. On her head, tied under her chin, was a black bonnet with white-and-black bows. Over one arm was a black woman's cloak, and in her hand her black doctor's bag. Her cheeks were pink as summer roses with excitement.

So were mine as I stood up.

Bokman had got up, too.

"Shall we go, Your Honor?" she asked him.

I looked from her face to his. He looked as if he couldn't believe his eyes.

"You're not who I thought you were!" was what finally came out of his mouth.

"Not quite, sir. I am Doctor Jeanette Marah and rest assured that I am a qualified and licensed physician."

I watched her put down her bag and throw on her cloak. The judge came over at once, reaching for the bag, which was next to me on our sofa. Doctor Marah picked it up before he could get his hands on it, though. "No, Judge Bokman," she told him. "You would not ask me to carry your gavel for you, and I shall not ask you to carry my bag. And once we're outside, I shall not require your arm to lean on. I make my own way in life, thank you. Let us go now, Your Honor."

I sat right where I was for a full five minutes after they had left. I wanted to cheer and shout, but I'd wake Papa and Davey up, so I shouted inside myself. It was nice, but it made me feel a bit stuffed and choked up and brought tears to my eyes.

Naturally I didn't sleep all night thinking about Doctor Marah's going out at last in a lady's gown and about the baby, too. What would it be? How was Mrs. Bokman?

When I heard Mama come in at dawn, I got out of bed and came at once to the kitchen, not even bothering to put on my wrapper. I asked, standing barefoot and shivering next to the almost-cold stove, "What was it? How's Emerald?"

"Just fine, both of them. It was a girl, Hope, a beautiful little girl, who looks a lot like you when you were born." Mama smiled at me and told me softly and a bit wearily, "Ottenberg's first baby is a girl."

Aha! A girl! That would please a lot of folks and not please some others! I was happy it was a girl, though. I told Mama, "You know, we ladies certainly have made our mark here in the year of 1875." I felt like using flowery language. All that poetry of Mrs. Bokman's must have gone to my brain. So had lack of sleep. I went on, "It comes to me now to wonder what the ladies will do in 1876 to better the lot of the town. It should be something to shout about, too."

She muttered as she sat down and unbuttoned the side of one of her boots, "What I suggest is that we rest for a good long time, Hope. My feet hurt."

I sat down across from her. "I hope you won't rest too long. We ought to get that $1250 back from the Territory for the school building this spring, shouldn't we? That will give us quite a bit of money to start something else with, won't it? Maybe it could be used to start a lending library or even to build a hospital, and we could collect more the same way we did for the school."

"Maybe, Hope." Mama had both snow-soaked boots off now and was wriggling her toes in front of her. She looked too tired to be excited about my dreams for next year.

So what could I do?

I knew. I'd wait until Doctor Jeanette came home, and then I'd take it all up with her and see what her thoughts were. And after that I'd ask Miss Willis.

There'd be something to shout about in 1876, too—I just knew it!

AUTHOR'S NOTES

First of all, I believe young readers will be interested in knowing that Doctor Jeanette Marah is based on a real frontier woman, who was forced to masquerade as a man in order to study medicine under a male doctor. Unlike my fictional Doctor Marah, Doctor Lillian Heath wore guns, as well as trousers, coat, and a vest. There were other pioneer women who were involved in work that was considered suitable for men only, although their number was very small. There were a few female lawyers, newspaper reporters, mayors and councilwomen, professors, policewomen, and engineers. More than a few Western women were forced to pose as men in order to keep their land safe from trespassers. Someday I hope to write about some of these other gallant ladies.

The concept of a chicken-coop school may seem incredible as well as laughable, but there was such a school. During this period schools were held in all manner of places—from mine shafts to dry wells.

Unlikely as it may seem, prefabricated houses were manufactured in the 1870's. It is true that the precut boards for a schoolhouse could be shipped out West by train or wagon for the sum of $1250. A church complete with a spire cost $4000. A one-room house, a modest $175. I've used the exact prices that were listed in an 1870 advertisement from Chicago.

Ten cents an hour would have been considered a handsome wage for a young girl doing household work in 1875. Wages were, of course, much lower than in today's society, though prices and incomes in a boom-town mining camp were much higher than those in other towns.

I've used the word *shebang* throughout as a term for a general store. This was a common slang term of the day. "Pass Under the Rod" was a favorite song of the era, and "Blessed Be Thy Courts Above" a well-known hymn.

The tale of the ladies collecting money in saloons and obstructing saloon business is one that actually did take place. It came about, however, in various ways in different locales, and I have brought these incidents together in *Something to Shout About,* inasmuch as Ottenberg is a fictional town.

Wives and mothers sometimes collected cash for worthy causes in saloons all over the American West. In one city, in the year 1874, they invaded saloons in great numbers. The city was Portland, Oregon, the scene of one of the funniest, wildest feminine revolts the West has ever witnessed. There the ladies tormented an uncooperative saloonkeeper, who would not go along with their nondrinking views, by sitting down out in front of his place of business. They were taken off to jail after he complained, but not before they had created a sensation and obstructed his trade. Ladies in 1874 Oregon—or anywhere else in the nation—were not supposed to act in such a bold manner.

Like my Ottenberg women, these Portlanders were brought to trial. They chose to remain overnight in jail rather than pay a fine. But they were ejected that evening by the Chief of Police at eight o'clock and had to make their way home through the rough street life they so despised.

The Portland women were inflamed to action by a

AUTHOR'S NOTES 253

movement from Ohio urging not only temperance but women's rights. Neither the Ohio nor the Oregon women achieved their aims—the closing of the city saloons and the vote—but they succeeded in breaking the spirit of the saloonkeeper who had insulted them and thrown some of them out into the street. This model for Mr. O'Hare came to a rather peculiar end. After he sold his saloon, he left Portland to sail to the peaceful South Seas but died on the voyage.

My lady reporter is based on the real-life Abigail Scott Duniway, publisher of the weekly Portland newspaper, *The New Northwest*. She was an active seeker of suffrage for women and a prime mover in the 1874 Oregon ladies' crusade against saloons. Mary Sissen Leonard, a woman lawyer of the 1870's, is the model for Miss Carruthers. Mary was an intelligent and colorful woman, who shocked others by her scandalous behavior.

A person wishing to read about the Oregon women and their ferment will find a booklet printed, in 1969, by the Oregon Historical Society most interesting. It is called *The War on the Webfoot Saloon and Other Tales of Feminine Adventures*. In its pages are a Shoo-Fly Saloon, a Dolly Varden Saloon, and an Oro Fino. I place a billiard table in Ottenberg's Shoo-Fly. Billiards was played in England in the sixteenth century, so I presume Portland, Oregon, and Montana Territory knew the game by 1874.

In this book for young readers, I have referred now and then to the fact that women could vote in Wyoming Territory in the 1870's. In 1869, primarily as a way of attracting a supply of future brides to the woman-scarce country, the women were given suffrage. In 1871, the men of the legislature tried to repeal the law, but the attempt failed by one vote.

I have referred to the very old custom of settling differences by dueling. Though prohibited by law in most places in the United States, duels were not uncommon in the last century, though they were always held in secret. A number of men prominent in American history—one of them a president of the United States—were involved in duels. Fortunately, dueling with swords and pistols has fallen into disuse nowadays, though no young reader or teacher needs to be told that grudge fistfights are still a frequent feature of school days and school grounds.

Writing about the early days of Montana proved a great challenge to me. As far as I can tell, there is a dearth of printed material on the subject, and I personally would like to see more books published about this state's fascinating nineteenth century.

Montana became a territory in 1864 but did not enter the Union until 1889. Although Ottenberg is a fictional locale, it is based on a town in the northwestern part of the state, not far from the Idaho border. Anyone who has endured winters in that area knows what to expect from late October through March.

As always, in writing my books for children, I owe my gratitude to the librarians and staffs of the Riverside Public Library, Riverside, California, and to the University of California libraries, both at Riverside and Berkeley. It was a librarian who first told me that shoo-fly is an incorrect spelling supposedly derived from the popular song of 1869, "Shew! Fly, Don't Bother Me."

Patricia Beatty
December, 1975

ABOUT THE AUTHOR

Now a resident of Southern California, Patricia Beatty was born in Portland, Oregon. She was graduated from Reed College there, and then taught high-school English and history for four years. Later she held various positions as science and technical librarian. Recently she taught Writing Fiction for Children in the Extension Department of the University of California, Los Angeles. She has had a number of historical novels published by Morrow, several of them dealing with the American West in the 1860 to 1895 period.

Mrs. Beatty has lived in Coeur d'Alene, Idaho; London, England; and Wilmington, Delaware; as well as on the West Coast. She and her late husband, Dr. John Beatty, co-authored a number of books. One of them, *The Royal Dirk*, was chosen as an Award book by the Southern California Council on Children's and Young People's Literature.

JOSEPH T. WALKER UPPER SCHOOL
700 ALLGOOD ROAD
MARIETTA, GEORGIA 30062

F
Be
79-187

2-16-79	DATE DUE		
OCT 1 79 KO			
FEB 8 '81			

79-187

F   Beatty, Patricia
Be
      Something to shout
      about